THE BEST LAID FLIGHT PLANS

PLANS

A MODERN PRIDE AND PREJUDICE VARIATION

LEIGH DREYER

To my children.

CHAPTER 1

*T*he clouds burst below and wispy peaks spiraled out as the plane surged through the sky. Captain William Darcy gazed at the horizon, crimson ribbons blazing across the sunrise. These peaceful moments were the only time he participated in anything resembling prayer. He checked his altitude and trimmed up.

> "Oh! I have slipped the surly bonds of Earth
> And danced the skies on laughter-silvered wings..."

DARCY RECITED these lines from "High Flight" to himself as he scanned his surroundings and instruments again, his situational awareness high.

This mission was bittersweet. His last in the F-22. He would miss the deep alien whistle from the engines as it flew over the base, close enough to wave at families walking near the harbor. This sortie was an easy ride, nothing but practice and war games, but he took it seriously. He knew a few meters off perfection meant life and death. A slight left bank and the deep green mountains were to the east as he approached the runway for a quick touch and go.

Those jade Hawaiian mountains rising from the blackness of the earth were what he loved most about this base. Oddly, they were quite alien to his upbringing in Central New York. The woods surrounding Pemberley were green but never quite this other-worldly, tropical color. Somehow Pemberley's hills and forests were more *real*, and he missed seeing the horizon curve over the gentle hills of his land. Here, that prospect was only available in the sky and he ached for it. He loved that feeling of being alone in the world and watching it go on forever.

Pushing forward on the stick, he felt the quick descent in a tactical approach before touching the runway for a split second— up on the thrust and away again, off to his place in the clouds and his head. He ran through the memorized checklist he needed to complete on this ride... *Touch and goes: check. Ship car: incomplete. Go to the TMO office: incomplete. Schedule movers: incomplete.* He blinked, staring unseeingly at his controls. *Damn moving checklist!* He halted the intruding checklist and reoriented to task. *Tactical approach: check.* One more turn and then in for landing.

He could not allow himself to think about moving again as he had spent enough energy on it already. He would have a quick Pilot Instructor Training in San Antonio and then the three-hour drive to the Mexican border to Longbourn City and Meryton Air Force Base to train America's best and brightest student pilots. He loved flying more than anything in the world but wondered if that love extended to the staleness of helping brand new pilots grasp the basics of the T-38 Talon.

Darcy hated moving; it was the worst aspect about the air force. Having grown up at Pemberley, near the Finger Lakes, Darcy always knew his place in that perfect, idyllic world. He did not understand how anyone would ever want to leave where they had grown up. Pemberley was the place his soul lived. He looked again at the green around him as he flew, but it was not the right shade —nothing like the bright emerald leaves at home. Pemberley had the best views the world had to offer: brilliant green trees in the summer, vibrant fall colors in autumn, winters full of snow and sledding, and fields of wildflowers to rival any florist shop in spring. There were lakes for swimming, canoeing, or fishing. There were large rocks and mountains to hike. Darcy had never known a bored moment in his childhood.

His father had taught him to fly at twelve, first in a small Cessna and then later in the Bonanza. Together with his father, Darcy had grown up looking down on the prospect of his family's holdings and missed them every time he was in the air. Flying was the only thing that kept him connected to his father and, thus far, the only reason he continued to tolerate moving by whim of the air force.

Meanwhile, Meryton, Texas was stuck in the middle of a desert. When he looked up information about the base, the pictures only showed brown dirt, brown grass, brown sage bushes, and brown mesquite trees. The only positive was that there were ranches nearby. Bingley had even talked about leasing a little working farm and maybe living together when he arrived. Perhaps this move would be fun if he could put himself back in wide, open spaces where he belonged. He might even mentor Bingley in the business of agriculture along the way.

William Darcy and Charles Bingley had become best friends at Cornell despite Bingley being a couple years junior. Both had been business majors and in the challenging program, Darcy's reticence had balanced Bingley's natural exuberance; it was a relationship that worked well for them both and followed into their military careers.

Darcy shook his head brusquely. He could feel his precision lagging as he pulled back from his daydreaming. Bank left, roll right. He held the stick just a little tighter and felt the metal, hot and slippery in his hand. It was hot. The cockpit was always hot, regardless of the external temperature, and as he pulled his damp flight suit away from his sticky chest, he smelled the musk of his sweat. It would be even hotter at Meryton. Hotter than Pemberley, to be sure. Possibly hotter than Hell itself, if his friends were to be believed.

On the upside, at Meryton, he would be able to go home to Pemberley occasionally as Meryton was near an airport and the ops tempo was significantly lower. As an instructor, he would be able to enjoy holidays, a luxury he had not experienced in the last four years; he might even be able to get other leave approved for once. Hawaii was too far to go home often and when he did go, he just depressed himself. Georgiana deserved more than a brother who moped around the house, seeing ghosts around every bend, and hearing voices that could no longer be heard. Besides, he missed Mrs. Reynolds' meals. He added "Enjoy a glass of Pemberley cabernet franc" to his moving checklist.

"Tower, this is Fitz 27. Request five-mile initial for the overhead."

"Fitz 27, this is Tower…" Darcy listened and noted the vectors to begin his landing. After breaking, he threw down his landing gear and banked right, watching his speedometer and began to slow to two hundred and fifty knots after breaking over the numbers.

"Fitz 27 in the Break." Darcy spoke clearly into the mic, adjusting the mask slightly closer to his lips in an effort to maintain clarity for the air traffic controllers watching the field.

"Fitz 27 Clear to Land," the tower replied through the scratchy radio.

"Roger. Clear to Land."

Darcy snapped the aircraft right again and applied the slightest of back pressures to the stick continuing his turn through the perch. He crossed the runway at fifty feet and grimaced as he felt the thud of a harder than usual landing. He pushed on the brakes and began his taxi to park. The runway was smooth, and he felt the muscles of his long legs flex as he steered toward the hangar.

Per tradition, with his last flight in the F-22, his squadron would be waiting for him with ice water and champagne, ready to dump it over him in celebration before his move. He was not ready for the fini-flight celebration and began to recite another checklist to calm his rising anxieties. *Smile during taxi to park.* He promptly raised the corners of his mouth into what he hoped was a look of glee. *Check. Take everything important out of flight suit pockets: check. Done before even leaving for the flight.*

The plane slowed and stopped smoothly while the air traffic marshaller crossed his arms in front of him signaling the stop. Next to the controller, a tall teenage girl echoed his movements, blonde hair blowing in the morning breeze. Darcy's plastered smile grew as his lips turned into a real grin when he recognized his sister, Georgiana. As she crossed her arms in front of her chest, he put the brake on and stopped the plane's rolling.

His flight stood with pressurized water hoses, coolers, and champagne bottles at the ready. He threw off his belts, helmet, and mask and opened the cockpit. As he stepped onto the ladder, the deluge started. The other pilots laughed and hooted in celebration. He closed his eyes to the onslaught of water and champagne and blindly stumbled down the ladder to the runway.

Shouts assaulted his ears while the pressured veins of water stung his skin beneath his flight suit.

"Fitz!"

"Darcy, you call that a landing?"

"Don't spray the cockpit!"

"Hooray!"

"Fitz!"

"William!" His teenager sister's voice rose out amongst the tumult.

Darcy ran toward Georgiana and as Darcy reached her, he felt the cool, sticky flood of champagne down the neck of his flight suit. Her thin frame was crushed and soaked by his hug. The cascade continued, sending chills down his spine and his legs and into his boots. The sweet smell of the alcohol mixed with his sweat and Georgiana's perfume. He released her and turned to his cousin and was grasped in a bear hug.

"Richard!" Darcy's shout was muffled over the water spray and ear-piercing shouts.

The two men laughed, Darcy patting the back of his shorter cousin. The hug was interrupted by Georgiana jumping on his back as he grabbed her legs and spun her around. Onlookers clapped and cheered at the small family's overt affection.

"You have a real career in air marshalling, G," Darcy said while lowering Georgiana to the ground.

Richard performed large sweeping hand motions in a teasing echo. "All those dance classes really paid off. Glad to see Will's money wasn't spent in vain."

Georgiana blushed. "I can follow directions. It's not that hard. Besides, I've never been allowed to do it before, so I was just excited they would let me even try."

Darcy shook hands with his flight mates amidst the revelry.

"Good luck, Fitz."

"Better you than me, old man."

"If you see Hammock there in Meryton, tell him 'hi' for me, would you? He's great to get a drink with. I think he's in the 15th so you'll have to keep an eye out for him."

"Next time we gas up at Randolph over a weekend, I'll give you a call!"

A helpful lieutenant took a group photo of the soaked but smiling faces, and Darcy escorted Richard and Georgiana back across the privileged-access runways. The rest of the squadron drove golf-carts and maintenance trucks and travelled quickly back to the unremarkable brick squadron building.

"Rich, I had no idea you would be here! How on earth did you swing it?" Darcy looked at Lieutenant Colonel Richard Fitzwilliam with a gleam in his eye. He noted Richard's short auburn hair stuck up in a variety of interesting directions from the sticky champagne and cold spray.

"I had a little *use or lose* leave left, stopped by Mom and Dad's, grabbed Georgie, and flew here. It was a near thing. We almost missed our connection in LA."

Timid and mouse-like, but exuberant, Georgiana said, "Will, you should have seen us! We were running all through the terminals. I thought for sure we would pass out before the second one. We were wicked fast. I love to fly, but if I never go through LAX again, it will be too soon."

"Oh, Fitz—"

"Richard, you know I hate that nickname." Darcy grimaced and rolled his eyes toward the heavens. Georgiana giggled as she looked between the two.

"Fitzwilliam is a perfectly fine nickname. Besides, Mom loves it."

"She loves it because... She thinks it's cute." Darcy sighed.

"It is pretty cute." Richard pinched Darcy's cheeks as Darcy pulled away, smacking his hands, despite also carrying flight bags and his helmet.

Georgiana jumped in. "You are pretty cute, Fitz..." She burst into a fit of squeaking giggles.

Richard's grin grew wider before sighing. "Anyway, Mom and Dad say 'hello' and I'm supposed to tell you that they think you should hurry up and get married so they have the hope of seeing a new generation of Fitzwilliam children before they die. I do believe they have finally given up on me."

Richard was good-looking enough, if not handsome: dark auburn hair, green eyes with an ever-present hint of mischief, and a stocky build. He never seemed to lack a date but never seemed to want to settle down either. With his elder brother Preston's marriage to a woman who does not want to have children, Richard was Aunt and Uncle Fitzwilliam's only chance at grandchildren.

7

Inwardly, Darcy frowned despite his outward smiles. He would love to find someone to share his life with. He had been lost after his parents died; and a lasting love while in the military was difficult. Besides, Darcy could not fathom even *introducing* any of the women he had met to his younger sister. "Well, I'll work on that"—tossing a flight bag at Richard's head—"and maybe I'll just mail-order one. Do they still do that sort of thing?"

"Are you excited about your new station?" Richard asked.

"Meryton? It's not my number one pick, but I suppose it will be okay. I'll be on the mainland, but I'm not looking forward to teaching know-it-alls who have never even been near a big boy plane, let alone in one." Darcy clenched the straps on his bag as he picked it back up and swiped his security tag against the panel that opened the large, grey metal door.

"You mean know-it-all brats, like you?" Richard winked quickly at Georgiana and rushed down the stark hallway before Darcy could respond.

CHAPTER 2

*E*lizabeth Bennet smoothed her hands down her starched camouflage ABUs once more and reached absently to the pins in her brunette hair, exhaling nervously. Again, she rehearsed what she would say, muttering under her breath. Putting her hand on the large, wooden door, she paused, stretched out as tall as her petite frame would allow, and walked in.

"Major Warby, sir," Elizabeth said crisply.

The major did not look up from the papers on his desk, his hand hovering over one particular sheet, and staring back at his computer. Over his slouched frame, she could see the top of his bald head reflecting the cheap fluorescent office lighting.

"Major Warby?" To her dismay, Elizabeth's voice lilted higher in question.

The major let out a noisy sigh and looked up, rolling his eyes as he did so. As he rustled the papers on his desk, tiny dust particles danced into the air.

"Hmm?" He grunted the question. Elizabeth hated when men grunted that way. They tended to do it a lot to her. And sighed. The sigh, especially, was always a sign she had disappointed them. The difficulty was however, she could never figure out *precisely* what she had done to offend. She persevered, thinking it would be best to have this sorry excuse for an interview over with.

"Sir, I've shredded and replaced the regulation binders as you asked. It took a little while because it was difficult to find all of the appropriate AFI's for each flight when no one could tell me where the binders were exactly. You should be ready for inspection next week."

"Thanks." Major Warby grunted his response and gave her a bored look that seemed to politely invite her to get the hell out. She stepped forward, fidgeting, but ventured forth regardless.

"Sir, is there any other work I can complete?" She hoped against hope that there would be a task, *anything*, for her to do. Elizabeth Bennet hated to be idle. She was a useful sort of person who thrived in activity and one more day of mediocrity might just kill her.

"Bennet, look"—Major Warby spoke to her like he spoke to his three-year-old at the last Family Day picnic—"You're in *casual* status. Do you know what *casual* lieutenants do?"

"Yes sir. They complete all work assigned to them and are available to their commanders for additional assignments as needed. Sir." The sarcastic answer dripped from her lips before she could stop herself, so she smiled as she spoke to ensure it sounded more polite than she felt.

"Bennet. That was a lovely book answer, but really, do you know what you guys do?"

"Umm." Elizabeth glanced at the white-painted cinderblock wall to her left and saw the clock ticking. She could almost hear its silent taunting.

"Bennet." Elizabeth could hear the sigh as he said her name. "You wait. That's it. Nobody cares about what you do or don't do because you don't have a real job. You just sit around waiting for your slot to come up. Now, can I do anything for you or are you just here to distract me from what I'm trying to finish before I can go home and have a drink?" He punctuated his question by raising his eyebrows, the wrinkles on his forehead becoming deep creases.

"No, sir. I'm sorry to have bothered you. I'll just go sit at scheduling in case you need me."

The major grunted in reply as Elizabeth exited, letting the door slam behind her. Her boots squeaked as she strode down the dull, tile floors. Oh, but she was bored. The assignment the major had given her had taken her two days. Two whole days that she was not sitting, bored, at the scheduling desk waiting for life to happen to her.

She turned left down the hall and looked at her favorite picture in the squadron. It was small and in a cheap, plain black frame, but she loved it. A loaded A-10 aircraft flying right above the cloud line where she could see the colors of the clouds. Most people thought clouds were big, white puffy cotton balls in the sky, but Elizabeth Bennet knew better. Clouds were a million colors: white and pale yellow with streaks of bright cerulean and cornflower blues, sparkling like pearls in the sunshine or darken in a sinister instant. This picture somehow captured what Elizabeth was so anxious to see for herself.

Elizabeth had only ever had one dream. She wanted to fly. When she was eight, she wanted to bend her legs, jump, and take off swirling through the skies. When she was twelve, she met a pilot during career day at school and decided to do everything she could to become one. She worked hard and blasted through her classes as fast as she could. And now, here she was, not quite twenty-one...and stagnant. Stuck as a casual lieutenant in a squadron that did not care whether she showed up to work or not. Elizabeth took another long look at the painting and sighed. She hated to wait.

SWEET GLISTENED as it collected on Elizabeth's temples. Her

gait adjusted as she swept damp hair out of her eyes and off her forehead. Elizabeth focused her breath and lengthened her stride down her favorite path to Oakham Mount. The little path up the hill was lined with trees shimmering in the sun. Leaves rustling softly in the breeze, the shade shielded Elizabeth as she padded rhythmically on the trail and let her mind wander.

Elizabeth's training start date was only a week away and she was filled with nervous excitement. She would need to find somewhere in town to study. Living with her parents at their bed and breakfast during training was great for her wallet but not for learning to fly.

The property had been in her family's possession for over one hundred years. The original land holdings had been home to more than five thousand head of sheep and goats during the area's wool and mohair boom. The land had been largely profitable until the 1960s when prices plummeted, and Elizabeth's grandfather was forced to sell off all but fifty of the home place acres. The home and outbuildings ran into disrepair until Mr. and Mrs. Bennet had renovated and opened the Longbourn Inn. Mrs. Bennet, known for her polished ability to entertain, doubled as party planner and chef, ensuring that no one left hungry. The main house, of course, was inhabited by the seven Bennets, but the outlying buildings had all been converted into various suites for guests. Longbourn was always full to bursting, either with guests or with any number of the twenty-four prominent families of Meryton.

Her sisters would always be difficult to study around; with four sisters, there was never a quiet moment in the house. Jane, the eldest, would be her greatest ally, willing to help her outside of her work schedule. As the most perfect example of both decorum and service, Jane had already announced she was willing to help Elizabeth study, make flash cards, and quiz her, for which Elizabeth was eternally grateful. She was not likely to get help from most of her flight of ten male pilots. Between being somewhat precocious—and a woman—she was almost guaranteed to be placed into one of two slots: amazing or awful. There was very little for women in between and she did not plan on being *awful*. Excellence would require more precision and devotion than her flight mates, and she knew it.

Mary, the most serious of all her sisters, had also stated that she would dedicate some time to her cause, but Elizabeth was loath to spend that much time with Mary's preaching. Mary loved the Bible and she loved music. Unfortunately for Mary, she was awful expressing either. Her piano, though well-practiced, always sounded strangled. Her Bible was not only often misquoted, but quoted so often that it was universally ignored. However, Mary's attention to detail had made her an important cog in the running of Longbourn as she was best able to coordinate services and attend to guests' tacit needs. These strengths could be an asset, but her personality made the point almost moot.

Elizabeth knew she could never count on Kitty or Lydia to be serious for more than thirty seconds at a time, and thus, had not even asked for their help. Elizabeth excused their behavior, remembering how at seventeen and eighteen, only time—and parents who took them in hand—would temper her youngest sisters into something resembling sense.

Her parents *could* possibly be of greater assistance, but Elizabeth knew they would not. Elizabeth's mother, covered in flour and frequently nervous, tittered about the house, but was an asset when it came to helping her daughters, especially if it involved handsome, young men in flight suits. Fanny Bennet was nearly mercenary when it came to requisitioning suitable husbands for her daughters to take care of them financially and ensure that Fanny could happily enjoy a long retirement—preferably on cruises featuring older morning talk show hosts or Barry Manilow impersonators.

Thomas Bennet, on the other hand, was a scholarly man and though he valued the solitude of his office and the friendship of a good book, he looked to the day his girls moved away with dread.

Jane and Elizabeth were undoubtedly his favorites but even the three younger girls brought life and effervescence into his home. He could only look on the day of their weddings and eventual departure with a sense of despondency.

Elizabeth had long known she was her father's favorite. Jane was always with her mother, demurely following directions while Elizabeth was wildly climbing trees and scraping her knees. Her father raised her as the son he never had. When she was little, he told her exciting tales about Chuck Yeager, Buzz Aldrin, and Gus Grissom while the rest of her sisters listened to *Cinderella* and *Sleeping Beauty*. As she got older, Mr. Bennet added the un-princess stories of Susan B. Anthony, Amelia Earhart, and Sally Ride while her sisters danced with Snow White and tamed a beast. Elizabeth often wondered about the differences in their bedtime stories. *Maybe that's why Lydia and Kitty are so ridiculous? If they only heard tales in which the princess did nothing but sit and wait for a prince to rescue her, wouldn't they emulate that behavior? That doesn't necessarily explain their total lack of rules or respect, though. Jane is well-behaved, but then, Jane had the most princess material to work with. And if anyone in the family could convince a squirrel to do the dishes, it would be Jane.*

Despite his vast intelligence and quick wit, Mr. Bennet was a lackadaisical parent. He had allowed her the use of his office during busy times at the inn and, for him, that required monumental effort.

With a stitch in her side, Elizabeth stopped to catch her breath, her hands on her knees. *You can do this crazy thing.* Pilot training should be a breeze even with the challenges she would face. Her town loved "Home Grown Heroes" and she was eager to begin flying, achieving her dreams. *Maybe I'll get my own "Elizabeth Bennet Day" like the silver medalist bobsledder a few years ago.* Snickering at the thought, she took a deep breath, picked up her pace again, and felt relaxed for the first time in weeks

CHAPTER 3

*T*he blue Volvo jolted as Darcy made his way down the dusty road that was lined on both sides by deep ditches and wire fencing. After nearly a mile, an avenue of cottonwood trees graced the roadside, their shiny leaves, not yet touched by autumn's magic, reflected the sunlight even while they threw the road into shadow. A shabby white sign proclaimed he had arrived at Netherfield Ranch and the farmhouse rose into view.

A two-story brick house with blue shutters on the windows and a large wrap-around porch loomed over the large driveway. Bingley's truck and also a two-seater were parked near a neat, white fence and a grass-covered yard. A small gate led to the walk and the front door.

Darcy stepped from his car and took off his aviators. He squinted and covered his eyes as the brilliant fall sun glared down on him, covering the dirt driveway with golden rays. He glanced at the house in front of him and inhaled deeply. Smells of the earth, grass, trees, and animals filled him. It was not Pemberley, but it might do for a brief spell at this awful base.

Netherfield Ranch was an operating ranch with a few hundred cattle, chickens, horses, and the occasional show goat. When

Charles Bingley had driven to Meryton to "window shop" for possible rental homes, he had found the small house "quaint" and thought the land "intriguing." Ignoring Darcy's concerns about time management with his military duties and unsolicited advice to cease listening to idyllic Louis L'Amour audiobooks, Charles Bingley had found an Ag major from the local community college, hired him as land manager, and put down the rental deposit before Darcy had even reluctantly agreed to be housemates.

Bingley was full of his picturesque visions of running a ranch from Darcy's stories of Pemberley, the winery and other extensive property owned and operated by the Darcy family. Bingley had asked Darcy to teach him the ins and outs of owning and operating land. Bingley was a city boy, born and bred, but he wanted nothing more in life than to buy some land out in the country and raise a family, trying his hand as a gentleman farmer. While Pemberley was technically being run day to day by an operating board, Darcy continued to be highly involved in the business decisions and could not see how to tell Bingley he could not help. With few deployments and only short cross countries, there would be time to get their hands dirty. After mulling the matter over, Darcy determined that it would be better for Bingley to drink from the fire hose of agriculture business knowledge than have too little information and kill everything on the land. Besides, he missed the country after being crammed into a cramped house in a congested city with the one million other residents of Honolulu.

"Darcy!"

Darcy looked up and saw Bingley walking towards him with arms outstretched. He closed the car door and grasped Bingley's hand in a firm handshake.

"It's been a long time! How are you, old man?" Bingley clutched Darcy's hand and slapped his arm in greeting.

"As well as can be expected, I suppose." Darcy said flatly, glancing at his old friend. Bingley's red hair was blowing in the gentle breeze, looking more like the fire Darcy felt rather than the easy calm Bingley exuded.

"Come on, Fitz, it can't be that bad. Your stuff arrived last week. We got it all put in your room. And you're here now. What can possibly be better?" Bingley smiled as he rambled on.

"You know I hate that nickname, and what do you mean, *we?*" Darcy glared sideways at his friend.

"Need any help with your bags?" Bingley quickly popped open Darcy's trunk.

"Bingley, what do you mean *we?*"

"Is it just this one?" Bingley grunted as he lifted the large, blue suitcase out of the trunk and began wheeling it toward the front door.

"Bingley... *We* who?" Darcy put out his arm to stop Bingley's progression.

"Well, you see, Darce, I couldn't just leave her..." Bingley looked down at his dust covered shoes.

"Do you mean to say that Caroline is here?" Darcy's face was a mask, but Bingley knew him well enough to know that a lack of expression could only mean one thing: Darcy was irritated.

"Well, I needed someone to keep house for me, and Caroline just graduated and is out of school and doesn't have any job prospects yet. Mom and Dad are on their cruise—"

"Oh yeah, I forgot they were doing the year-long QE2 thing. How is that going?"

"Queen Mary 2. QE2 was retired a few years ago. They're doing great, I think. Every email I get mentions whatever awful white wine was available at the Duty Free store. Certainly not what they've been used to since knowing you and getting all the good Pemberley Riesling. I suppose drinking their way through famous tourist destinations of the world was the plan, so I'm sure they deem it a success."

"And Caroline can't stay at their house because?"

"Mom's renovating. So, I thought she might stay with us for a few, and Louisa and Hurst are in the Hamptons until after Christmas and you know how much Hurst hates Caroline. When I happened to mention that you were coming to share the house with me, she said she would love to come and—"

"Bingley, you know how I feel about Caroline."

Caroline Bingley had been chasing Darcy since they had met; at first a simple flirtation, but it had escalated quickly into predatory, guerilla warfare. Caroline had been invited to Pemberley one Christmas with Bingley. After that incredibly trying holiday, Caroline continued to throw herself at Darcy. She had plied him with homemade treats, dominated conversations to ensure he spoke to her, insinuated to others that they were dating, came to his room at night, and arranged times when they would be alone, which he had learned to assiduously avoid.

Darcy was exhausted of his frequent run-ins with Caroline's antics and her insatiable appetite for his company ruined what once might have been a friendship. Instead, their relationship was best defined by the covetous, monopolizing conversation of Caroline and Darcy's inattentive silence.

"I know, I know. She's awful, but just think of it this way. We will always have a clean house and home-cooked meals."

"I can cook."

Bingley put his hands together into the universal gesture for begging.

Pinching the bridge of his nose, Darcy sighed. "Bingley, as long as you know I can't stand your sister, and keep her out of my way, I guess its fine." Darcy was greeted by a wide smile.

"Excellent! We'll have a great time. Tonight, we were invited to the current class's Drop Night, so we can go and scout out some new friends and neighbors."

Darcy rolled his eyes at Bingley's inability to handle his sister before taking two large strides to open the heavy farm door. *Thank goodness, Georgiana is easier to manage.*

"Darcy? Is that you?" Caroline Bingley peered into the hallway wearing a bright orange Tennessee Vols t-shirt and jeans.

"Hello, Caroline," Darcy said gruffly. "Bingley, where did you say my room was?"

"Oh! I'll show you. I have it all set up for you. I don't want you to think I would let my brother loose in an old house like this. It would probably fall down around our ears without my help. Besides, I wouldn't want you to think me a poor hostess." Caroline grabbed Darcy's arm, letting her hand slide down to his hand and led him down the hallway.

Darcy extricated himself from Caroline's clinging grasp and grabbed his suitcase. He turned around to roll his eyes to the ceiling before crinkling his nose at Bingley who responded with a shameless smile and two thumbs up.

Caroline prattled all the way up the stairs, discussing the finer points of the home including some curtains she had purchased and showing him different rooms along the way.

"Here is the guest room, like for sweet Georgiana if she comes. How is she? She hasn't answered my text from last week... Obviously, we don't have the views we did back East, but there's nothing I can do about that. That door there is Charles'. And this here is my room." Caroline pointed to a room with a wide, open door. Darcy peeked in and immediately wished he still wore his sunglasses. Vermillion décor and the smell of cinnamon, wafting out of the room, nearly choked him.

"Here is your room! I hope you like it. I went through your boxes and got the bed set up for you." Caroline fluffed a throw pillow he had never seen before then turned back to Darcy with a pageant queen smile plastered across her face.

Darcy, refusing to imagine Caroline creeping through his things, placed his suitcase on the bed without looking and somehow managing to keep his tone free from annoyance: "Uh, thanks." He pointed toward the door indicating she should leave, and as soon as she cleared the room, he shut and locked the door.

Alone, at last. Darcy made quick work of unpacking and going through his remaining boxes. Looking out the window, he decided he was grateful for this opportunity to live outside of town. Longbourn seemed small and quaint. With less than ten thousand people, it boasted only a few stores and no large chains. He would have to travel three hours to San Antonio if he wanted anything of real quality, but he enjoyed the city's hometown feel.

Netherfield was certainly no Pemberley, but the house seemed to be in good repair and he was excited to go out with Bingley on his next day off to inspect the fields and fences. He loved his job and he loved flying, but he lived for the bucolic life. He longed to be home, riding through pastures and smelling the earth in the dew of the morning. He missed the birds chirping and wind whispering through the fields. On second thought, he was lucky Bingley was so spontaneous and had thought to rent out here.

A knock interrupted his reverie, and Caroline's cloying voice invited him down to dinner. Looking back at his sanctuary, he briefly considered hiding the rest of the night, but ultimately, stirred himself to join his housemates.

CHAPTER 4

*a*fter taking a shower, Elizabeth sat down to relax and attempt to read a book. The sounds of her parents bickering, her youngest sisters fighting, and Mary practicing the piano assaulted her ears. Elizabeth lounged in her favorite over-stuffed chair, one leg draped over the arm of the chair while the other leg was propped up on a coffee table. Jane sat across from her on the couch, ankles neatly crossed, flipping through a magazine in her lap.

"Thomas, we simply must go tonight!" Elizabeth's mother shrieked from the family dining table as she set out the dinner plates.

Elizabeth's father strolled into the room and planted himself firmly in his high back arm chair. "Fanny, it is my understanding that it is still a free country and I am privileged to not be required to do anything. That freedom gladly includes the freedom from attending social events that I despise." Thomas smiled at the scene of relaxed feminine bliss around him and picked up a newspaper.

"Where do we have to go?" Looking up, Mary ceased her plucking at the piano.

Fanny Bennet was a determined sort of woman. She had grown up in the South and could best be described as a debutante who never moved on past her cotillion. Raised on manners and fried pickles, her focus was getting her girls married and building the perfect home with the best food in the county. She had a short, plump frame and her white-streaked curls shook as she glared at her husband with indignation.

"Thomas, you know perfectly well that your influence on the base allows us to go to these events and that we can't go if you don't. I don't know why they never see fit to put my name on the invitations. Couldn't you call security forces and put my name on the list instead of yours? My contributions here are every bit as valuable, after all. Don't you care about your daughters' futures? Don't you have compassion for my feelings?" Mrs. Bennet's ample curves jiggled as she stomped her foot on the carpeted floor. The sound dampened to nothing. "Nonsense, Fanny. I have every compassion for these feelings of yours. They've been married to me as long as you have." Mr. Bennet winked at Elizabeth who smirked and giggled lightly at the joke.

"Daddy, we're going, aren't we?" Elizabeth's youngest sister, Lydia, spoke up, her alto voice rising high as she almost whined the question.

"Where are we going?" Mary once again raised her voice to be heard but was ignored.

"Dad, I heard there are a few new instructors coming in this week. Maybe we could meet one and then marry them and move away!" Kitty tremored as she spoke, whether from excitement or in excessive punctuation to her statement, no one could be sure. Eighteen-year-old Kitty and the seventeen-year-old Lydia covered their mouths, leaned close, and descended into conspiratorial whispers as to exactly where in the world they would move if given the chance, their words accentuated by high-pitched giggling.

"Because a single pilot must be in want of a wife." Elizabeth jested and watched her father's newspaper quiver as he chortled from his hiding place.

"Why anyone would want to date an instructor pilot is beyond my comprehension." Pointing her chin at the two youngest—"I guess we are going somewhere on base if those two can't control themselves," Mary said glumly, returning to her piano stool.

"Just because you don't have a spark of adventure, doesn't mean we don't." Lydia stuck her tongue out and Kitty copied.

"Besides, who doesn't love a forty-inch zipper?" Kitty murmured.

"Girls!" Mrs. Bennet clucked, all the while, looking fondly at her two youngest who seemed energized by the prospect of hand-some young men in long-zippered flight suits. She wiped her hands over her apron, clearly daydreaming too, before Jane caught Elizabeth's eyes and looked to the heavens.

"Are we going, Dad?" Jane asked.

"Of course, we're going. I've had the tickets to Drop Night for days. And Kitty is right. There are a few new IPs for you girls to moon over." Mr. Bennet smiled and stood up. "If anyone needs me, I'll be in my office, working on something far less silly than anything happening in here."

The girls laughed while the room's noise level increased a hundred-fold. Mrs. Bennet pouted just a little at the tease before bursting into laughter in anticipation of the party that night. Mrs. Bennet quickly began directing the traffic of her daughters as they moved about the house doing their daily chores for the inn. Lydia and Kitty chattered as they went to search each room for items guests left behind and refitted each room with fresh linens and towels. Mary dutifully cleaned the bathrooms while listening to self-improvement podcasts. Elizabeth cleaned the common areas and made some small repairs in one of the guest rooms. Jane greeted the new arrivals and checked them in at the front desk. As soon as the tasks were completed, the sound of five girls deciding what they were going to wear, borrowing each other's clothes, and bargaining with each other for makeup or longer showers, rose in a crescendo until they left for the Meryton Officer's Club.

~

THE OFFICER'S CLUB, a remnant of the former glory days of the military, when enlisted and officer personnel were separated by rank, was made of the same utilitarian brown brick as every other building on base. The only differentiating characteristics of the club were a round covered driveway in front of the double entry doors and a long, rectangular parking lot to the side of the building that was either packed full or completely empty, depending on the occasion.

When the Bennets arrived, the party was in full swing. After handing their tickets to the staff, Mr. Bennet led the female Bennets through the doors to the main ballroom where they were met with loud music blaring over the speakers and the hum of small groups. A large projector in the front of the room presented a loop of a variety of aircraft and the current flight in their uniforms in both official pictures or candids around town. Several rows of utilitarian metal folding chairs were arranged around the projection screen and the standing bar was set up in the back of the room.

Behind the bar, large decorative mugs with names of pilots, long since moved on, were lined up on rows of wooden shelves. The walls to the left and right of the bar were covered in old class patches and patches from when the base only housed combat squadrons. Flights from yesteryear were forever memorialized in five-inch-wide Velcro squares glued to the wall. Several pictures of the planes that flew from Meryton interspersed among the patches told a history of the base and its role in former battles. Memorials to fallen soldiers and a large Prisoner of War flag also brought bitter remembrance that all missions do not safely arrive home.

The Drop Night guests wandered about in various attire. The

honoree flight wore their flight suits and an impressive variety of brightly colored plastic fedoras atop their heads and sequined gloves on their hands as part of the 'Eighties Dance Off theme. Instructor pilots and student pilots wore flight suits, if they were late getting off work, or casual civilian shorts and t-shirts, if they were able to change at home. The women, mostly spouses and girlfriends, wore everything from cute dresses and high heels to jean shorts and tank tops. Children of all ages ran through the room, their laughter ringing through the dull roar of a hundred people. The vast array of dress styles and participants made Drop Nights special. Graduations, Awards, and other assemblies on base required pressed uniforms and a firm code of conduct, but Drop Nights were a celebration and the evening reflected it.

Elizabeth and Jane stuck together as their parents greeted other local business owners including their aunt Evelyn and uncle Jonathon and training class sponsors. Mary, not one for idle gossip and too efficient a person to participate in small talk, sat down in a row, pulled out a Bible study, and began her evening evangelical studies. Lydia and Kitty immediately found someone in a green flight suit and began outrageously flirting. Lydia modulating her voice into what she likely thought a coy simper, flipped her hair from side to side, loudly elaborating on her upcoming eighteenth birthday plans. Kitty interrupted every few sentences and attempted to draw each pilot into a discussion on the various planes on the screen. She tried hard to impress, squinting her eyes and creasing her forehead as she called each plane the wrong number and could never remember which base was which, alienating each pilot quickly. While some men took their bait, others seemed to realize quickly that their age did not lend itself to equal maturity.

Elizabeth, tired of wearing her uniform and doing nothing all day, had come casually dressed in a flowing white shirt and jeans and her favorite silver sequined ballet flats. Her brunette hair was pulled into a high ponytail, a remnant of her afternoon run and the cold shower after her four sisters. Arm in arm with the blonde Jane, Elizabeth looked around the room for her best friend, Charlotte.

Charlotte Lucas was the daughter of Meryton's former wing commander, William Lucas who after his retirement, had decided to stay in town. He was a bit of a local celebrity having formally met the Queen of England during a Royal Air Force ceremony. After repeating the story at multiple graduations and during an interview with the local paper, a legend was born. Military members and residents alike had begun referring to him as Sir William.

Charlotte was finally found standing near Sir William, listening to him regale yet another new trainee with the story of being at Court. "Lizzy! I didn't realize you were coming tonight!" Charlotte held out her hands to clasp Elizabeth's.

"Yeah, Dad got tickets and after listening to Mom whine for an hour, here we are." Elizabeth shrugged and pointed at Jane who nodded her agreement.

"Have you heard if anyone is getting an exciting Drop?" Jane's lyrical voice asked while looking about the room. Weeks before, each student had submitted their dream sheet which listed what plane they wanted to fly and what base they would like to go to and tonight they would learn of their "Drop." The students' excitement for finally learning their fate was palpable.

"No, nothing really. Remember Snell? He supposedly is getting KC-10s to Travis," Charlotte said, sighing, obviously wishing for some excitement.

"Exactly what he wanted. That is nice." Jane, who had a sweeter than honey demeanor and never thought anything but the best about anyone, was truly excited for Lieutenant Snell. He had wanted to fly the big tanker jets in California for as long as he had been in training. Jane had gone out with him a few times after college before becoming a teacher at the local elementary school, and she knew how hard he had worked in order to deserve his new assignment.

"Lydia and Kitty said there were some new IPs, is that true?" Elizabeth queried after nodding her agreement that Snell would be happy.

"Oh, there are a few new instructors! Two cute ones! You can see them over there." Charlotte pointed just as the crowd around them parted to reveal a tall, dark man and another, somewhat shorter ginger.

"Do they have names, or should we get out duck calls and see if they respond?" Elizabeth asked slyly, her eyes meeting Charlotte's and gleaming with mischief.

"The one on the left is Charles Bingley, a new captain with the T-6's, I believe, and on the right is his sister, Caroline."

Elizabeth glanced again, having not noticed any women. On her toes, she observed a red pony tail and a violently orange shirt.

"Yikes," she said, raising her eyebrows while Charlotte snickered. "And on the left?"

"His friend, Captain Darcy."

"He looks miserable, poor man." Elizabeth grimaced as she saw the captain scowl at his surroundings, his brow drawn and his neck straight.

"He might be miserable but certainly not poor." Charlotte leaned in conspiratorially and continued. "Apparently, his family owns half of the East Coast and the Pemberley Winery. Someone told me he was a distinguished graduate from every program he's taken and was brought in by special request of the commander."

"The Commander of Misery?" Elizabeth broke in with a grin.

Elizabeth, Jane, and Charlotte descended into a fit of laughter as Sir William shushed them, ushering them toward the chairs.

"Good evening!" The emcee spoke heavily into the microphone before backing off a bit to temper the volume. "Welcome to Drop Night, the highlight of everyone's pilot training time here at Meryton. As most of you know, the flight is split from the T-38 fighter trainer who will hopefully be assigned to their favorite fighter jet and the T-1 trainer who will receive a tanker or cargo plane. Both are awesome, so let's get ready to cheer!"

The crowd let out a cheer and raised their drinks. The three friends sat down in the middle of the room as the lights flashed to quiet the crowd and start the program. Drop Nights were always full of laughs, a few earth-shattering disappointments, and a few surprises. Each student pilot was called up one by one, roasted by their friends, and then presented with their first assigned base and plane. Elizabeth knew most of this class—from her time sitting bored at scheduling—and loudly cheered and jeered with the rest of the audience.

Elizabeth enjoyed seeing her friends separate from the class and stand next to their name and picture on the screen. Each pilot received a story of introduction, typically raunchy, and a nickname presented to the audience. The group waited with bated breath as the emcee would announce the location and plane. During Snell's turn, Elizabeth watched his look of surprise when the KC-10, a large tanker plane, flashed on the screen. Snell exploded with excitement and was tackled by four of his friends. The dogpile of flight suits on the ground writhed as they tried to get up, made somewhat more difficult by their slightly inebriated state.

After the fifteen graduating pilots received their assignments and were all a little worse for wear, the Drop Night's official festivities were over, and the large party recommenced. The smell of beer and spirits surrounded the crowd and the thrumming bass of the electronic 'Eighties music could be heard rhythmically throughout the room. Most happily participated in general carousing, drinking, swaying to the music, and enjoying the occasion. Elizabeth felt a detachment from her fellow pilots. She had few friends outside her own class. Even her classmates froze in conversation *if their girlfriends or wives were nearby.* The women ostracized her for being a pilot, unable to talk about the latest manicure styles in town or engagement rings. Some of the men resented her taking another man's spot. But she could not allow it to phase her. She put on a smile and resolved to enjoy her evening.

Soon after, the red-haired Bingley politely introduced himself to all three, but it seemed he only had eyes for Jane. He stammered as he asked to buy her a drink and followed her closely to the bar, his hand hovered protectively over, but never touching, the small of her back. To anyone observing him, it was plain Bingley was firmly besotted before they had finished sipping their first drinks.

With Jane thoroughly occupied with the engaging Captain Bingley, Charlotte and Elizabeth fell into a lull.

"Seems like it was a good Drop," Charlotte said.

"Mm-hmm."

"Bingley seems nice."

"Jane certainly thinks so."

"I wonder if Adams will enjoy Creech. You said he liked Las Vegas, right?"

It was at this point that Sir William tapped Elizabeth on the shoulder to introduce the new officer to the women.

"Captain Darcy, Caroline Bingley, may I introduce you to Lieutenant Elizabeth Bennet, a student in class 18-13, and my own daughter Charlotte, of course, you've met."

"Very nice to meet you both." Elizabeth extended her hand to shake Caroline Bingley's. Captain Darcy however had already turned to follow his friend. Elizabeth noted the snub but hid her embarrassment with an awkward high-five to Charlotte. Caroline excused herself and followed Darcy.

Caroline Bingley, in Elizabeth's brief observation, appeared incapable of cheer. Caroline squinted her eyes at the décor and crinkled her nose when Lydia and Kitty ran past, laughing boisterously. The tall, raven-haired Darcy did not talk to anyone. He hovered near the wall and looked over the gathering, clearly unimpressed by the "locals." He did not smile and did not frown; he simply looked. His expression was unapproachable, unfriendly, and intimidating and soon the crowd around him accepted him as part of the wall and ignored him.

Charlotte and Elizabeth enjoyed drinks with some of their friends and some of the new pilots and instructors who also attended. Caroline hovered near Darcy and both appeared busy looking down their noses on the entire body of guests. Elizabeth and Charlotte were not left to their own devices long, soon they were approached by an enthusiastic Charles Bingley holding Jane's hand, leading her back to her sister.

"Come grab a drink with us, Lizzy!" Jane said, her eyes pointing obviously at the hand holding hers and back at Elizabeth, a wide grin appeared on her face.

"What can I get you, ladies?"

"White wine," said Jane.

"I'd love a Tom Collins," said Charlotte.

"Okay, wine, Collins. And Elizabeth? Anything for you?"

"If they aren't busy, a mojito, but if they are, then just a beer would be great."

After Bingley left to order the drinks, Charlotte was the first to speak.

"He seems very nice, Jane. He was sweet when he came over to introduce himself a few days ago. Even Maria was entertained. You know how she is normally so shy, but he just brought her right out of her shell. It was nice to see."

"He just asked me questions the whole time. I feel like I still don't know anything about him."

"What kind of questions? Questions like, 'Are you free next Saturday?'"

"Just about where I work, and he loved hearing the stories about the kids. He asked where we lived and, when I pointed out Mom and Dad, he asked all about the inn and if I liked it. It was nice. Most guys spend so much time talking about themselves— he's a nice change of pace."

"That's because most of the guys you date have to be focused on training over everything else."

"Obviously, Lizzy, but Jane should have someone interested in her as a person, not just as entertainment while they are here at Longbourn before moving on, shouldn't she? Honestly, Jane, you should claim him before anyone else has a chance."

"Bennet, good to see you away from scheduling," Lieutenant "Shadow" Riviera said to Elizabeth as he walked past. Elizabeth walked with him while Jane and Charlotte excused themselves to the restroom.

"You too! Where's Chunk?"

"Didn't you hear? Went DNF. Broke his leg last week at the lake, so he stayed home tonight."

"He didn't want to get drunk here for a change?"

"Said he couldn't drink with the pain meds they gave him."

"I guess that's a good enough reason to stay home."

"Hey, hear about the FNG? Apparently, he's loaded."

"That's what Charlotte told me."

"Yeah, Garcia told me his family is crazy famous."

"That doesn't make him good."

"Bennet. I can't wait till you get in the seat. It'll be the biggest piece of humble pie you've ever eaten."

"I'll dry your tears when I, a lowly girl, kick your ass in every flight."

"They're importing girls now? The air force must be getting desperate."

"Shut up"—hitting him playfully on the shoulder.

Elizabeth walked through the crowd and initiated conversation with several students from other flights. Some of them wanted to know about the upcoming schedule, some discussed the Drop and the finer details of the F-16 to Nellis versus the F-16 to Holloman. One had heard a rumor that an F-35 had dropped to another class out of Shepherd—a mind-blowing event that caused several minutes of boasting about who *really* deserved an F-35. Another reported that only RPAs to Creech would be available for the next three classes to a collective groan from any pilot in earshot. Elizabeth bounced between conversations, smiling and laughing, but always just on the outside. She made relevant comments and showed more superior knowledge than several of the men around her, but she could feel their resentment toward her if she corrected their misapprehensions or dared to look too intelligent.

Elizabeth, determined to sit for a minute or two, went back to her seat across the room where they viewed the drop assignments. Hearing voices, she looked up to spot Darcy and Bingley just a few rows ahead of her, obviously unaware of her. The low hum of their masculine voices rolled over her as she closed her eyes.

"She is the most beautiful creature I've ever seen, Darce." Bingley's gentle tenor voice rang out exuberantly.

"She is pretty. Certainly the prettiest in this crowd," Darcy's lower, clipped tones responded.

Elizabeth smiled at the compliment to her favorite sister.

"What about her sister, Elizabeth? She is very pretty as well."

"Tolerable, I suppose. She's a seven in a crowd of fives." Elizabeth's eyes and mouth dropped open in indignation. "I am not interested in these local girls pretending to like me to get out of Hickville, Texas. Besides, no other guy here is talking to her about anything other than flying. Why would I want to waste my time on someone practically ignored by nearly everyone who actually knows her? Anyway, go back to your angel. You're wasting your time with me."

Seven! They certainly were not referring to her. Jane might have been a ten, but she certainly was an eight. *At least!* She smoothed her shirt and looked down at her jeans. She crossed her legs and then, uncomfortable in her own skin, uncrossed and crossed them again the other way. She fixed her gaze at the back of the dark head, narrowing her eyes and rolling them before standing and shuffling down the row. She looked immediately for Charlotte and Jane, her eyes darting across faces in the crowd. Distracted, she tripped over the leg of the last chair in the row and caught Bing-ley's glance back at the dull clunk of her shoe on the metal. Her cheeks burned, and she turned away sinking as quickly as possible back into the crowd.

Elizabeth went back to the bar and ordered a shot of tequila, deliberately making a show of gathering flight mates to drink with her to toast the dropping class. Then, finding Jane in the sea of male faces, she replayed the entire episode through gritted teeth. Charlotte looked properly appalled while Jane suggested that maybe Elizabeth had misheard. Elizabeth had been insulted before, of course, but for some reason, being slighted by the hand-some, supposedly rich, and recently arrived stranger, stung her pride more than she wanted to admit. Elizabeth consoled herself by thinking, "One cannot account for taste. Obviously, Captain Darcy has little and is not worth knowing"—and tossed back another drink.

To add to her misery, Kitty and Lydia skipped about the crowd, making spectacles of themselves by shamelessly flirting with every officer in a uniform. Mary was at the piano in the corner of the bar but had failed to account for the Eighties pop music blaring over the club speakers. Her clearly inebriated mother was loudly proclaiming Jane and Bingley to be the most adorable couple the world had ever seen while her father stood back, watching the chaos, and not taking the trouble to check the actions of his daughters towards the young officers.

Elizabeth, now thoroughly mortified, glimpsed Captain Bingley and Captain Darcy witnessing her family's absurd behavior and she felt herself turn a deep shade of pink. She whispered to Jane her desire to go home. After a quick glance at Bingley, agreed to speak to their parents and convince them that their night should end. Elizabeth went about the unwelcome task of gathering Mary, Lydia, and Kitty from their revelry and pushed them toward the exit doors.

Shuffling through airmen crushing class patches to the other's shoulders and wading through rough games of crud, Elizabeth ran headlong into the one she most wished to avoid. She looked up into dark eyes which regarded her with incredulity and annoyance, making her cheeks burn in humiliation. Darcy muttered "excuse me" before he stepped deftly around her and proceeded to the wall near the bar.

Like herding cats. Elizabeth hid her self-conscious blush as she corralled her siblings to the car, where Jane and her parents met them a few moments later. Mrs. Bennet declared the night a success, the youngest sisters laughed boisterously, and after what seemed an eternity, the car backed out and drove into the night.

CHAPTER 5

*D*arcy stretched out in the armchair, leisurely propping his long legs on the matching ottoman in front of him. He settled his steaming mug of coffee on his leg and let out a sigh of contentment. The Drop Night had been *interesting*. In fact, Darcy was beginning to think that maybe Meryton would not be so bad after all. There were certainly *some* attractive girls in the crowd— even that Elizabeth Bennet—and the men he was going to work with seemed amusing and genuine.

"Darce, you really need to figure out how to be happy at these social things. You'll be going to quite a few of them here," Bingley said, sitting across from him examining his water bottle.

"William was obviously disappointed in the behavior of these people, Charles." Caroline walked in from the kitchen and draped her long legs over the edge of the arm of the chair opposite Darcy's. She kept her toes pointed and sat up, arching her back ever so slightly so that her chest puffed out, showing her figure off to its greatest advantage.

Bingley rolled his eyes.

"I was no such thing."

"It's okay. I know you are unaccustomed to vulgar behavior

and a complete disregard for manners." Caroline stared at Darcy through her thick eyelashes, making him shift uncomfortably in his chair.

"Who are you talking about, Caroline? It was a Drop Night. *Everyone* was being ridiculous."

"Well, if you must be told"—she huffed—"the student pilots were absolutely idiotic, wandering around in those stupid hats and gloves. And *why* must they tackle each other every minute throughout the night? Another thing," she said, ticking off offenses on her fingers, "those Bennet girls running around flirting with any man in sight."

"I found the Bennets perfectly lovely company."

"Well, you would." She hesitated, as her eyes traced up Darcy's legs before she added, "Jane was nice enough, but the other Bennet sisters... Eliza thinks she is smarter than everyone around her. The ugly one...Maria? Martha? MaryAnn? Something"—waving her hand—"ruined everyone's night banging on the piano. And the two idiotic teenagers. They literally threw themselves at every man they could find. I'm surprised they didn't jump on you or Darcy."

Darcy listened to Caroline's tirade and thought, *Elizabeth Bennet did not act above anyone at all.* In fact, of all the conversation he had overheard throughout the night, Darcy was certain that hers had been the only fascinating discourse. She had shown an uncanny understanding of air force politics and even an impressive knowledge of available flying options, where they were stationed, and their pros and cons. Most women he interacted with could hardly identify a Cessna from a B-52 and there was something about her clever and quick remarks, especially in the face of men who barely tolerated speaking to her, that made his stomach flip over on itself whenever she was nearby. Darcy was not ready to admit it to anyone, especially in front of Caroline, but Elizabeth Bennet intrigued him, and he *almost* wanted to see her again.

"Well, that's because Darcy stood in the corner moping and stopped being noticed after very long."

"I wasn't moping. I was just taking in the sights."

"Caroline, I don't know why you insist on looking down at the world around you. Everyone I met was wonderful and you might see that if you stopped looking down your nose so often. Now, tell me more about Jane."

"Her family lives three miles north of here at a place called Longbourn Inn. They run some sort of bed and breakfast on an old homestead that has been handed down to her father. Jane and Eliza apparently help their parents run the place and keep the surrounding grounds working."

"Very industrious of them. I wonder what else the property does." Darcy wondered if there could be potential for the creation of a winery. *There would have to be some experimentation with the grapes, and the relatively unpredictable weather might make it difficult...*

"I suppose. Honestly, I think it is rather degrading for them all to have to rent out their own home."

Darcy frowned at the irony of Caroline, currently living on the good graces of her brother, shunning anyone for working hard, while living in a rented house. He stirred his hot chocolate and ignored Caroline, instead choosing to imagine a pair of laughing brown eyes and dark lashes gazing at him over a grape vine.

"What else do they do?"

"Jane works as a kindergarten teacher in town and Eliza is a student pilot."

Reminded she might soon be one of his students and thus, strictly off limits, Darcy dropped his spoon, splashing hot chocolate on himself and the chair. Caroline jumped from her perch on the chair and rushed to the kitchen. She returned with what appeared to be the smallest towel in the house and attacked Darcy with it. Instead of handing the towel to him, Caroline tried to employ long, caressing strokes to Darcy's torso. Darcy snatched the towel from her hand and stepped away, turning his attention to the mess on the chair.

"I don't think she's started yet. One of the majors thinks she is an impertinent, spoiled brat and complained about her being casual in his squadron." Darcy knew full well Caroline's opinions of women in the military.

"Well, I think they are lovely. Caroline, you should invite them over. I think it would be good for you to make some friends in the neighborhood. It looks like you might be here a while and I want to make a good impression."

"Charles, why don't we move to the city rather than live near this tiny town? You could easily commute, and I would have access to all the stores and do something more than sit around folding laundry."

"I'm sure you could be sending out resumes to put that college education to work."

Caroline ignored her brother's jibe and doubled down. "Besides, this house isn't really what you need. Don't you want something bigger with a little class? Somewhere with decent coffee?"

"Caroline, I've already told you. I like this house and Darcy's going to teach me about living in the country. Besides, I had to listen to you compliment Pemberley for months after we spent Christmas there last year and I thought you'd like living out of town like this."

"Really, Charles. This is no Pemberley." Caroline had the decency to blush at Charles' very pointed remark about pursuing Darcy.

"Well, I am off to bed. It's going to be a long day tomorrow if you want to go look at the fences, Bingley." Darcy stood and stretched.

Bingley said, "By the way, we have been invited to Sir William's party."

"Whose party?" Darcy look incredulously back at Bingley.

"William Lucas? They call him Sir William..." Bingley watched Darcy for any sign that he might recognize one of the pillars of the community before giving up and continuing. "He throws a party for all new IPs once a month and the next one is tomorrow evening. You were otherwise engaged—moping against the wall—when he talked to me about it, so I accepted the invitation for both of us."

"Thanks, Bing." He exhaled slowly in a great sigh. He hated parties.

WHEN THE NETHERFIELD party arrived at Sir William's plantation-style home the next evening, a large, printed sign on the front door instructed them to go through the side gate and into the back. Around the corner was a lovely landscaped lawn and a dimly lit pool. A grand covered porch stretched out into the yard and allowed for patio seating and a buffet table.

Charles worked the crowd effortlessly, as he always did, giving rise to Darcy's longstanding wish that he too had the talent to make friends quickly. He introduced Darcy to the various locals that he had met at the Drop. Darcy shook hands politely, but remained aloof, allowing Bingley to keep up the flow of information and witty commentary.

Even more than his successes in the military, Sir William was known for and cultivated a reputation of friendliness. It was obvious William Lucas and his wife enjoyed entertaining. He manned the grill, calling out to his guests grabbing drinks out of coolers. Darcy smiled at the familiar sight, grabbed himself a drink, and took up his place against the railing on the porch.

Being a tall man, Darcy immediately spotted the Bennet sisters. If he was honest with himself, Darcy spotted one Bennet sister. Elizabeth's brunette ponytail swayed from side to side as she laughed at something Charlotte Lucas said. Darcy caught Elizabeth's fine eyes, but she looked away and then began chattering quickly to Charlotte.

Jane and Charles retired to the edge of the pool, putting their heads together in a long tête-à-tête. Bingley had been in love every six months since his sophomore year in college, always referring to his angels as the "love of his life." Jane appeared to be a nice girl, and Darcy hoped neither were hurt by Bingley's inability to commit.

He overheard one of the other Bennet daughters, Molly or Marion he thought, educating Caroline on the history of the Epistles and laughed to himself, knowing Caroline's disinterest in the Bible. After a few minutes, Caroline rolled her eyes at this unsolicited information and walked away, however, the young zealot followed after her. The two youngest Bennets were dancing *vivaciously*, if not inappropriately, with two new IPs near the speakers.

Mr. Bennet joked on the porch with other business owners including Sir William, his lawyer brother-in-law, Jonathon Phillips, and the Longs who owned the local hardware store. Meanwhile, his wife, Mrs. Bennet, soaked her pudgy legs in the pool with other gossipy wives, nodding knowingly towards Bingley and her daughter.

Darcy left his post to fill a plate and returned to lean against the rail. Elizabeth happened past and before he could stop himself, he found himself speaking. "Are you looking forward to starting academics?"

Elizabeth nodded, and before Darcy could venture further, Sir William appeared beside Elizabeth, clasping her shoulder in a bear-like grip.

"Ah, Captain Darcy. I see you've found our Elizabeth. Not a finer flyer at Meryton, mark my words."

Darcy watched as Elizabeth's cheeks took on a becoming shade of pink.

"Not many women pilots in the air force. In fact, one of the first woman fighter pilots was just a class or two behind me. She was terrible, of course, one of the types that really connive their way to the top. Not sure how she passed pilot training. She always used gender to get her positions, but she really paved the way for others."

Darcy watched Elizabeth's smile falter slightly as she looked down at her shoes.

"The first pilots were the Women Airforce Service Pilots in World War II. They're hardly mentioned, even in history books, but had they received the recognition they deserve, I'm sure women would be in a different place in the profession," Darcy said.

Elizabeth lifted her head and said, "The WASPs quite literally gave their life, same as any man in the Force at that time. It really is a shame."

"Well, obviously, they couldn't have been used in theater, so they only did what they didn't have enough men to do, but their contribution deserves notice at the very least."

"Those women died testing planes that men would later use to further the war effort, and you think they only deserve notice?"

"It's not as if they were Aces, were they? Other than a few test flights, what did they actually accomplish? Had there been enough men, their tasks could have easily been redistributed back to the real pilots. Of course, they need to have their achievements lauded as a footnote in aviation history."

"They were much more than a footnote—"

Warmed by her passionate speech, Darcy stared at Elizabeth's eyes and noticed the tiny golden halo in the center, almost like the sun peeking out behind the clouds. Before he could register all she had said, Sir William grinned and clapped Elizabeth on the shoulder once more.

"Now, Lizzy, did your mother make her famous mac and cheese again? I thought I saw her bringing in a casserole dish, but I just want to make sure. Darcy, you really should try this mac and cheese. It is to absolutely die for. Lizzy, would you lead me to it? I simply must have some before it's all gone."

Elizabeth's eyes flashed in Darcy's direction before she led Sir William off in the direction of the food.

Darcy startled by a sudden hand on his shoulder and Caroline's low voice behind him.

"I believe I can guess what you are thinking."

At this exact moment, Elizabeth's laughing eyes caught his.

"I seriously doubt it, Caroline," Darcy said acerbically.

"You are thinking how ridiculous this whole town is. How it is filled with nothing but hicks and hillbillies who wouldn't know a party if it hit them in the face. It's like these people seem to think that some cheese cubes on a toothpick amount to class."

"Not at all, Caroline. I was just thinking about a pair of pretty eyes." Darcy stared ahead before quietly adding, "How they can sparkle when they look at you."

Caroline preened and put her arm around Darcy's back.

"And who's flashing eyes have brought about this great introspection, William?"

Side-stepping Caroline's pernicious web, he said, "Why, Elizabeth Bennet's."

CHAPTER 6

t's not as if they were Aces, were they?" The words echoed in Elizabeth's head as she lie in bed. She could already hear muffled fighting from Lydia and Kitty's room, presumably over clothes, and the closing of a door in the hallway as Jane left her bedroom. Mary had started practicing the piano in the family room at seven before being harshly reprimanded by Mrs. Bennet. Elizabeth sank deeper into her pillow and roughly pulled her blankets around her as she thought through the night before.

Elizabeth and Charlotte had walked the perimeter of the fenced yard, Sir William's latest party in full swing.

"Jane seems to enjoy Bingley's company. What about his friend? I didn't get to talk to him at all last night."

"You know, I talked to one of my friends about him. They said he was stuck up at his last squadron too. Greg said he went to a squadron-wide briefing one time with Captain Darcy presenting. Some guy in the back was looking for the slides on his laptop and Darcy stopped in the middle to say, 'Hey! Mr. Tippee-Typee! Pay attention.' Yeah, that happened. He's a conceited jerk."

"Now who's being petty? That's just an instructor demanding

your attention. That's not conceited. I think his wounding your ego at Drop Night has clouded your judgement."

But later, when Sir William and Darcy had both taken their turns insulting female pilots as worthless uniform chasers using their gender rather than talent to get ahead... Elizabeth groaned as she climbed out of bed and dressed for the day.

Mrs. Bennet shaded her eyes from the sun pouring into the kitchen, barking shrill orders and making Challah French toast and fresh fruit for the guests. The sisters served in the dining room and ensured the comfort of the guests. Mr. Bennet hid himself away in his office, presumably ordering supplies and managing the day to day of the business.

Around eleven, after the last guests had been served, but before the first of the daily chores, the family began to eat the leftovers for brunch along with eggs fixed by Jane. Mrs. Bennet took her eggs raw in an awful looking concoction, while the rest of the family enjoyed them fried. Jane's phone *binged* and she looked down at it, unable to hide the blaze of hope in her blue eyes.

"Who is it?" asked their mother.

"It's Caroline Bingley."

"Caroline? You didn't give your number to her brother? How many times do I have to tell you that the quickest way to landing a man is to get his number and invite him over for dinner? Your voice is so soothing, the men flock to you."

Jane read the text, responded, then proceeded to clear the table.

"Well, Jane, what does Caroline want? Why did she text? You must have made a tremendous impression on her for her to contact you so soon."

"Caroline is asking me over to Netherfield to have lunch."

"Oh! What a marvelous opportunity to be so close to her brother! Of course, she must have seen what a handsome couple you both made."

"What about his friend?" Lydia asked.

"Ugh, the pompous one? Captain whats-his-name? Wasn't it something French? Maybe D'Artagnan?" Kitty chimed in.

"Captain Darcy. He wasn't pompous. I think he was just shy," Jane said.

"I can't believe you actually know what pompous means," Mary interjected.

"I know what it means because I know you," Kitty murmured while scrubbing a pan.

"He wasn't shy. Just proud, rude, inconsiderate, and insensitive. Definitely pompous." Elizabeth spoke through clenched teeth as she put the guest china back into the cabinet.

"It doesn't matter. Jane didn't sit talking with *that man* for more than an hour. She sat talking with *Captain Bingley!* First Bingley seemed shy and could hardly glance in my Jane's direction, because Jane is so beautiful, of course. Then, Jane must have shown him encouragement, because it wasn't ten minutes before he could not look at anything else!" Mrs. Bennet sighed. Her mother's imagination was wild with dreams for her oldest, most beautiful daughter.

Mr. Bennet, who had stepped into the kitchen for a cup of coffee, interjected sarcastically, "It would have been better for me if Charles Bingley had broken his ankle at The Drop. Then, maybe he would have stayed home, and I wouldn't have to hear this rundown of the evening."

"Oh Thomas! You seem very sure of yourself. You know how small this town is and you know no one gets out. When you die, Thomas, which may be very soon, your daughters and I will be stuck here, and we won't even have base access to find suitable husbands for our poor girls."

Mr. Bennet interrupted. "Lizzy is getting out, aren't you, Lizzy?" He smiled briefly at his favorite daughter, causing the wrinkles near his eyes to deepen before he turned on his heel and left the room.

"Well, not all of us can go flying about like Lizzy." Mrs. Bennet glanced at Elizabeth grimly. Elizabeth knew well how her mother felt about women in the military.

Jane looked from Elizabeth to her mother. "In any case, Mom, the men won't be there. Apparently, they are going to lunch with the other officers out in town."

"Well, I never. How can they just go out like that? Of course, they want to see you. I saw how that Charles was looking at you all last night. Mark my words, we will have a wedding by Christmas!" Mrs. Bennet crooned above a pile of freshly folded tablecloths in front of her, magically delivered of her previous headache, likely plotting the wedding of her eldest, most beautiful daughter.

"Well, I'm going. We won't be meeting until around one anyway, so I'll just take the truck out."

Elizabeth, proud of Jane for being so resolute, offered, "Would you like to just borrow my car? It's newer and a little nicer than you're old truck."

Despite her typical annoyance of Elizabeth's life decisions, Mrs. Bennet leapt at the chance to make Jane look even better. "Of course, you will take Lizzy's car! It's not like she has anywhere to go today. No one wants her. And you will take some truffles! You can leave them for the men. They always say the way to a man's heart is through his stomach and I have just the recipe!" Mrs. Bennet fluttered off to begin the creation of the world's best truffles, quietly whistling the wedding march.

"Thanks for that vote of confidence, Mom." Elizabeth's eyes twinkled, and her sisters laughed.

～

JUST TWO MORE MILES. Two more.

Elizabeth's running shoes pounded against the pavement. She was tired and knew she really should have gone to bed much earlier the night before. These last few miles were killing her. She only had two more miles and refused to walk the rest of the way home. Turning up her music, she headed down the road.

Unbeknownst to Elizabeth, behind her, the puffy, white clouds that had accompanied most of her run began to build into massive columns of grey and black. The first few pat-pats of sprinkles were a shock on her hot skin. When the sprinkles transformed into fat drops, Elizabeth finally saw the dark curtain of the downpour in the distance. She picked up her pace and made it through the front door of her home just as the skies opened and dumped buckets of rain, banging on the roof and causing the other inhabitants to be grateful they had not ventured out of doors.

CHAPTER 7

$\mathcal{H}$ail bounced off the truck and the soft ground outside. The rhythmic metronome of the windshield wipers fought a mighty battle to keep up with the cascades of water and still, it was nearly impossible to see the ditch from the road. Bingley's truck maneuvered deliberately down the slick, muddy road.

"Bing. Look at these tire tracks in front of us. Can you see them?"

Bingley pointed at a set of twisting tire tracks to the front. "Those deep rivets? Yeah, why?"

"I think someone came down this road during the rain storm. Caroline wasn't planning on leaving the house, was she?"

"No, she just said she was going to invite someone over for— Darce, stop the truck."

They skidded to a halt.

Bingley shot out of the F-250, running towards the ditch where a car rested, leaving Darcy to stare after him. He strained to see more than a few feet in front of him. Small balls of hail stung his skin and he covered his face with his arms in an attempt to protect himself. He clambered into the ditch and upon reaching the car, rapped sharply on the window and looked down to see a blonde-haired, blue-eyed angel gaze up at him with tears in her eyes and the gentlest, most hopeful smile he had ever seen.

"Are they okay?" Darcy called out from the truck.

"It's Jane!"

Bingley wrenched open the car door and pulled Jane out and into his arms. She squinted up through droplets of tears in her eyelashes as the noise of the storm drowned out his words. Laughing in relief, he grabbed her hand and they both made a run for the truck. The mud squelched under their shoes and Jane's flats turned out to be no match for the slick ground. One shoe sunk into the mud and as she pulled the shoe up, she slipped and landed hard, one leg crumpling beneath her.

"Are you okay?" Bingley shouted as he felt her hand slip from his. He only needed to see her face before he picked her up and carried her the rest of the way to the truck.

The truck door tugged against the wind while Bingley helped Jane into the seat that Darcy had covered with a workout towel and some spare clothes from his flight bag. Darcy handed Jane a microfiber cloth for drying the truck to dry her face while Bingley climbed into the backseat alongside Jane. Darcy put Bingley's truck back onto gear and proceeded slowly toward Netherfield.

"I can't thank you enough for saving me. I've been there for over an hour and I tried to call Caroline, but the phone lost signal. I had just pulled onto your road when the storm turned bad. It was just sprinkling when I left my house." Jane looked gratefully at Bingley, obviously on the edge of more tears.

"We're lucky to have stumbled upon you. You would have had to walk out in this mess. Besides, Charles is quite the knight in shining armor."

Charles glanced sideways and smirked. "That's me."

"You'll want to elevate that leg until we can get inside and look at it."

"Of course, I should have thought of it." Bingley placed her legs over his, gently moving her ankles across his thigh. Her skin was soft and slick, and he marveled at the feeling of it under his hands. Swallowing hard, he looked up from her shapely legs. Her soaked linen shirt now accentuated her soft curves, outlining perfect breasts. Her clear blue eyes caught him staring and he could not help but return her shy smile.

At last, just as the hail turned back into rain, the truck pulled back into the drive at Netherfield. Darcy and Bingley were the first to step out of the truck and despite Darcy's offer for help and Jane's assurances that she could walk, Bingley reached into the truck, gathered her into his arms, and carried her to the door. Caroline met the sodden group and ordered the men to "Stay where you are. I'll be right back"—then helped Jane to the guest bathroom. "Darling, you look positively drowned. Let's get you out of these clothes. I'll go look and see if I can find anything of mine that you can fit in."

Towel in hand, Caroline returned. Her eyes travelled slowly from Bingley's soaked hair to his mud caked shoes.

"Can I have a towel, Caroline? It's freezing."

Caroline clutched a white towel to her chest and handed him a ripped, brown rag.

"Do *try* not to get mud everywhere. Go upstairs and take a shower. Immediately! For God's sake, Charles, take off your shoes! Darcy, I know you share a water tank with Charles, so if you need hot water, you are more than welcome to use my shower."

"Uh, thanks."

"He's fine Caroline." Bingley threw his boots out onto the front porch. "I'm sure Darcy's can handle a cold shower."

"Well, I wouldn't want our guests to be uncomfortable."

"He's not a guest, Caroline. *You* are."

AFTER CHANGING INTO DRY CLOTHES, the four sat down to

a lunch originally meant for the two ladies while the storm continued to rage outside.

"Thank you so much for letting me borrow your dress, Caroline. It really is lovely, such an unusual color."

"It's my signature. I fell in love with a Peter Dundas' dress in the same color on Jasmine Sanders. It was amazing. Since then, I've tried to put that color into every piece. It's just so vibrant and alive. Tommy Hilfiger did a dress for her also in almost the same shade last year at the pre-Oscar dinner."

"That's wonderful that you could find something you love so much."

"Yeah, too bad it's also the color of construction safety vests," Darcy said under his breath.

"You look beautiful in it, Jane, though I'm sure you would look good in anything of Caroline's—I mean, you would look good in anything you wear. You're so beautiful."

Jane blushed and looked at her plate. "Thank you, Charles."

"Are you feeling okay? Can I get you any ice or a heating pad or a pillow? Anything?"

"I'm fine. I've always had kind of weak ankles. I'm sure it's just a sprain and will heal quickly. I'm honestly more embarrassed to be putting you all out than about the ankle. I'm sure we made quite the picture outside though, you carrying me like a drowned rat."

"I've never met someone decidedly less like a rat."

Bingley stared into Jane's light blue eyes and failed to notice that there were still others in the room. He did not hear Darcy clear his throat loudly and he ignored Caroline's inability to stay still in her chair. Bingley had found the person he wanted in his life and even in his sister's god-awful orange dress, Jane was the most beautiful creature he had ever seen.

Jane and Bingley talked amongst themselves in the near privacy Caroline's attitude afforded them and leaned closer across the table as they listened intently to the other.

"WHAT DO you mean the car is in a ditch? Are you all right?"

"I don't know if I hit anything. I don't think I did. Just slipped into the ditch, but I was too scared to really know for sure."

"Don't even worry about the car, Jane. Isn't that why I pay all that money for insurance? Are *you* okay?"

"My ankle is swollen and a little bruised, but I'm sure it's just sprained. Charles thinks I'll have to stay off it for a few days."

Jane quickly told Elizabeth all about her knight in shining armor coming to her very wet rescue. She also mentioned that Caroline had graciously offered to let her stay over at Netherfield and that hopefully by the morning, the weather would clear, and they might get her car towed out of the ditch.

"That is great news, because there's no way I can get to you today. Mom and Dad have me here manning the desk, waiting for the new arrivals to check in, while they and the girls are over at Sir William's. But, it's only a few miles over there. I bet if I took the back way through the pasture, I could just run there, and at least bring you some clothes. I ran that way sometimes before it was rented out. Based on Caroline's awful orange shirt from last night, I can only guess what awful pumpkin outfit you must have on."

Jane laughed as she looked down at the orange and white striped dress Caroline had let her borrow.

"No pressure, Lizzy, I'm fine here. And again, I'm sorry about your car."

"I'm just glad you are okay. I'll see you in a bit."

LIZZY FLITTED AROUND LONGBOURN, finishing up a few essential tasks and packing a small bag to tide Jane over for the night. She called her parents and her mother almost fainted when she heard about Jane's ordeal. She quickly recovered, however, when reminded that Jane was spending the night at the home of an eligible bachelor.

After she checked in the new arrivals, Elizabeth left the house with Jane's backpack and a cold bottle of water in hand. A chorus of birds seem to join her after the storm had passed and she walked through wet grass, the crisp air brightening her cheeks.

Longbourn was only three miles through the back pastures to Netherfield and was easily accomplished within an hour. Elizabeth's well-worn boots were muddied, as were six inches of her jeans. She laughed to herself—"*I* must *look positively wild*"—and she knocked on the door of Netherfield.

The red door creaked as Charles Bingley opened it, smiling. Leaving her boots at the door, he showed her into the dining room where Darcy, Caroline, and Jane sat, eating an early dinner. As Elizabeth entered, Darcy stood, as if to clear his plate, but instead he simply stood still, staring at her in her unruly state. Though the wind had died down, she could only imagine her appearance. Her hand went to her windburned cheeks and then to the tangles in her long, curly hair. She looked back at him, cleared her throat, and pointedly ignored his examination of her person, remembering his insulting speech at the Drop Night and then his disparagement of all female pilots as social-climbing bimbos who should have left the real flying to the men.

"Good heavens, Elizabeth, did you walk here?" gasped Caroline.

"I did." Elizabeth smiled slightly at Caroline's look of dismay. Darcy had not looked away after he put the dish in the sink. She assumed that he too must be offended by her muddy appearance.

"Jane, I brought some stuff for you." Elizabeth handed her sister the backpack after a quick embrace.

"You're my hero! Not that I haven't appreciated Caroline's generosity in sharing her clothes." Jane smiled graciously at Caroline and started rummaging through the pack.

"How's the ankle feeling?" Elizabeth asked, noticing that Jane had not placed any weight on one leg while she pulled a shirt and jeans out of the bag.

"I can't really stand on it, but eight hundred milligrams of ibuprofen later and it isn't throbbing anymore."

"I'm so sorry, Janey." Elizabeth turned to Bingley. "Thank you so much for taking care of Jane. I'm sure she's in good hands here; just don't let her do too much. Jane tends to try and hide her pain."

"Charles has been quite the doctor. He won't let me move without his assistance and has been so diligent about getting me ice and whatever else I didn't know I needed. I really can't imagine anyone more helpful."

He grinned as he helped Jane back into the chair, his hands lingering on her back and shoulders longer than necessary. "You must stay, Elizabeth! We can play cards or brood out the window like Darcy. Our television went out in the storm and hasn't come back on yet, so you see, you are our only entertainment."

Darcy, who was indeed staring out the window now, started at his statement and looked over the others in the room. Caroline, who had been complaining about the inability of the town to maintain power said, "I'm sure Elizabeth has other, more important things to do than stay here and keep us company, isn't that right, Darcy?"

Darcy ignored her.

"Well, actually, my first day is tomorrow, so I really need to go home and get a few things ready." Elizabeth shifted her feet slightly.

"Starting T-6s tomorrow?"

"I am. Well, academics, at least."

Bingley interjected, "Excellent! I wonder whose flight you'll be in. You know, I'm a T-6 instructor. Darcy is T-38s."

Elizabeth nodded and was about to respond when Caroline interrupted:

"All these letters and numbers. I don't know how you can keep the planes straight. They all look exactly the same."

"Caroline, they are nowhere close to the same. You came to my graduation! We toured around! You watched the flyovers! Stop acting like a bimbo."

"Charles, I mean it. They all look the same! Boring grey." Caroline glared back at her brother. Darcy's eyes met Elizabeth's across the room and she noticed they were wide and his head was slightly tilted. She read her own irritation at Caroline's total lack of intelligence in them, and for a moment, she felt a quick flash of understanding pass between them.

Darcy sighed and gripped his nose between his thumb and forefinger. "Caroline, they are all totally different. Only the T-38s are grey, by the way. The T-6 that Charles teaches and Elizabeth will be training on first is a prop plane with a propeller. It's the trainer plane that everyone starts on. Then, she'll either fly T-1s, like Charles did, which are a white jet that looks like a private jet with several seats and windows or she will fly T-38s like me which are sharp, fast, pointy, jet planes." He gesticulated with his left hand attempting to show her the difference. *Maybe she comprehends sign language.*

"Well, of course you would fly the fast planes, Darcy. You are the best at everything you do," Caroline cooed, flashing her pageant smile.

Biting her lip, Elizabeth could not help but ask, "And are you the best, Captain?"

"I was number one in my class, distinguished graduate at every training I have attended." He said it as fact, which only annoyed her more.

"Darcy is most definitely the best." Caroline stood and rubbed her hand down Darcy's arm. "Darcy has accomplished more in his career than anyone else I have ever known. From awards to successful deployments to running Pemberley. Darcy is highly successful because he expects the best and surrounds himself with the best."

Darcy flinched. Elizabeth shifted where she stood, and she could feel the beginnings of a smile on her face.

"I didn't realize we were in the presence of a great American hero. Do you not have any faults, Captain? I'm doing my best to not act awestruck as your friends would have me believe you are a walking demi-god."

A booming laugh erupted from Bingley as he pointed at Darcy and sang, "You're welcome!"

Darcy spared him only a quick glance before answering. "Only that I cannot forgive those who hurt my family or friends."

Their eyes locked, and Elizabeth realized while she had been teasing, Darcy had not. He had a vulnerable look in his eyes, but she was almost afraid to recognize it. She cleared her throat.

"I suppose that I can't laugh at that. Which is really rather unfortunate. I could use a laugh after my muddy trek this afternoon. Other than at myself, of course"—pointing to her muddy attire. His eyes seemed to darken as they studied each other. Elizabeth struggled to be perfectly serious in even the most trying of situations, looked away in her disquiet, and rolled her eyes at Jane.

"Well, I think I must be off. I have things to do. I'll come back tomorrow after work and maybe the road will have dried out and between Captain Bingley and I, we can tow out the car." She turned on her heel and started off down the hall, not noticing that more than one pair of eyes followed her progress toward the front door.

CHAPTER 8

*E*lizabeth's first day of pilot training, while an improvement from casual status and Major Warby's sighs, was almost a non-event. She showed up to her assigned classroom in her neatly pressed blues, shiny second lieutenant *butter bar* glittering on her shoulder and proceeded to spend the day in various mind-numbing welcome lectures from base officials and she picked up an armload of books and checklists and signed administrative paperwork. The air force excelled at bureaucracy and seemed to ensure that pilot training students really understood their place in mounds of paperwork.

As promised, after work and just before dusk, Elizabeth drove Jane's truck carefully down the not quite dry road to Netherfield. Still in her blues, Elizabeth knocked on the front door. The door was thrust open by a somewhat flustered Darcy, flight suit unzipped to his hips and the arms of it tied around his waist revealing his taut undershirt. His shiny dog tags swung against his broad chest as he stared down at her.

"Oh. Good evening," Captain Darcy said in a tone of voice that did not match the tenseness of his body.

Elizabeth shoved down a quick appreciation for the male form, remembering that the captain was a jerk, and recovered her equilibrium.

"Yeah, hi. I was just looking for Jane and a place to change so we can tow out the car. I came directly here from the base." She pointed to the empty hallway and held up her large tote bag.

Captain Darcy ran his fingers through his hair, causing it to stick up at odd angles before he smoothed it back down and sighed. "Sure. Come on in."

"Thanks." *It really isn't fair that this jerk is so hot.* Elizabeth walked past him, breathing in the scent of pine and earth and man. She spotted Jane stepping gingerly out of the living room, assisted by Caroline.

"Jane! I just need to change. Maybe you can grab Captain Bingley and we can run out and grab the car."

She looked around at several closed doors.

"First door on the left," said Caroline, pointing past her.

After changing, Elizabeth found Jane hobbling out to her truck on the arm of Bingley. She looked at the other truck in the driveway and saw Darcy staring back at her. Elizabeth let out a disgruntled breath. After Bingley got in the cab with Darcy, Jane offered:

"Oh, Darcy volunteered to help out."

"Probably to show us all how perfect he is at it."

"Lizzy, that's not very kind. He did grow up in the country. Maybe we should give him the benefit of the doubt."

"I don't think we should give him the benefit of our company, let alone the benefit of thinking him perfect. Miss Caroline Bingley already compliments him enough for all of us put together."

"Caroline just has a huge crush on him. We have to take everything she says with a grain of salt."

Elizabeth shook her head at her sister's determined ability to look for the best in everyone.

"Jane, you are really too good for the rest of us here on Earth."

The sisters laughed as they drove down the road until they found the car. Once there, Elizabeth jumped out of the truck to grab the tow strap. Darcy took the strap from Elizabeth's hand and began strapping it to the back of the car.

"I actually do know how to do that," Elizabeth said, standing akimbo.

"I'm sure you do. I just wanted it done right," Darcy said without even looking back.

Elizabeth swallowed a sassy retort and her eyes threw fiery daggers at the back of his dark head.

Dropping her hands and giving an exaggerated shrug, she stormed back to her truck and gripped the wheel, turning her knuckles white.

Bingley took his position in the driver's seat of the car to help steer it during the tow and waved at her. Hearing a tap on the side of the truck bed, Elizabeth looked in the rearview mirror to see Darcy, again not looking at her, motioning for her to begin moving forward. She pressed gently on the gas and felt the truck shudder as it pulled against the car. After several minutes of careful maneuvering, heaving, and adjusting of the strap, the silver car was finally righted on the road.

Bingley stepped out of the car and, together with Darcy and Elizabeth, inspected it for damage. Finding none, Darcy placed himself in the driver's seat, driving it down the road to ensure the car was drivable and responsive. He reversed back to the group and Bingley helped Jane into the car. As Elizabeth waved her thanks, Darcy stood ankle deep in the mud; she secretly hoped mud sprayed him from the tires. *I know how to tie a strap to the back of the car. Serves him right. Even if he does have a very nice chest.*

At Elizabeth and Jane's triumphant return to Longbourn, their mother greeted them with arms outstretched. She peppered Jane for details about Captain Bingley, and it was not until dinner when her father asked about Elizabeth's first day that anyone in the family acknowledged her small milestone toward her life dream.

Elizabeth had always felt she was her mother's least favorite daughter. Although Elizabeth learned how to cook at her apron strings, she gravitated towards her father's approval and away from the kitchen, distancing herself from her mother. Her mother seemed to thrive on criticizing her while pouring compliments on the rest, especially Jane or Lydia.

Her father, on the other hand, adored Elizabeth's quick wit and intelligence. They enjoyed sharing books and discussing philosophy and playing chess. Unlike her mother and three younger sisters, Elizabeth's head was not filled with silliness or husbands and that made her father love her all the more. He loved that she aspired to bigger and better things and was her constant source of support at Longbourn.

While the ladies cleared plates, her father coolly sipped at his drink and said, "Fanny, I hope you have a few good meals planned for our guests this week."

"Of course, I do. That's what we're known for after all." Her mother tittered and sat down in a chair near her husband.

"Well, I have good reason to believe we will have a relatively famous addition to the Longbourn guestbook." At this point, all five daughters stopped what they were doing and turned to their father.

"Oh, who?"

"You see, Meryton is apparently up for closure and the entire place is being investigated by this man—Collins is his name. And he will arrive tomorrow."

At once, the room became a boisterous scene of frantic activity. Her mother threw a fit of epic proportions about the cruelty and absolute absurdity of anyone closing the base and shutting down the inn. Who would come to stay if Meryton was gone? Who would she plan parties for? After this outburst, it appeared that she realized that her planned menu for the week contained nothing appropriate for a pivotal life-changing guest and she ran off to re-plan the entire week. Jane immediately attempted to calm her mother with platitudes while Mary waxed philosophic saying that perhaps this calamity was all for the best: "That which does not kill us, makes us stronger." Elizabeth, could only stare at her mother's antics and rolled her eyes toward her father who sat equably, taking in the scene.

Her mother retired early to rise and make appropriate culinary preparations for the man she dubbed "he who shall not be named." The next day, the girls returned home as soon as possible from their school and other jobs to support their mother and welcome Mr. Collins at check-in.

William Collins was a short, corpulent, sweaty man. The best that could be said about him was that his greasy hair might be confused for hair with too much gel in dim light. He carried a handkerchief with him dedicated to wiping his damp forehead in five-minute intervals and seemed to require sustenance in the form of a sugary snack almost every time the handkerchief was placed back in his pocket.

The first interaction with Mr. Collins required the sustained attention of everyone in the room. Mr. Collins not only introduced himself but praised the various architectural masterpieces, interior design choices, and choice of pen for the Longbourn guest book.

"I am so glad that I could be here while on official business for my most excellent supervisor. I cannot tell you enough how eager I am to get to know you. My supervisor, Senator Catherine de Bourgh, I'm sure you've heard of her, has often imparted to me that familiarity is the best way to understand the inner workings of a business or a community. 'Collins,' said she, 'You must get to know these people. How can we help them help themselves?' Of course, she is absolutely correct. So here I am. Here to make your acquaintance and hopefully get a better understanding of how Meryton and Longbourn coincide."

This speech was met with a hacking cough, covering giggles from Lydia. Her father smirked and welcomed Collins to Longbourn while her mother chirped and fluttered about the reception area with a tray of hors d'oevoures.

"Senator de Bourgh has given me the task of evaluating Meryton Air Base's continued suitability for remaining open in the face of congressional cuts and budgetary setbacks. You see, in this time of limited funding and uncertain voting, we need to ensure that all defense spending is properly allocated for the most efficient use of tax-payer funding. It is my job, therefore, to evaluate all possible base closures for this round of discussions. I evaluate the weather, tasks, and base housing allowances to determine which bases remain most advantageous to the government."

"That is quite fascinating, Mr. Collins. I do hope you will continue to regale us with your adventure over dinner," said her father.

"I am ever so glad to be invited to dine with you and your fair ladies. Most invigorating to get to acquaint ourselves on a more personal level and build a better relationship."

"Dinner will be at six in the main house," her mother said in the calmest manner, defying her previous anxiety.

At dinner, Mr. Collins, whose loquaciousness was tolerated with a droll sense of boredom, continually complimented the meal, chairs, décor, table, plates, bowls, and even the serving utensils until the family could take no more.

"What a beautiful room and what excellent boiled potatoes." At once, Elizabeth could see how incensed her mother was becoming as her "cacio de pepe potatoes" had been reduced to "boiled potatoes"—she could hardly wait for her retort. "I can't remember a time when I've had such a superb vegetable. Which of your beautiful daughters should I compliment for the excellence of the cooking?" Fanny Bennet flushed from the top of her large hair to the tip of her polished toes.

"Mr. Collins, I am the chef here."

The pudgy Mr. Collins looked at her mother with awe and adoration.

Her father cleared his throat. "Mr. Collins, you possess such a talent for flattery. I simply must know. Do you offer whatever compliment comes into your head at the moment or are they the result of previous study?"

"Well, occasionally I write down a compliment or two, especially if I think they will go over well with friends or associates, but when I deliver them, I do try to make sure they don't sound memorized."

"Believe me, no one would ever believe that." Elizabeth smiled behind her drink while the other girls attempted to cover their snorts and snickers by coughing into their napkins.

Collins continued, apparently unfazed. "I know it is important for women to feel significant. Women, much more than men, are highly disposed to enjoying various little commendations. I have found in my own life that it is absolutely necessary to ensure that women in my sphere of influence feel self-assured and self-confident in order to make the best decisions and continue on the best path in their lives. Senator de Bourgh is always mentioning how vital *appropriate* self-esteem is to the work of women and how too many of them are assured by those around them when they need honest evaluations of their work."

"How fortunate to surround yourself with strong connections."

"Ah, forgive me. I forget that many are unfortunate to not have such vaulted connections. You see, Catherine de Bourgh is not only a very powerful senator as the head of several committees, but she is a woman with uncanny vision for the future and such leadership abilities. She lives in the Rosings Park area of Hunsford, which, as you know is very fine. Why, her windows alone were recently replaced to the tune of fifty thousand dollars. Who, but Senator de Bourgh, would have foreseen the importance of energy efficient windows? All to show how our climate scientists are continually supported."

"Who indeed?"

Elizabeth was anxious to return to her studies, and after this odd speech by their strange guest, Elizabeth murmured, "Excuse me," and cleared her plate while Mrs. Bennet spoke to Collins over the clatter of the silverware against the china.

"Oh, our Elizabeth has so many things that she needs to do. She is a pilot training student, you see, so she must study, study, study. Day and night, it seems." Her mother took a sip of her drink and continued. "We hardly see her these days."

"What a perfect coincidence! I need to go to the base tomorrow to begin my inspections."

Her mother clapped her hands together and began to twitter enthusiastically.

"Why, Lizzy would love to take you! It is a bit of a drive out to the base and, of course, she will need to sponsor you on, but of course, she would love to make it easier for you to do your job. How lovely that we could come together so unexpectedly!"

Elizabeth rolled her eyes at her mother, knowing full well arrangements were already in place without her assistance.

"Elizabeth! Why that would be perfect. I can only imagine that the Honorable Senator de Bourgh would be most pleased with utilizing your services. Of course, I would love to interview you to determine a new student and local business owner's daughter's perspective on the Meryton base closure. Perhaps you could also introduce me to your commanders and allow me to accompany you throughout your work day. Obviously, I have all the appropriate security clearances necessary and I can fax them to your supervisors as necessary."

"Great," Elizabeth said in a clipped voice. "We leave at five in the morning, so I have time to study there before report."

"Excellent!" was the last Elizabeth heard as she trudged up the stairs.

~

THE NEXT MORNING, Elizabeth dragged the torpid Collins from the house ten minutes later than usual. Lucky for her, Collins was not a morning person, so she was able to consume her coffee in relative peace. With the window rolled down, she was not half-offended by the smell his overpowering cologne-covered body odor. How this man was a professional was beyond her and she turned her mind to bigger, more important things. She was still stuck on formal release, working in twelve-hour shifts, and dressing in uncomfortable blues until Lieutenant Hall flew his solo ride at the end of November. Tomorrow, the dollar rides would begin and Lieutenant Porcelli was first of her flight to get an artistically decorated dollar to his IP. Three weeks later, when he finished his solo ride he would be thrown in the dunk tank by the flight-mates as a rite of passage. Her own turns would come the day after, but she had more studying and could not begin to daydream about that now.

Elizabeth dropped off Collins at the Wing building and proceeded to the large parking lot for the squadrons. She parked and made her way to the two-story cinderblock building where her show time was six o'clock. She found her flight mates standing in a huddle outside of the double glass doors. The clock started as soon as they crossed the entry way and they stood vigil outside the building in the crisp morning air.

"Six," said Lieutenant Graves and flight entered the lobby. Elizabeth picked up her bag and walked to the door. She spotted Captain Darcy just ahead and he opened the door for her.

"Thank you." She removed her cover and placed it in her right leg pocket. She looked at Darcy once more and on impulse, she smoothed her hair. She walked left, and he walked right. She climbed the stairs and found her flight room, entering just seconds behind her flight mates. Hall flipped on lights and Lieutenant Porcelli, as the senior ranking officer, started assigning tasks. Each member of the flight moved into action.

"Bennet: coffee. Thornton: weather. Graves: NOTAMS. Valdez:

popcorn. Hall: power point. Martin: down range MOAs. Cook: brief data. Am I missing anyone?"

"No, sir," Elizabeth said as she threw old coffee grinds into the trash.

Within ten minutes the students were not quite ready but as ready as they were going to be. The sound of men laughing greeted them from just outside the door, boisterously heckling a lieutenant from Joker flight who had been air sick on his ride the day before. The IPs were imitating him, asking for the air sick bag and making vomiting noises. The door was wrenched open by their flight commander striding into the room followed by the assistant flight commander, the lead instructor pilot, and the other available IPs.

The students stood at attention until the flight commander dropped himself at the end of the long work table facing a white projector screen and brusquely told them to take their seats. The students sat at attention, back straight, away from the back of the chair, ankles touching, toes apart, hands in a fist and touching their thighs.

"Brief." Lieutenant Graves hopped out of his seat, still at attention and made his way to the opposite end of the table to begin.

Graves informed the day's slides on the weather, auxiliary fields, scheduling conflicts, who had which gos, applicable NOTAMS, and more. The instructors listened closely to find fault with the brief and the students remained at attention, their backs beginning to ache and their posture growing uncomfortable. Elizabeth determined that if she had to sit this way, it must be more comfortable to wear a corset like one of those fainting women in romance novels. After ten intense minutes, Graves came to the last slide and looked at the flight commander. A long, uncomfortable pause

"In pattern, you think you should have a wide downwind, perch late, and pull power early?"

The flight commander stared expectedly at Graves who fidgeted with the computer remote and said, "Yes."

"No, you aren't understanding the winds..." The flight commander proceeded to dress down Lieutenant Graves, the victim who had been offered up by the students for today's meal. They were each mocked, ridiculed, derided, and lampooned for their—or other's—mistakes. Just when they had really started to feel sufficiently sub-standard, the flight commander stood (causing a ripple effect of the students to stand at attention) and turned them over to the lead IP. "They're all yours"—and muttered something about their pathetic level of general knowledge and their certain road to failure.

"Porcelli," the IP said without even looking at the students, "if you aren't too stupid to screw this up, let's get to work."

The students then again sat *at attention* as the IP dragged a podium across the room and started in the middle of a lecture. Sitting in this attitude, Elizabeth was unable to look at her notes to ascertain their exact location.

"You are in Military Operating Area number six practicing a downwind patter and you see a light. Lieutenant Bennet, you have the aircraft."

Elizabeth did not break her perfect posture but could feel sweat begin to slick her palms. She gathered her materials, a laminated cutout of the jet interior, her DASH-1, in-flight guide, and notes that would be allowed on the jet and headed to the front of the room and set up, thinking furiously about the problem at hand.

"Sir, are there any other aircraft around me?"

"What do you expect to see?"

"In Longbourn MOA, I would expect one, possibly two other aircraft in the vicinity."

"There are two jets in nearby areas."

"Where are they?"

"Areas 4 and 7."

"What is my fuel state?"

"What do you expect it to be by now?"

Elizabeth calculated the distance from the runway to the operating area and said, "Half."

"Great. It's half." The IP looked bored and, at the same time, imposing. Elizabeth knew she could not fail this stand up evaluation without delaying her solo ride.

At attention, Elizabeth struggled to maintain her focus. She struggled not to fidget as was her nervous habit; too many movements and she would be told to sit back at the long table —and fail.

"What does the Hog Log say?" she asked.

"The maintenance log was routine."

"What is the weather?"

"Same as today."

Her eyes moved of their own will to meet Thornton's who had put together the weather for the briefing. "I am ready to go through MATL."

"You sure?"

She had spent half of the night memorizing general knowledge, like the numbers on every knob, switch, and meter in the T-6, and she felt the cold sweat of stress slowly run down her back as she continued to answer every crisp question. "Yes, sir."

"Maintain aircraft control."

"Sir, in order to maintain air craft control, I am going to set proper power and pitch." She hoped her voice sounded more confident than she felt.

"What is that?"

"Thirty-five percent, two degrees nose high, wings level. Sir, am I able to do that?"

"Yes, you are."

"Sir, in order to analyze the situation, I look down at my gauges. What do I see?"

"Clever, Bennet. What do you expect to see?"

Elizabeth proceeded to describe various levels for oil, RPMs, throttle positions... Eventually, she made it through the *Take proper actions* step and *Land as soon as conditions permit.* The stand up evaluation seemed to last forever, and her thoughts were racing as fast as her heart.

"You brought the aircraft to a safe conclusion." Relieved, Elizabeth returned to her seat at the table.

After being harassed, bullied for information, and mocked when they did not know the answer, the class was released for lunch. A few of the students had flights in the afternoon which were exciting and terrifying all at once, but for Elizabeth she would spend the next six hours of her shift studying as if her life depended on it—because at this point, it did.

Elizabeth glanced at her phone to check the time and was greeted by a text message from Lydia: *Come to the bowling alley for lunch. Our treat.*

Weighing her options, lunch with her sisters at the bowling alley beat eating junk from the *snacko*. At least she would not be hungry.

CHAPTER 9

$\mathscr{D}$arcy's boots thudded down the sidewalk toward the tall brick building with a set of glass double doors beneath windows adorned with the words "Through these doors pass the best trained pilots in the world." He pulled open the first door and feeling the presence of someone behind him, held it ajar, and stepped to the side. Elizabeth Bennet muttered "thank you," slipping through the door and tucking an unruly curl behind her ear. Darcy, followed her, allowing the door to close on a male lieutenant who took a tad too long. He nodded in greeting and the two parted ways—Elizabeth to the T-6 wing and academics, and Darcy to the T-38 hall, where he would teach and do paperwork.

He hoped this day would be better than his first day as an instructor. He hated having to hook a student for a flagrant error but failure in the plane came with real costs and he could not tolerate anything but excellence in those he taught. An error, like the one in the cockpit the day before, could have cost them the jet, if not their life, had it not been for Darcy's quick action at the controls. At Pemberley, he was known for competent management and quick thinking. His training there had come in handy as an officer and he found himself easily able to adapt to new jobs within the squadron.

He walked past the operations desk and glanced at the white board displaying the locations of all IP/student combinations. Darcy waved to the lieutenant behind the desk. Upon arriving at his grey cubicle, he sat at his non-descript government desk and jotted a checklist. *Email sorted/replies sent: check. Complete computer-based training: check. Review slides for next academic day: check.*

Soon his stomach reminded him about lunch and he headed to the bowling alley, the only decent place on base. The walk was an easy distance and he met Bingley on the way. In his usual jovial manner, Bingley discussed the trivialities of his day and his most recent favorite subject, Jane Bennet.

The bowling alley was full to the brim with pilots, spouses, mechanics, children, finance personnel, civilian office personal, and contractors. Most, like Bingley and Darcy, were eating a quick lunch before returning to their duties, others however were taking advantage of free lunch time bowling with a meal purchase. After receiving their food, the pair were hard-pressed to find a seat together but eventually found a small corner in the dining area.

One bite into his bacon cheeseburger and a burst of hysteric giggles attracted Darcy's attention. Two teenage girls doubled over with glee at an all too familiar face. Darcy stiffened, and unadulterated hatred roiled through him.

Bingley followed Darcy's gaze.

"Ah, the Bennet girls! I wonder if they are here to meet Elizabeth for lunch?" Bingley stood to greet the small party. Darcy stayed obstinately in his seat and continued to eat his cheeseburger, his face a mask to his closely bridled rage.

"Lydia, Kitty! It is so nice to see you. Darcy and I were just having lunch. I thought I should come say hello."

The two ridiculous girls burst again into a shower of giggles before the younger one was able to respond.

"Well, of course, Jane isn't here because she has to work, but we did find some new friends, Lieutenant Wickham and another new captain, Captain Denny."

Bingley nodded. "Nice to meet you."

Denny shook Bingley's hand but quickly turned Kitty's attention to a conversation about the latest movie they had both seen. Wickham however, met Bingley's eyes and stood. George Wickham was taller than Bingley and his ash-brown hair was a little too long for regulations.

"Charles."

"George." Wickham spoke while their hands pumped once in a firm grip.

Wrinkling his brow, Bingley turned to see Darcy still seated. Just then, Elizabeth Bennet arrived at the table. Wickham smiled like a cat and Darcy clenched his teeth as Elizabeth sat down.

Darcy stood, picked up the red plastic baskets of food from the table in both hands and said "hi" while eyeing Wickham now seated next to Elizabeth. Darcy forced his lips into a smile, which he hoped looked friendlier then he felt.

"George." Darcy nodded and continued speaking to the rest of the group, not allowing his eyes to grace Wickham's face again. "It seems your group is in need of another table. Bingley and I would love it if you took ours. We were just headed back to work anyway."

Wickham glanced at the burgers with two bites missing and the mound of steaming fries and smirked. Darcy watched him curl like a content snake, waiting for his opportunity.

Bingley, looking somewhat confused, quickly about-faced, and followed as they picked up to-go containers and exited the building.

~

WICKHAM—THE lieutenant with a devilishly handsome face, glittering eyes, and a strong jaw—leaned into a tranquil posture against the metal chair. He grabbed one of Lydia's French fries and flirted smoothly with Kitty. Elizabeth picked up an onion ring and said, "What got into him?"

"Who, Fitz? Oh, he's always in a mood." Wickham slathered a fry in ketchup and popped it into his mouth.

Elizabeth's curiosity piqued. "How do you know Captain Darcy?"

"We grew up together, Darcy and me. My dad used to work for his up at Pemberley. We've known each other since we were babies. You might not believe me, considering Captain Crabby's greeting just now, but we used to be best friends."

Lydia who had been distracted by Denny, took this moment to change conversation partners. "What on earth happened that he hates you now?"

"Well, it's kind of a long story. Maybe some other time."

"Pffft." Lydia rolled her eyes, flipped her hair, and leaned one arm on the table. "Tell me about your last assignment. Where did you come from?"

"Well, I was with Darcy actually. We were in the same squadron."

Elizabeth's eyes widened in surprise.

"Really? How unusual for you both to come from the same place and be assigned together twice!"

"Yeah. Anyway, we were deployed together and aside from his holier-than-thou attitude and moodiness, he's not all bad."

"Well, Darcy certainly hasn't made any friends here. He hooked his first student and spends every event moping around or insulting people."

"Not especially surprising." Wickham leaned in conspiratori- ally. "You know, when his dad died, I was supposed to receive a big inheritance from him to help me get my education and start my life on the right foot. Instead though, when the time came, he passed me over. Completely refused to give me anything. It was awful, not only had I lost my godfather, a man who had been as close to me as my own dad, but I had lost everything I had been counting on. So instead, I wound up as a poor, neglected airman who keeps getting crushed under Darcy's big, fat thumb."

The girls sighed at the injustices. Denny shook his head either from the loss of Kitty's attentions or the loss of Wickham's inheritance.

Elizabeth quickly recovered. "Wasn't there a will or something? He can't just have done that! How completely awful!"

"There was a will, but I guess my inheritance wasn't put in quite right and wasn't legally binding. Believe me, I looked into every possible way to make sure the older Mr. Darcy's wishes were fulfilled, but there was nothing I could do."

"La! At least now you can be here with us! Now, let's talk about my birthday party next week!" Lydia crooned and then changed the subject to much sillier topics. Thirty minutes and several cheeseburgers later, the group dispersed. The two boy-crazy teenage girls promised to see them all later, and Elizabeth, sharing a smile with Wickham at their nonsensical attentions, headed back to the T-6 building.

IN A SILENT FURY, Darcy completed his afternoon checklist. His desk now shone, having been straightened, organized, and cleaned. Turning to his tasks and away from thoughts of his former friend, he regained control of his emotions. And yet, thinking of Elizabeth sitting next to Wickham, his fists clenched over the soiled paper towel.

Since meeting Elizabeth Bennet, thoughts of her seem to fill his imagination. Her dark, curly hair flowed past her shoulders and fluttered when she moved. He imagined her smirking at his tantrum as he cleaned and organized his desk, and he shook his head. In his mind, her face lit up when he looked at her and unfortunately no amount of drinking, PT, reading, or work could exorcise her from his thoughts.

Finally, the mocking hands of the clock arrived at their places. He was finally able to leave his godforsaken office and look forward to suffering in the comfort of his own home. Shutting the door behind him, Darcy started off to find Bingley, aching to return to Netherfield as soon as possible.

He located Bingley at the T-6 scheduling desk. Behind the lieutenants working the desk, the large monitors noted Elizabeth was still in academics for another hour, so Darcy was safe from her *dangerous* company. Darcy also noticed Wickham's name graced the list of Elizabeth's flight's instructor pilots and cringed. Wickham should never have been a pilot, let alone an instructor. Wickham had only made it through pilot training on a wing and a prayer and should never have been selected for training.

Finally, Bingley was ready to go, and Darcy was glad for the quiet ride home. Caroline met them smiling brightly, wearing a shirt cut far too low for anything but trouble. After dinner, the trio retired to the living room, television blaring. Bingley reviewed his DASH-1 and Darcy read a book by Antoine de Saint-Exupéry who always included a pilot.

Darcy wished Elizabeth was beside him, her hand on his thigh as she read a book too, her feet curled under her, making her petite frame even smaller. Darcy slammed his book closed and stood up suddenly. Caroline and Charles both looked at him askance.

"Are you all right, Darce?" Charles asked while picking up the book dropped during Darcy's sudden rise.

"Perfectly fine. I'm just going to go to bed." Darcy shook his head, grabbed the book from Charles' hand, and marched from the room.

Darcy took the stairs two at a time to his room, muttering. "You're going crazy"—*fantasizing about this girl who has an insane family and wants to be a hero! They have therapists for this and probably some sort of pill for it too.*

CHAPTER 10

The following Saturday, Aunt Evelyn and Uncle Jonathon Phillips hosted a dinner for the Bennets to celebrate Lydia's eighteenth birthday, accompanied by Mr. Collins, the Longs, the Lucases, and two other student pilots from Elizabeth's training flight, Lieutenants Graves and Hall. Denny and Wickham had been included by the begging insistences of Kitty and Lydia. All in all, the group made a merry party. Everyone ate well and enjoyed cornhole, and conversation.

The Phillips were renowned for their excellent table. They loved to barbecue and presenting the best spread in Texas available to their guests. Uncle Jonathan, a successful lawyer, had inherited his father's law firm at age thirty when his father retired and moved to Miami. Aunt Evelyn had never been blessed with children and had, in turn, been a second mother to the Bennet girls. A sister to Mrs. Bennet, Aunt Evelyn loved her nieces and frequently conspired as secondary matchmaker with Fanny, dreaming of weddings.

The spicy barbecue was placed on a long table in the dining room accompanied by buttery corn on the cob, baked beans with bacon, potato salad, creamy mashed potatoes, jalapeno corn bread, hush puppies, coleslaw, pasta salad, and greens. Mr. Collins, who was particularly fat, piled his plate high and returned no less than three separate times *to taste* the pecan pie, homemade ice cream, and berry cobbler. At the end of the line, Elizabeth, humming to herself, began creating a volcano of potatoes with baked beans as the lava. Wickham chuckled lightly.

"I see you've created Mount Vesuvius there. Are those ribs all the poor Pompeiians?"

Elizabeth started at the unexpected question and then laughed, meeting his grey eyes.

"Well, I was going for Mount St. Helens, so I suppose my artistic skills are somewhat lacking."

"Where are you sitting?"

"I was planning on sitting in the living room near Charlotte Lucas. Have you met her yet?"

"I think we were introduced when we first walked in, but I'd love to meet her again. I'm sure any friend of yours is a friend worth knowing."

George Wickham grabbed her plate and, dodging an attempt by Collins to sit with them, followed Elizabeth. Plates perched precariously on their knees, Charlotte amused them both with tales of Elizabeth's tomboy childhood.

"She's been playing pilot since she was eight! She had the Thunderbird pilot Barbie! One time, my parents remodeled the kitchen. She stole the box our new fridge came in and made up this whole plane. She had drawn all the little dials and was using a spatula for the stick. We were forced to play passengers in there for weeks while she piloted us to all sorts of exotic locations like Timbuktu and Beijing and Nicaragua. We had to disembark and pretend to be natives while she found the different parts to fix the plane in each land."

Elizabeth blushed while Wickham's charming laughter roared. After the fourth or fifth story, Charlotte said she needed some lemonade and returned to the buffet. Wickham smiled at her, with his remarkably straight white teeth. She always had a thing for good teeth.

"So, how is training going?"

"It's great, I guess. Just doing academics right now. We should be on the flight line soon though, in just a few weeks. I've been going through the systems this week and we'll be onto instruments next week."

"Excellent. I hope the other IPs are being nice to you. I'm with your class in a few weeks as soon as this current flight graduates. Maybe I can do your dollar ride!"

Charlotte returned. "Wait. When is your first ride?"

"Should be in three weeks or so."

Charlotte again picked up the conversation. "George, I heard you were friends with Captain Darcy, is that true?"

"I've known him and his sister since birth, but we've drifted apart."

"Probably because he is a pompous, proud, pushy, crabapple," Elizabeth muttered gruffly while attacking a piece of brisket with fork and knife much more aggressively than the tender meat warranted.

Wickham nearly spit out his current mouthful of food and quickly covered his mouth with a napkin. Charlotte smirked at Elizabeth while Wickham snickered behind his napkin.

"He always did tend to insult everyone around him, except his sister. Georgiana would very likely call him the best brother, but of course, she is very young and lacks comparison."

Suddenly, Kitty and Lydia appeared by their sides as though gossip was their siren song. Lydia leaned on Wickham's shoulder, fawning over him.

"Oh, George, what is Elizabeth saying that is keeping you over here? We were wondering if you would come teach us to play cards. Now that I'm eighteen, I want to go play in a casino somewhere and I'll need a few lessons..." Lydia's flirting voice seemed to raise three octaves. After a well-timed hair flip and a hand placed gently on Wickham's arm, Lydia continued, "Well, Georgie Porgie, are you coming with us?"

Elizabeth's first impulse was to gag, then plug her ears, and then smack Lydia's hand from the much older Wickham. Instead, Wickham winked at Elizabeth, mouthed the words "it's okay," stood to his full height, and said, "Lead the way, little lady."

Lydia put her arm through Wickham's and led him to another room for cards with Kitty trailing behind, as always.

Charlotte looked at Elizabeth and said, "So, I heard about Jane staying over at Netherfield. Does Bingley like her?"

"I think he likes her very much. You should have seen him. He was practically tripping all over himself to talk to her and make sure she was comfortable with her ankle sprain."

"Does she like him?"

"Of course, isn't it obvious?" Elizabeth turned to view Jane who was standing with Charlotte's sister, Maria, but very clearly was not paying attention; her eyes glazed over as she scrolled through her phone.

"To you and me, of course. We know her. Bingley, though, doesn't. His sister's a snob and based on what little we've seen, doesn't like you and wouldn't necessarily want Bingley tied to Jane. Jane needs to be more obvious and snatch him up while she can."

Elizabeth's face flashed with frustration. "That's ridiculous. She's just shy and modest! If Bingley can't figure that out, he's a fool."

"We are all fools in love." Charlotte nodded sagely before standing up to take care of her plate. "Lizzy, we all want to get out; and some of us are stuck here biding our time until marriage or money can get us out. I don't want Jane to miss her chance."

Elizabeth watched Charlotte's retreat to the kitchen. She studied her family scattered around the room. Mary was waxing philosophic in a dull monotone to Uncle Jonathan, who nodded politely, never taking his eyes off of his food but randomly inserted himself into surrounding conversations. Mary, however, continued droning, apathetic to her partner's total lack of interest.

Alternatively, Lydia was flirting outrageously with any male in the vicinity of her card game. While still gripping Wickham's arm possessively, she patted Denny's thigh, flicked her hair from side to side, and her teasing whine could be heard throughout the house. Kitty also flirted shamelessly. Though, Kitty, being slightly smarter than Lydia, had not laid a hand on anyone.

In between bites, Mr. Collins was speaking enthusiastically with her mother and aunt about the various architectural design aspects of Rosings Park, the fabulous manor owned by the fantastical Senator de Bourgh. After detailing the number of windows, buttresses, pillars, and couches, he moved on to the more fascinating comparison of Aunt Evelyn's sitting room to the second parlor of Rosings. Apparently, the color of the throw pillows somehow matched a main color scheme of the parlor, and the favorable comparison resulted in blushes and smiles from Aunt Evelyn. Eventually, Charlotte joined their group and was also regaled with the fine pattern of the curtains and number of side tables in each room. Elizabeth's father sat away from the group, nose buried in a book, thoroughly tuning out the party around him.

She wandered aimlessly for a few moments and ultimately ended the night sitting near her father, listening to the clamor of the party spin around her.

CHAPTER 11

*D*arcy woke with a headache. He had slept little having been besieged by dreams of a certain woman he would very much like to forget. He stumbled blindly to his shower. After standing in the hard stream of steaming water until the water ran cold, he ran his hand over the mirror's fog to look at his drawn face. Dark circles rimmed his eyes and the few creases on his face had deepened into hard lines. This assignment was getting the better of him, something which had never happened in the past. Darcy prided himself on his ability to be in control of every situation since his father's death.

That control had earned him his nickname. Darcy had been raised with the expectation that he would go and return from university, live at Pemberley and learn the ropes and then take over at thirty when his father retired. Everything changed when he was twenty-two and freshly graduated from Cornell. His father had been cooking breakfast that morning, as he had done every day since Darcy's mother died when he was twelve. If he thought back, he could still smell the bacon sizzling in the pan. Darcy had just come in from checking the livestock and had stopped in the kitchen. They had chatted about the blonde Darcy had taken out the week before, some recent news from town, and a dozen other small things. His father had gripped his shoulder affectionately and sent him off to take a shower. When Darcy had returned, his father was dead on the kitchen floor. Heart attack, the doctor had said. The bacon burned and made the kitchen stink for weeks. Still, years later, Darcy was unable to eat bacon.

He had run away and joined the air force soon after. He could not bear to stay and had always loved the sky, lazily spending most of his childhood looking for cloud shapes while taking care of the land with his father. Three weeks later, on the first full day of basic training, they had served bacon and eggs. Darcy was inconsolable as soon as the scent permeated the air. He had a breakdown the likes of which the men he trained with had never seen. As they had yet to learn anyone's names, they began to call him "Fitz." Darcy hated the nickname and all that it implied, and when the others he worked with saw his impeccable self-control, the name stuck harder than it ever would have otherwise. The name had been passed from basic to pilot training and from squadron to squadron during his service and when his cousin Richard had heard it, his family as well. It was almost laughable now, so many years later, but every time he heard it, he could hear that bacon popping and feel the tight squeeze on his shoulder.

HE FLEW FIRST GO and his student performed well. He landed and spoke briefly with his maintenance crew chief before seeing a flash of familiar, curly hair slipping into the hangar behind the crew chief. He told his student to go back to the briefing room and that he would be right behind him for their post-flight brief and followed Elizabeth Bennet through the large sliding metal door.

He stepped into the room and followed her to a corner where she was gesticulating wildly, her voice giving away her frustration.

"I just need a yard of flight line," she said to the maintenance worker.

"Yeah, you can't get that here." The worker responded without so much as a glance in her direction, though Darcy could clearly see the stifled laughter of the crews standing near the scene.

"Okay, where can I get it? The Step Desk told me to go to Scheduling. Scheduling told me to go to Training, and then they told me to come here."

"LT, I don't know where you need to go, I just know, ain't no one in this hangar got a yard of flight line for ya."

"Why doesn't anyone have it?" Her intonation rose with barely suppressed fury.

"Lieutenant Bennet, can I speak to you for a moment?" Darcy raised his eyebrows in silent comradery to the maintenance crew member.

"Sir?" Elizabeth turned on him, eyes flashing.

"Who sent you down here?" Darcy spoke softly, but somehow that spun Elizabeth rancor to new heights.

"One of the IPs."

"And, where is the flight line?"

"Out there." Elizabeth pointed outside of the hangar.

"How do you think you would go about getting a yard of the tarmac out there?"

Silence. Elizabeth crossed her arms and fumed but did not speak.

"Someone is playing a practical joke on—"

"Oh, they will pay for this!" Elizabeth stomped off without another word.

"Heaven help that officer." Chuckling to himself, Darcy watched her lithe body practically vibrate as she stalked out of the hanger and back into the squadron building.

Upon arrival in his shared cubical office, he created his checklist and got on with his work. After completing item Number Two, Darcy opened his email. A number of pointless emails about various spouse activities, outlined base-sponsored trips, and calendared base library events were deleted quickly. One invitation sent by Bingley, however, did catch his eye.

United States Air Force Ball
Celebrating a Legacy of Valor
November 26, 1800
Meryton Air Force Base Officer's Club
Guest Speaker: Colonel Stephen O'Brian
Vietnam Veteran and Recipient of Air Force Silver Star
Military Uniform: Mess Dress, Semi-Formal Dress, or Service Equivalent
Civilian Attire: Black Tie, Cocktail, or Evening Gown
Tickets $75 per person
Please contact the following personnel for ticket sales:
SSgt Abernathy x2812, TSgt Carter x3372, SMSgt Grover x6593

THE AIR FORCE BALL was held every year in celebration of the air force's birthday on September 18, 1947. Darcy, who loathed going to large social events, was nearly ecstatic to have arrived after the date, as that would be one less event that he was expected to attend. Bingley, however, had been told that the Ball was postponed due to a water leak at the club, with no other appropriate venue in town. Bingley had immediately joined the committee to plan and hold the ball in November and, to Darcy's introverted horror, had been quite singular in ensuring it occurred.

Upon reading the invitation, Darcy's mind flew to an image of a petite brunette twirling in his arms while a band played a tune from days gone by. With one long blink, the vision was gone and sanity restored. Darcy determined to go, obviously, Bingley would want to go, and as he had been mooning about the house, most likely would be taking Jane. Caroline would expect him to take her, but Darcy could not even contemplate such a horrid idea.

Perhaps, just perhaps, Elizabeth would attend with her sister. Surely, they would make quite the grouping and it would be great to have the sisters together. Darcy's thoughts once again turned to her curly hair and brown eyes when he let out an audible sigh. Of course, he would not ask her to attend with him. She was an officer, he was an officer, thus far they were equal, but the world did not work that way. He was an instructor. There were rules regarding fraternization and it was too close a call for Darcy. He resolved to attend stag and remain in control, thus eliminating the guilt for ditching Caroline as a possible date and ridding of the option of Elizabeth Bennet.

ELIZABETH BENNET HAD GONE about her day in as routine a manner as possible. Instead of a flight suit, she was dressed in her light blue shirt tucked tightly into dark blue pants with shiny, polished black shoes. One of her flight mates had decided it would be fun to be stupid over the weekend and, despite the orders to stay local only, drove three hours to San Antonio to go to a club. He was found out when one of the instructors saw him driving around and now the whole class had been thrust back into *blues*, losing the precious privilege of comfort. Elizabeth went to academics, studied in her windowless flight room, memorized checklists, and ate a chicken Caesar salad for lunch. Flights would start tomorrow, so she worked diligently on her flight plans throughout the day. She knew her exact assignment would be given to her tomorrow, but competency in the planning program would assist her ability to quickly accomplish her pre-flight tasks and allow her a little extra time to chair fly.

Before returning to Longbourn, where she would be in charge

tonight while the younger girls and Mrs. Bennet went to the Lucas home for dinner, Elizabeth opened her email. She received an invitation to the Air Force Ball and felt excitement well in her chest. Elizabeth loved to dance. While she had wanted to be a pilot, and thus was often called a tomboy all her life, she really loved to dress up and pretend to be a princess ruling over a kingdom. Of course, this military ball, as an officer, she would be in a blue Mess Dress skirt and jacket with her hair pulled back in a bun, which would feel decidedly less like a princess, but that would not spoil the night.

After fulfilling her evening duties at Longbourn, she studied for her flight the next day. As her first flight, it would be a simple one with only a few tasks to execute, but in order to maintain her status at the top of the class, she would need to be perfect. At the breakfast table the next morning, her father winked and said, "Don't worry, honey, you'll do great." Lydia and Kitty gave her happy *thumbs up* from across the table and Mary told her to "trust in the Lord." Jane had hugged her tightly, letting her physical affection speak her words of hope. Only Elizabeth's mother had not joined in the family's wishes of luck. Mrs. Bennet ignored Elizabeth and all the well-wishing at the table and was strangely quiet, choosing instead to focus hard on her glass of sweet tea and toast.

Mercifully alone as Mr. Collins, unable to wake up before six-thirty, would drive himself, Elizabeth drove to the base, muttering flows, checklists, and mnemonic devices before showing her ID at the gate and then falling silent during the short, anxiety-filled mile to the squadron building. Ten minutes after she arrived, she was notified that she would be in the first flight group of the day and her brief began in thirty minutes. Captain Dashwood would be her instructor pilot and Elizabeth could not have been more pleased. He always had a calming demeanor.

Instructors varied like the colors of the rainbow. Some were incredibly strict, asking for perfection. Others were loose and practical, asking that they not wreck but not much beyond. Many preached different techniques and each had their own peculiar quirks as they flew. Captain Dashwood was a fair instructor who was praised by his students for his ability to explain procedures. Typically, the only complaint lodged against him was his propensity to hum during flights.

The briefing went well. As it was Elizabeth's first flight, Captain Dashwood would be flying the majority of the mission. Other than a few NOTAMS and procedural discussions, the most important thing he imparted was how to pass the stick back and forth. The T-6 was a small propeller plane that had enough power to do acrobatics and was equipped with two seats, one behind the other. The instructor sat in the back while the student took the front seat. The sticks of the aircraft were connected so when the student flew, the instructor could feel what they were doing and vice versa. Captain Dashwood spoke confidently during the brief and ended it quickly.

"Bennet, you look well prepared. It's your dollar ride. Let's just go out and have fun."

"Yes, sir." Elizabeth sat up a little straighter, her seriousness attempting to dampen her obvious excitement for the flight.

"Bennet, relax. Look. If you take nothing else from me today, here's what I want you to remember. When I shake the stick, I want you to take control, okay? I'll shake the stick and say, 'You have the aircraft' over the comms. In response, I want you to shake the stick and say, 'I have the aircraft.' That way I know you understand. Just have fun. Have a blast. There are so many people who would kill to fly one of these and you are one of the lucky ones. Enjoy it."

Elizabeth smiled widely and took a deep breath. He was right, of course. She was the envy of half of her ROTC group when she received her pilot slot. She had worked her whole life to fly and this would be it. Her stomach churned in a ball of anxiety and excitement as she briefly pictured diving in and out of clouds, the sun shining through the cockpit. She released her breath and suddenly, she was calm. Ready. She looked at the grinning Captain Dashwood, motioned to the door, and said, "Let's get out of here."

The two gathered up their things and headed to the equipment room where they both picked up their helmets, G-suits, and a coat for the November chill. Stopping briefly at the step desk, they received the go-no-go procedures and the tail and row number of the plane they would be flying. Much more swiftly than Elizabeth expected, the duo stepped out to the brilliant, morning sunshine and the white, concrete runways.

They boarded the bus to take themselves and the other pilot pairs to their planes and chatted briefly about the perfect weather and the day's flying conditions. Elizabeth glanced around her as they passed silver-grey T-38s, shiny white T-1s, and finally to the blue and white row of T-6s. She had not flown since finishing Fundamentals in Colorado, but the feeling remained the same: nothing is more thrilling than the sight of a plane shooting through the sky, except for the sight of a plane that one is about to fly. The most beautiful plane in the world right now was this small, propeller plane with a black painted tail number of MT-9805.

Elizabeth began her walk around looking for damage, maintenance issues, and safety concerns, following the checklists provided her during training. Captain Dashwood spoke to the maintenance crew chief and examined and signed various maintenance forms.

"All right, Bennet? Ready to get this show on the road?"

"Yes, sir!" Elizabeth responded, overjoyed at the first step to her life's goal.

"Ladies first," Dashwood said as he motioned to the ladder up to the cockpit. Elizabeth climbed quickly and began nesting in her seat, placing her bag and other items where she liked them, and began her flow: checking instruments, settings, dials, and switches while checking her work against her printed air force checklists.

Captain Dashwood checked her work and her harness straps and then climbed into his own seat.

Before she knew it, Dashwood was starting the engines. She could feel the deep rumble beneath her as the propeller in front began its dizzying spin. The air marshaller in front of her pointed at the plane and spun his hand near his head, fingers pointed to the sky, and the flight operations check began. The flaps were moved up and down, spoilers checked, and the speed break examined. Soon, she could hear Captain Dashwood's baritone over the radio:

"All right, Bennet. Take us out."

"Uh... Okay."

"Bennet, that radio is a push to talk, not a push to think! You are holding everyone up."

Elizabeth glanced to the planes around her and saw other pilots chuckling at her mistake. Embarrassed, she tried again.

Radio static.

"Yes, sir."

"Try again!"

"I said, 'Yes, sir.'" Elizabeth thought through her next words before pushing the button to speak to the Tower. "Tower, this is Dollar-05, row B, Tail MT-9805. Requesting taxi to inside runway."

A static, scratchy voice responded, "Dollar-05, this is Tower. You are approved for taxi to inside runway."

Dashwood signaled to maintenance to pull the chocks from the front and back of each wheel. Elizabeth, her helmet feeling heavy and awkward on her head, watched as everyone did their jobs. This was all a dance. Each move choreographed to perfection with every dancer making up a small part of the whole, only visible if one looked at the bigger picture on the stage. It would be easy to say that, as a pilot, she was the most important, the most vital part of flying a plane, but it would be patently untrue. Each maintenance worker, each marshaller, air traffic controller, and even every factory worker that built the plane was a backstage worker who made this flight possible.

Chocks removed, the plane pushed forward toward the runway like the smoothest car ride she had ever experienced. On the taxi way, Captain Dashwood led the instrument checks until the Tower broke through on the radio. "Dollar-05, hold short."

The plane's progress stopped, and Elizabeth took this last opportunity to calm her stomach and nerves. She took a deep breath and straightened, her hands sweating with nervousness inside her green flight gloves despite the cool air.

The tower burst through her musings: "Dollar-05, line up and wait."

The plane crawled into line at the end of the runway. Time seemed to stop and then accelerate as the tower said, "Dollar-05, cleared for takeoff." The plane sped up, throwing her back into the seat and pressing her as they rolled faster and faster. The world blurred by in blots of green and black and blue, and then, they were slicing through the air as they climbed.

Captain Dashwood began speaking on the radio, explaining procedures and demonstrating the nuances of the aircraft, but Elizabeth was unable to focus. Instead, she exhilarated in flight. She watched as the thin, wispy clouds came closer, then covered them like a blanket, before they burst through and into the blue of the sky. She squinted as the sun burned through the cockpit and felt her stomach sink and rise with minor turbulence.

When they arrived at their Military Operating Area, the imaginary box she was to stay in while practicing her maneuvers, Elizabeth was given her first go on the stick. She hit the stick and travelled a full three hundred and sixty degrees, pressed hard against the seat as she gritted her teeth and strained at the pressure of the Gs. Though she had only had the stick for her pressured circle, Captain Dashwood put the plane through its paces, demonstrating all sorts of acrobatics and showing them both a good time. They looped and rolled, sped up and stalled. Elizabeth was in heaven, even if she was a bit queasy.

Elizabeth had been flying in a small Cessna available for lessons at the local airport since she started working and was able to pay for private lessons. She had been to IFS before pilot training and was used to the feel of a stick in her hand and watching her instruments. But this was different. Elizabeth felt as if she had never truly flown before this moment. Giddy, she could feel the pressure of the plane from her eyelids to her smallest toe as it dipped and dived. The clouds slipped in and out of sight and the sound of the propeller hummed in her ears and chest. She had been on roller coasters, but nothing compared to climbing softly up and shooting straight down, hurtling toward Earth and then climbing again in safety. Grinning, she took a thousand mental pictures to recall for years to come.

Dashwood continued circling, scooping, and twirling around until Elizabeth was finally downright sick.

"Bennet, getting sick?"

The stick shook in response, Elizabeth not trusting herself to open her mouth without vomiting.

"You have the controls, just keep your mind off being sick, okay?"

The stick rocked, and she took control, keeping the plane level and matching the nose to the horizon. She searched her mind for something else to think about other than the nearest airsick bag when a tall, dark, and overconfident man presented himself to her mind's eye. Why was she thinking about Darcy at a time like this?

"Bennet, you all better? You about ready to head home?"

"Not at all," she answered sarcastically, still trying to rid herself of thoughts about Darcy's dark, piercing stare.

"It is pretty great, huh? The only time Meryton ever looks pretty in my opinion."

The tower burst through the radio waves. "All flights, we have a weather recall. Clouds moving into airfield. Return to base immediately."

"Well, that was good timing. Let's get out of here. We can do some cloud surfing on the way since they're moving in."

"Cloud surfing?"

"Haven't you ever seen a movie where the hero flies through the skies and they touch the clouds as they slip past them?"

"Yeah, but those are just movies."

"Oh, Bennet. Just you wait."

The plane streaked through the sky on their way back to the base. Large marshmallow clouds began moving in and around the plane. Large columns of cloud shot up into the sky. The plane banked and rolled through the pillars causing waves of white to surge around them. Elizabeth could not stop her burst of laughter as the plane continued its ballet through the blue.

When there was a ceiling of white above them and a floor of white below them, Dashwood got back on the radio.

"All right, Bennet, I want to show you something. Just down and to your left directly below the clouds is a red farmhouse. It is an important sight to remember because it is typically when we begin our initial for our approach back to base."

They dipped below and banked thirty degrees so that Elizabeth could see it well.

"Got it." Elizabeth spotted the red tin roof surrounded by a barn and outbuildings. The clouds rose up again and she sat back enjoying the ride.

"Bennet, I want you to do something for me really quickly. Just point up if you can hear me."

Elizabeth pointed directly above her head at the canopy.

"Now, look down at your instrumentation."

Elizabeth did as instructed and was shocked. She had pointed to what she felt was up, but they were still in the thirty-degree bank, doing circles above the farmhouse that was now invisible below the clouds.

"I'm glad these clouds moved in; I can make an important point. You have vertigo, when your ears and your eyes are telling you two different things. Especially when flying in clouds or where you can't see the horizon, like at night, it's important to check what you're feeling with what your instruments are saying. They call what just happened the 'death spiral' if it happens too long and you don't check yourself. You just keep turning, losing altitude slowly until there is nothing you can do, no amount of pulling up on the stick or pushing up on the throttles will help."

Elizabeth nodded in response and said, "Noted. Consider this one lesson learned."

The plane circled about and with the turn, Elizabeth refocused herself to the tasks at hand. She fought the whole world as it seemed to scream to her that she was turning, despite heading straight and level at the horizon. Despite her concentration, Darcy strolled arrogantly back into her thoughts during her vertigo. She maintained her concentration as best as she could under his dark level gaze until the wheels touched down and she found herself posing for pictures, helmet in hand, on the ladder of the plane as she stepped out of the cockpit.

Elizabeth was heady with the thrill of flying, briefly distracted by Captain Darcy who had strolled in. She walked past the step desk, oblivious to most everything else in her post flight bliss.

CHAPTER 12

*E*lizabeth rushed home, thrilled to tell her older sister the news of her successful flight. When she arrived, Jane was beaming.

"Charles just called. He asked me to go to the Air Force Ball with him. Oh, Lizzy! I am so excited! We have to go dress shopping. Mama said she will take me on Saturday, but you have to come. You know her taste is always so gaudy, and I just want something tasteful. I need you there with me."

Elizabeth, who had been grasping Jane's forearms and twirling and jumping about the room with her, shrieked. "Of course, I'll be coming! I have to wear a boring Mess Dress, but you will be absolutely lovely! Ready to run away to Netherfield with Mr. Bingley!"

The girls giggled together. "Jane, he is handsome and awesome and rich. I'm sure you'll have a whole pack of babies and make each other both incredibly happy!"

It was at this point that their mother's twittering rang around the family room contrary to their placid father, who sat in his chair and opened a newspaper.

"Oh Jane, we are saved! You will marry Mr. Bingley and he will take care of all of us when that dreadful Mr. Collins closes

101

Meryton and none of us have jobs! You will have a wonderful time. He's half in love with you already, but you must finish roping him in! You must have the best of everything! Maybe green silk to bring out your eyes? Or lace to keep him wanting more, hmm?" This statement was punctuated with a raised eyebrow, knowing smile, and seductive waggle of the shoulder.

"Fanny, if you act like that, you will surely draw the eyes of the handsome Bingley, and then where will I be?" Their mother blushed at her husband.

"I draw the line at talk of lace and husband hunting. I am going to my office." Their father stood, grinned at both daughters and tapped his wife on the shoulder with his newspaper as he went.

Simultaneously, Collins entered. Elizabeth had been relieved he had not imposed on her early schedule and opted to drive himself, sparing her his slimy company. His double chin wobbled as he surveyed the room's inhabitants and smirked.

"Marvelous. I am very excited to attend such an innocent diversion as a ball. You see, as an aid to Catherine de Bourgh, I am often held to standards which are much more stringent than that of the rest of society. A ball, however, and a military ball at that, will be a symbol of gaiety, of morale, and of good will, that I, as an emissary for the United States Senate, cannot *not* attend. Of course, with a personal invitation from the wing commander, how can I refuse? Obviously, I will also be able to escort you fine ladies and perhaps engage in a lively dance or two, hmm?"

Jane and Elizabeth stared blankly at the stout man before their mother broke the awkward silence, her debutante training never failing in her hostess duties.

"Of course, our dear Lizzy would love nothing more than to attend with you!"

Elizabeth could have kicked her mother, however, surprised herself by saying, "Certainly, I'm sure I could drive you." She prayed the vagueness of her answer would save her from the

THE BEST LAID FLIGHT PLANS

indignities that were sure to arise and stretched her mouth into a gracious smile and not the grimace she felt. Taking Jane by the elbow, she steered her out of the room as quickly as she could manage.

It didn't occur to her until she settled into her own bed that no one had asked her about her first flight.

The shopping expedition came and went, and the night of November 26 arrived much faster than anyone anticipated. Elizabeth had flown her first flights and other than a few rough landings and occasional difficulty with the stick, she remained first in her class. Meanwhile, Jane and Bingley had been texting, calling, and attending every activity their small town had to offer. Caroline was always with them, a constant third wheel, but still, Jane was happy, so Elizabeth was happy for her.

Elizabeth helped Jane curl and pin her hair into an up-do with cascading curls over one shoulder. Jane held up Elizabeth's dark blue Mess Dress jacket and helped Elizabeth slip it over her shoulders.

"Jane, you really are the most beautiful person I've ever known. Bingley will die when he sees you."

Jane's eyes lit up. "Well, I hope not *die*."

Bingley arrived at five thirty to pick up Jane and their mother immediately accosted him, dragging the poor man into Longbourn's sitting room and plying him with a glass of homemade lemonade and a lavish hors d'oeuvre tray.

"How delightful it is to have you at Netherfield, Captain Bingley. It is such a nice home after all. Such expensive furnishings. The last renters left ages ago and it is a drag on the neighborhood for the home to be left empty."

Though uncomfortable to all, her raptures were accurate, as Netherfield had been once considered one of the grandest homes in the county and only a man with a small fortune could afford the rent. The air force paid its pilots decently, but not *that* decently, and her mother knew it.

"It is lovely. My sister Caroline has done quite a bit of redecorating, and I quite enjoy it. There are fewer things to do here than in the city, but I find the country absolutely delightful!" Bingley was all smiles as Jane stepped through the door, revealing her forest green dress and long blonde curls. He reached for Jane's hand and stood, excited to be on their way and turned to politely say goodbye.

"Well, my Jane must not be showing you around town. There are events nearly every weekend! FFA and 4-H always hold several nice stock shows, and there is the First Friday art-walk through the galleries in town. In fact, I think there are at least twenty-four families here that are very welcoming and, of course, Meryton always hosts such lovely events. Drop Nights, graduations, and the like. Well, look at tonight, for example, the two of you make such a lovely couple!"

Bingley nodded as a blushing Jane ushered him out. Bingley's truck made quick work of the driveway, and Elizabeth left soon thereafter with a sweaty Collins in an ill-fitting suit. Wishing she could be alone with her radio instead of his incessant chatter, she counted the miles until they arrived at the O-Club and she could escape Collins' disgusting presence.

The club was decorated with air force blue and silver fabric, flowers, and confetti, transforming the same room where Drop Night had been. Round tables of eight were arranged around a large wooden dance floor. A local deejay played easy jazz.

Elizabeth swiftly ditched Collins at the reception line, while he toadied up to high ranking officers, and strolled around the tables looking for the place card bearing her name. Luckily, Collins would be seated at the head table near the wing commander as his personal guest, so she would not have to worry about listening to his blather throughout the night. She grabbed a Manhattan from the bar and found her name next to Jane's and Bingley's. She glanced at the card on the other side of her plate and slumped.

Captain William Darcy. Was there never a way to escape that man? Now she was to be subjected to his arrogant, know-it-all comments or his haughty silences. *No. I will not let his disagreeableness affect my night.* She was going to have a good time, regardless of the company. She looked again and noted that Caroline Bingley and her stares of displeasure would be seated at the other side of Darcy. *Lovely.*

Elizabeth walked around the table reading the name cards to see who else would be there. A pestering voice in the back of her mind told her to look for Wickham, as she had secretly hoped to be entertained by his quick wit. On her tiptoes, she peeked over the centerpiece at the next table. A shadow passed over her and she found herself staring at a white shirt and blue jacket tailored tightly over a broad chest. She dropped to her heels and looked up to see William Darcy's eyes boring down on her. His earthy cologne enveloped her, and she felt her blood pressure race next to his impressive physical presence.

"Looking for someone?" Darcy's quiet voice reverberated near Elizabeth's ear.

She shook herself out of her fog. *He probably gets in my personal space to disconcert me*—but she would not fall under his spell.

"No, uh... Just admiring the general splendor." She turned away and swallowed deeply from her glass, glimpsing Jane leading Bingley to the table. He carried their drinks behind her and seemed entranced by the cut of Jane's dress and her exposed back. Jane smiled knowingly as Elizabeth pressed her lips together and widened her eyes in attempts to convey her irritation at the presence of Darcy.

A bell rang and the emcee, a nervous major, clearly emceeing for the first time, called for everyone to be seated. The head table, including the guest speaker and an already wilting Mr. Collins, was herded into their seats by committee members. Five minutes later, following the national anthem, Caroline, wearing a vivid burnt orange cocktail dress, arrived and sat down next to Darcy.

Her tardiness was noted by the surrounding tables and more than one eye roll was hidden behind programs.

"Charles, you *left* me!"

"I told you when I had to leave, and you said you needed another thirty minutes. It's not my fault you didn't want to come with Darcy, besides you have a car."

"Darcy didn't tell me when he left."

"Well, I imagine he thought you would just come with me."

Caroline's grunt of frustration overpowered the speaker's lengthy introduction of the chaplain.

First, Collins, then Darcy is next to me, and now Caroline. Super. Elizabeth sighed thinking she would likely burn in Hell thinking such uncharitable thoughts during the chaplain's prayer over the proceedings. Immediately following this bleak thought, Jane leaned over and touched Elizabeth's knee gently.

"Lizzy, I've asked around"—in a hushed voice she continued —"I know you were hoping to see Wickham tonight, but someone said they've got him working some special duty. I don't know that he is coming. I'm so, so sorry, Lizzy."

Elizabeth's dreary demeanor had deflated further, and she decided to drown her sorrows in her cocktail. Of course, she discovered her glass empty, so water would have to do until she could get back to the bar. At this point, she expected rain to come pouring through the ceiling and wondered if she should have brought her umbrella.

The wing commander then stood and began his introductory remarks of welcome.

"Per tradition"—the wing commander rang out over the microphone in the room—"we will start our proceedings by toasting persons who are prisoners of war, killed in action, or missing in action. Please stand and raise your glasses.

> *'We toast our hearty comrades who have fallen from the skies,*

*And were gently caught by God's own hands to be with him
    on high,
To dwell among the soaring clouds, they have known so well
    before,
From victory roll to tail chase, at heaven's very door.
And as we fly among them, we're sure to hear their plea,
Take care, my friend, watch your six, and do one more roll
    for me.
To our comrades killed in action, missing in action, or
    prisoners of war!'"*

A RESOUNDING, "HEAR, HEAR!" was heard throughout the crowd.

The wing commander then introduced the guest speaker who gave an inspiring speech about his squadron during Vietnam and how they overcame their trials. During the speech, Elizabeth heard a low buzz of whispers between Jane and Bingley, leaning toward each other, foreheads almost touching. Elizabeth's heart glowed to see the romantic scene and she distracted herself through the rest of the speeches, imagining Jane's wedding. *You are as bad as Mom.* She reached for her glass. *Still water.*

"How are the flights going, Elizabeth? Where is your class right now?" asked Bingley as he accepted his plate from the waiter.

"Going well. I had my Dollar Ride with Dashwood—"

"I like him. Really knows his stuff."

"And did you do well?" Darcy asked.

"Well, I didn't hook, so I suppose that's the best any student could hope for."

"Lizzy is just being modest," interjected Jane. "She told me she had the best grade in the flight."

"I'm sure Eliza just didn't want the rest of the company to feel embarrassed about their own performance in the plane. Of course, William has no reason to blush. Always Distinguished Graduate." Caroline's voice purred as she reached out and brushed Darcy's arm from shoulder to elbow. Darcy maneuvered his chair closer to Elizabeth.

"Trying for 38s?"

"Of course." Elizabeth looked directly into Darcy's dark eyes and remembered his comments about women pilots and how they should leave the real work to the men. "I know we lady pilots seem demure, but I plan on being the best pilot the air force has to offer."

"I'm glad to hear that. I'm sure the WASPs would be proud." His mouth crooked into a half smile.

Elizabeth smiled sweetly back at him. *The WASPs proud that a woman actually gets credit for her contribution for once? Shocking!* She received her plate and immediately dove into her food, attempting to ward off more conversation with the man sitting next to her and listened to Jane and Bingley discuss the shows they watched together and whatever other trivial topics they discussed.

Eventually, dinner plates were cleared, and dancing music commenced, encouraging Bingley to sweep Jane to the dance floor for the first song. Caroline, Darcy, and Elizabeth meanwhile remained at the table. Caroline silently watched Darcy who stared straight ahead. Elizabeth yawned and fought the urge to lay her head on the table and let the evening wash over her. Mr. Collins, who had moved from the head table, had been following commanding officers around as they took flight from his greasy prattle. He ultimately landed in Jane's seat and began a running commentary on the events of the ball so far.

"I'm so glad you are here to witness what has been such a prestigious event. Never before have I attended an evening of such beautiful military precision outside of the purview of my wonderful manager, Senator de Bourgh. I find that that lady not only has the exquisite taste that comes with someone of high society, but she also graciously condescends to those who could never imagine the life of class that she is able to create. Despite being an employee of hers, I find that I am often grateful for what she has taught me regarding how to properly run an event. I flatter the organizers here by thinking that Senator de Bourgh would be very impressed how this ball has been run. My duties for the senator obviously take precedence over any sort of joyous occasions of celebration, but I flatter myself that I have been to one or two thus far in my employment."

Elizabeth, who had chosen to not pay attention to the former speech, nodded appropriately and Mr. Collins continued, this time, to Elizabeth's horror, speaking directly to Darcy and Caroline.

"I am William Collins. And who are you? Friends of the Bennets?" He looked at them expectantly and Elizabeth nearly bolted from her seat. She had intentionally not introduced him in hopes that he would not humiliate her.

"Caroline Bingley. How do you do?"

"Captain William Darcy."

"Oh, Captain Darcy? Not the famous Pemberley Wines, William Darcy?"

Darcy looked around as if to find another William Darcy had walked up and entered the conversation.

"I own Pemberley."

"Captain Darcy. I must tell you that your aunt, Senator de Bourgh, was well when I left her one month ago."

Darcy twisted his lip but maintained his stoicism that had come to define him in Elizabeth's mind.

"Thank you for that information."

Darcy turned away. Elizabeth pulled out her phone to check for messages while planning a quiet exit. She could not exactly abandon Collins, but maybe she could coordinate another ride through the wing commander's assistant. As she put her phone back in her purse, Darcy asked, "Are you having fun?"

Elizabeth rolled her eyes. "Oh, you know, loads."

"Would you like to dance?"

Anything to get away from Collins.

"Sure." Elizabeth was shocked to hear her voice and felt an overpowering urge to retract her answer and run but reminded herself that every attempt to intimidate her must be a reason for her courage to rise. Caroline scowled, and Elizabeth sensed the toady Collins meant to say something. Smiling graciously, she stood up. Despite her annoyance at Darcy's pompous existence, the man made her pulse quicken.

Darcy led Elizabeth to the dance floor without touching her, but still, she could feel the electricity sparking between them. What song played Elizabeth would never know because when he took her hand and placed his other hand on the small of her back, the music seemed to fade away. And all she could hear was her pulse in her ears and the pressure of his fingers on her spine.

"Well, Captain Darcy, it seems like the committee has done an outstanding job this year." Looking up to his face, Elizabeth acknowledged that he was a very handsome man. Beneath his dark jacket, she could feel lean muscle as he led her smoothly around the dance floor.

"I see you prefer to be unsociable and taciturn. But conversation makes this all so much more enjoyable, don't you think?"

"Well, please, do continue."

"I talked about the committee and program, maybe you can start with the attendees or the deejay?"

"In that case...seems like a good crowd."

Elizabeth scrutinized his expression but he pointedly ignored her eyes. She began searching the room again for Wickham to determine if maybe her night might not be a total wash.

"Looking for someone?"

"Yeah, actually. I thought George Wickham would be here tonight."

"Wickham?" Darcy practically growled the name.

"Yeah, he said you guys were once friends."

"Yeah, at one time. He certainly makes friends, but I wouldn't say he has ever kept any."

"I suppose he should be upset for losing your friendship?"

Darcy frowned. "What is it you Southerners say? Bless his heart." Sarcasm dripped off of every word and Elizabeth was stunned that she had ever thought Captain William Darcy handsome as he displayed his disgust.

The pair had stopped moving, both with hands clenched at their sides.

"You should stay away from him. He is nothing but bad news. He shouldn't be trusted." Darcy then left her fuming in the middle of the dance floor and stalked out of the room.

CHAPTER 13

*D*arcy stormed out into the dark, embracing the humid night air in his fury like a comforting blanket.

Why Wickham? Why can't Wickham just disappear in the light like the cockroach he is?

Breathing deeply, Darcy paced in the parking lot. He fidgeted with the keys in his pockets as he regained control of his emotions. Wickham has been poisoning her against him with whatever lies he had concocted this time! Wanting nothing more than to flee Meryton and everyone—*don't think about Elizabeth*—associated with *this damn base,* he mulled over a few options. After hasty deliberations, his mind clung to a new plan and he set off for Netherfield to put it into action.

He was halfway through packing a bag full of sand-colored flight suits when Bingley arrived home. Darcy heard his friend's elated voice drifting up the stairs before Bingley's head of red hair leaned against the door frame.

"Tonight was fantastic. I don't think I've ever been so happy in my entire life." Bingley walked to the bed and flopped down on it looking dreamily at the ceiling. "I think I'm going to marry her, Darce. Want to be my best man?"

"I may have to miss your blessed nuptials, Bing. I am deployed to Qatar in the morning, so I won't be around to plan your bachelor party." His voice was clipped but his happiness for his friend was real.

"What on earth do you mean, deployed?"

"Well, you see Charles, since 9/11 there has been a war going in Afghanistan and Iraq—" Bingley threw a pillow at his head.

"I know what deployed means, you ass."

"I got an email a few weeks ago looking for CAOC tour volunteers. Kelley volunteered to get a box checked, but he's been having a rough time. I called him up just now and I was able to take his spot, so he could stay here and take care of his personal issues. They pull chocks tomorrow, so I'm packing up tonight and then I'll be off around five in the morning. I'm catching a ride with Patrick Hammock who's headed toward the airport to pick up a friend."

Bingley's surprise by this sudden news was expected but not the range of emotions that flashed across his face: annoyance, sadness, and finally, acceptance. "Well, what shall we tell Caroline?"

Neither Darcy nor Bingley could hide their smiles and eventually doubled over with laughter.

THE NEXT MORNING dawned while Darcy sat in the passenger seat of Hammock's car.

"Miserable weather, huh? I hate it when it gets all cloudy like this," Hammock said as he squinted out at the skies around the car.

"Makes for nice sunrises though," Darcy said, pointing to the sky in front of them.

"I guess."

A few hours later, they arrived at the San Antonio international airport and Darcy caught the first flight to the East Coast and then another to Qatar. Forty-six hours later, he arrived tired, hungry, and cranky but relieved to have escaped Wickham and the haunting presence of Elizabeth Bennet.

After orientation at the base theater, Darcy found his trailer building, getting the lay of the land. The only concern he had was when to call Georgiana and Richard and inform them of his arrival. The old, rundown trailers had internet, of course, but it was spotty at best and would require all his patience to focus on the conversations and not just press the hang up button before his relatives were content.

He organized what he referred to as his "cell" and then fell blissfully asleep for fourteen hours. He awoke with a headache and the need for the restroom. He put on sandals and trudged outside the fifty yards, away from his trailer to the communal bathroom, blinded by the sun glaring off the rocks. He noted to get sunglasses for this awful routine as he was not quite up to relieving himself in a bottle to avoid the bright sun. Darcy brushed his teeth and readied himself for the day. On the way back to his room to change into his uniform, he grabbed a case of water from under a centrally located tent to place in his tiny room refrigerator.

Eventually, he made his way to the cafeteria where he gorged himself on eggs and purposefully ignored the distinct scent of turkey bacon (pork bacon being impossible to get within the Muslim nation). After breakfast, work was next. Darcy completed his twelve-hour shift, perfectly executing his check lists and eliminating Elizabeth Bennet from his thoughts for most of the day. He spent his evenings at "the bra", a large tent with two pointed domes which earned the recreation center its name, where he was allotted three alcoholic beverages for the day at the bar and could call family or play games with other soldiers.

Thus, his life went on through December, January, and February. The weather was moderate during the winter so for the first time he suffered through a deployment without his skin melting off in the heat waves of Arabian summers. His opportunities to communicate with Charles or Georgiana or Richard were infrequent due to time differences and scheduling difficulties and his unvarying shift work.

Despite his general pleasure in his work and his duties, every night, Darcy was troubled by the remembrance of Elizabeth's chestnut curls, her eyes flashing in laughter or wrath, the curve of her hips... Every night was the same: sleep, then wake up from vivid dreams of Elizabeth.

Darcy knew it was only a matter of time before he returned and would be near *her* again. As the New Year broke, he made several resolutions. First, he would forget that Elizabeth Bennet existed. Second, he would throw himself into being the best brother and guardian Georgiana had ever seen. Thirdly, he would find someone. All this being alone was going to his head.

In March, Darcy made the reverse trip back to Meryton. First to Germany, then the East Coast, and finally arrived to the fanfare of Charles, Caroline, and Jane Bennet who had driven up to meet him at the airport. Charles and Jane were inseparable, practically glued at the hip, but the peace on Charles' face was undeniable.

The next morning, Darcy returned to work, grateful that the ghost of Elizabeth Bennet chose not to accompany him.

CHAPTER 14

*A*fter the Air Force Ball, Elizabeth had arrived home infuriated and tired. Darcy was apparently too good to say goodbye to even the Bingleys after abandoning her on the dance floor. There was already going to be some gossip about her dancing with him as he had never participated in any social activity on the base. She was now afraid that gossip would now revolve around their evident argument on the dance floor and his quick exit.

She would not let Darcy and his bad manners dictate her behavior. She was used to the male pilots in her flight exhibiting shock and awe when she excelled; Darcy would be no different. She determined to fling herself into her studies and think no more of him. Elizabeth religiously avoided the T-38 hall, and three days after the Air Force Ball, Mr. Collins left as well, off to give his report to the grand lady herself, Senator de Bourgh.

Bingley and Jane's relation continued to grow, much to Caroline's obvious dismay, and Elizabeth's joyful envy. The day after the ball, Caroline left to visit her sister and brother-in-law, the Hursts, in Charleston, leaving Bingley blissfully alone to woo his angel in private. Since Darcy had volunteered for deployment,

Caroline no longer felt her presence necessary at Netherfield. With Netherfield quiet and Jane content, Elizabeth thrust herself into pilot training: studying, chair flying late into the evening, and practicing in simulators in the early mornings.

Though she had flown with him a few times and was still mesmerized by his presence, word eventually reached her that Wickham was now dating the freckle-faced Mary King. Mary was a sweet local girl who had recently received a large inheritance from her uncle. Lydia had decried the situation to be "the absolute worst" and moped around the house for several hours before determining she liked Captain Denny better anyway. Elizabeth decided men were too much of a distraction from her studies. Between her duties at Longbourn and continuing in the T-6, Elizabeth seemed almost manic as she not only powered through her responsibilities but thrived in the frantic pace of discovery.

The beginning of March brought back the irksome Collins for another report and the end of Elizabeth's peace. Jane was expecting a proposal from Bingley any day and her mother could hardly control herself. She was constantly in the kitchen concocting a dish for Bingley to try in order to reel him in further. Determined that two daughters wed was better than one, Fanny Bennet increasingly threw Mr. Collins in Elizabeth's path. To her chagrin, Elizabeth was forced to provide him rides, accompany him around town and to the base, and listen to his pretentions of Senator de Bourgh interspersed with senseless ramblings.

Lydia and Kitty continued to throw themselves at every officer in sight and Mary's preaching became increasingly doomsday. There never seemed to be a minute at Longbourn where Mr. Bennet was cloistered in his office—so tiresome were his silliest daughters and wife. Elizabeth frequently kept him company hoping to drown out their tittering, gossiping, and philandering. Between her family and Mr. Collins, Elizabeth's only quiet moments were flying.

As training progressed so did the work load. Trainees memorized entire texts about the plane, flying, the Bernoulli effect, weather, flight physics...to be able to recite at a moment's notice. She went to bed every night only when she could no longer keep her eye lids open and woke before she was ready. Both her body and mind were tired but so was everyone in her flight. She had no choice but to push harder. In her flight, only the slowest had missed a question on a test and she would not allow imperfection in herself.

The Wednesday before Easter, Elizabeth arrived at work, after dropping off the irritatingly loquacious Mr. Collins at the Wing building. While waiting for her slow, government-issue computer to open, Elizabeth amused herself by spinning in her large office chair. A flash of dark green caught the corner of her eye. Her brown boots scraped the floor as she stopped and placed both hands on the desk to give full attention to the flight suit in front of her. Dizzy, she felt her face burn to discover Captain Darcy looking down at her ridiculous spinning. And smiling.

"I didn't know you were back," Elizabeth stuttered.

"I was told to come here and escort you to a meeting with Colonel Forsythe," Darcy said evenly. She was surprised to see his dark eyes laughing at her playful antics rather than an officer in the air force.

Her stomach turned on itself when she heard his deep voice. By rank, she would obey but.... His voice seemed to brush past her ears and caress her hair and—*What are you thinking?* Lack of sleep and constant male interaction (without any *action*) was clearly muddling her head.

"What about?"

"No idea. I was sent and here I am."

"Let's get going then."

The two left Elizabeth's office, exited the building, put on their covers while squinting in the sunshine, and strolled the long sidewalk to the Wing building. Neither spoke. Neither looked at the other, though she could not help but wonder what he was thinking. A constant buzz of thunderous take offs and planes circling overhead made it difficult to converse even if they had wanted to do so. To observers, the two probably looked like they were marching on parade, feet in sync despite the marked difference in their statures. To Elizabeth, the only thing of which she was aware were the sparks ignited from being so near *him*. In fact, since their disastrous dance months before she had both arduously avoided even thinking about *him*, but somehow, now that he was close, every moment of that night came rushing back—she could almost feel his hand at her back once more.

She also could not forget how he left her on the dance floor or his treatment of his former friend. She wondered if he felt the tension between them or if she was only imagining it.

Upon entering the white, art deco era building, Darcy held the door to the conference room, gesturing for Elizabeth to go through first.

The droning sounds of Mr. Collin's voice filled the room and Elizabeth rolled her eyes and groaned. Darcy grinned at her dramatic deflation and collapsed into the first available chair at the conference table. The wing commander, Colonel Forsythe, cut Collins off.

"I'm sure y'all are wondering why I called you here today."

Elizabeth and Darcy glanced at each other and then back to Forsythe. After a short beat, Elizabeth decided to respond.

"Um, yes, sir. Especially since we aren't in the same plane or even the same squadron."

Mr. Collins, who had been bowing his head over and over, could not stop from inserting himself into the conversation.

"Captain Darcy, it is so nice to meet you once again. I must tell you that your aunt, the Honorable Catherine de Bourgh, was quite well when I left her in her office at the capitol building not two weeks ago. Her assistant Anne also fares quite well, but I am sure you must keep in touch quite often, so you would have no need of me to tell you that. The grand lady would, I am sure, be quite pleased to let me bring you this wonderful news and I am positive would add her glad tidings to the rest of you as she is the very model of benevolence and decorum."

Before he could continue further, the colonel, closing his eyes briefly, displaying his saint-like patience, interrupted.

"We have a very special assignment for the two of you. Apparently, Mr. Collins, here, is on a special mission as an aide to Senator de Bourgh and is to return with a report on whether Meryton base should continue to be operational or should be placed on the closure list this round. He asked for two representatives to attend the first committee session regarding these closures in case any of the senators have questions about the base. Captain Darcy, your familial connections to Senator de Bourgh will have no bearing on the case as, of course, the senator is impartial and above nepotism. Of course, being regularly ranked as the number one IP for your classes justly imparts credibility to your expertise and opinion. Lieutenant Bennet, you are not only a local who can brief about the community's involvement with the base and vice versa, but you were also the number one pick for your class' pilot slots and are currently number one in your class. Of course, both of you pilot different aircraft which lends itself to a broader sense of diversity and ability to answer any technical questions which may be addressed to you."

Darcy nodded.

"Mr. Collins will also be bringing along a"—he lowered his glasses and checked a list in front of him—"Miss Charlotte Lucas, whose father is an important local and former commander here. As a civilian, she can speak to the importance of the continued operation of Meryton, the impact on the community, and past issues of which Lieutenant Bennet may not be aware."

Elizabeth's lips turned up into a wide smile upon finding out that her best friend would be travelling with them. Perhaps, despite Darcy's moods and Collins' longwinded chatter, she may actually have an enjoyable time.

"Of course, Collins and Miss Lucas, as civilians will be travelling separately and Darcy and Bennet, the two of you will take one of the u-drives and run up. The senate committee meetings will apparently all be taking place at Rosings, Senator de Bourgh's compound. Do you know how to get to Hunsford?"

"I do. I've gone there every Easter since my uncle died," he said so rapidly, the words almost spilled from his lips.

"Let me know if you need help finding the forms for the u-drive or the non-availability slips. I know the MPF isn't always on their game when you need them.

"You will be expected to arrive in casual dress but be aware that you will have several dinners which will require appropriate dress. See my secretary for the details. I'm told you should expect to be there for up to two weeks so pack accordingly. Janine has the lists from the Senate, so just stop by her desk on the way out."

Two weeks? Elizabeth stood to argue. "But, sir. What about training? If I'm away, I won't be able to keep up, sir."

"Don't worry, Bennet, if you need to wash back, I'll make sure you get a special bullet for your promotion boards discussing the vital nature of this assignment."

"But, sir..."

"Bennet. This assignment is above me, so I'm not the one to complain to. In point of fact, if you figure out who to complain to, let me know. I don't like being told where my pilots should go."

Elizabeth was incredibly pissed. She had worked too hard to get to the head of her flight. She had done nothing but eat, drink, and sleep pilot training for months and would be damned if she did not graduate on time. She had even defied her mother and given up dating (not that she had had any time for a social life!) And when she did go out with her flight mates, all the guys talked about was beer, sports, and women. At least they stopped degrading women in front of her, but she still had to listen to more than her fair share of detailed sexual encounters. She had dealt with the challenges her family presented and the ridiculous image her officer-chasing sisters presented. She was going to get out of this assignment come hell or high water.

When they were dismissed, she left the room with a cold, indignant gait.

Darcy led the way out the door and she sped up, passing him while trying to walk off her anger before getting back to her flight room. She heard his clunking boots on the tile behind her and then the sidewalk, easily keeping with her furious pace.

"If Aunt Catherine wants you there, nothing you do will keep you here." Darcy spoke gently, cooling the flames of her indignation. "You might as well channel whatever it is you are feeling into training. You'll be a better pilot for it."

Elizabeth stopped the retort on the tip of her tongue. He *was* trying to be nice to her.

"Great." She sighed. "Just great. And what exactly am I supposed to do between now and then? Just study? How am I going to get my hours if I'm forced to be off rambling around the state with that ogre and his boss?"

Elizabeth swore she saw Darcy's mouth hint at a grin.

"I can help you while we drive. T-6s were a long time ago for me, but I'm sure I remember the basics."

Elizabeth let his voice wash over her, weirdly calming while causing her temperature to rise a few degrees.

"That would be great." She quickly realized she had acquiesced without so much as a word and her resentment rose again. She swallowed it down and muttered, "That would be helpful. Thank you."

"Let me grab your number so I can call you after I talk to Janine. She'll be out for lunch by now, but I can run back by this afternoon and figure out the plan. I've got an office day today."

"That would be amazing," Elizabeth said as she pulled her pen from her flight suit sleeve and wrote her number on Darcy's outstretched palm, ignoring the current pulsing through her fingertips. "I've got a sim at two and then an academic test tomorrow and I have to go review some emergency procedures."

"Eps, huh? Who's running the sim?"

"Bear, I think."

"Make sure you state your case firmly. He likes it when the students are confident, even if they are wrong."

"I heard he was a bit of a stickler."

"That's why he's called 'Bear,' but really, as long as you state your case, he's more Teddy than Grizzly."

Elizabeth looked at Darcy for a long moment while he opened the building door for her. "Thanks again." She smiled at him and walked through the doors, removing her flight cap.

"My pleasure. I'll, uh, call you later, then"—and then turned down the T-38 hallway. Elizabeth returned to her flight room depressed at the idea of going to Austin and the impact it might have on her training, but, for some strange reason, her mood became increasingly light as she studied.

CHAPTER 15

*D*arcy pulled up to Longbourn Inn a week later in a blue sedan. Elizabeth climbed in before her family could say farewell and they were off. He tuned the radio to the only English radio station in the area and country music filled the car. Darcy had always preferred other musical genres but had to admit that country was fitting considering the barren South Texas surroundings. He settled into driving and let his mind drift to the woman beside him.

After a few miles, Elizabeth said, "This is a nice car for government issue. Normally they give you those awful cars with the manual windows and locks. Did you know those are actually more expensive? I guess civilians get cranky when they see government cars with auto-locks because they think we are living in the lap of luxury or something, but yeah, the air force gets all the auto stuff taken out for a *higher* cost, so we don't look rich."

"It's my car, actually. I didn't feel like driving one of those until we had to."

"That seems like a smart plan." Elizabeth quietly returned to looking out the window at the world as it passed, humming familiar tunes as they drove.

He rarely had seen her in civilian clothing. She wore tight jeans which showed off her muscular legs, and a loose-fitting button-down shirt tucked into her jeans further accentuating her figure. He could never describe her as curvaceous, but she was, without a doubt, sexy. Small, plump breasts hinted a perfect décolletage at the V of her shirt and her polished, bare toes peeked out from her jeans in strappy sandals.

"Where are we going?" Elizabeth finally asked when she noticed they were going in the opposite direction of Austin.

"Rosings."

"Thanks," she said sarcastically. "You're going the wrong way. Hunsford is that way." Elizabeth pointed behind her.

"I know where I'm going." Darcy felt his smile reach his eyes beneath his sunglasses.

"Sure you do." She leaned back, brought out her study materials and began reading, murmuring as she read and frequently moved her hands about an imaginary instrument panel.

Staring straight ahead, Darcy interrupted her review. "Where are you guys these days? You should be doing low levels soon, right?"

"Yeah, we've been a little slow with some weather, but we should get there within the month. Although, maybe not me with this little delay I have going." She smiled at him, her eyes sparkling.

"What are you studying now? If you want, you can chair fly out loud. I'll tell you if you miss anything."

"That would actually be amazing. I'm struggling with the timing of clock to map to ground."

"That will be easy to work on in a minute."

"Well, honestly, I think it might be a little hard in the car since I've got to figure out the new maps and times, and I know I'm from here, but surprise, surprise, I actually don't know every possible threat on the road."

"Good thing we won't be on the road then."

Darcy looked at her over his sunglasses and turned the car into a parking lot. She was astonished to find they were at the small county municipal airport. A rusting, white metal sign spelled "Hertfordshire County International Airport" in black, block letters.

"Are the T-1 guys taking us up to Austin on an out and back or something and then we just go from there?"

"No, Bennet, I'm flying us up." Elizabeth snorted as he took their suitcases out of the trunk and began walking to the double doors of the miniscule terminal.

"In what? Your private plane?"

"As a matter of fact..." He grinned and motioned through the small hallway to the windows opposite them. Outside on the ramp stood his glistening Beechcraft Bonanza A36.

Clearly stunned, Elizabeth stopped. The Bonanza was a propeller plane that could seat six. The belly of the plane was painted white, while the top half was grey. The nose of the plane and the tail were both jet black.

Walking through the terminal, he waved to Chance and Jared, the air traffic controllers and terminal caretakers. When he reached the next set of double doors leading to the runways, she still was several feet behind him.

"Bennet? You coming?"

"In that?" Elizabeth began walking, looking at the plane.

Darcy took her bag from her and began his ground checks, walking slowly around the plane. Elizabeth was oblivious to him as she strolled to the open door and peeked inside.

Darcy climbed in and began his checklist. As she crossed the threshold, he *felt*, more than saw, Elizabeth sitting, her back to him, glancing around at the plane's amenities. Plush, leather seats, small pullout tables and large windows. Darcy granted Elizabeth some time to take in everything around her, signaling to Chance that he was ready to go. Chance waved up at Darcy and pulled out the chocks from around the wheels. Elizabeth merely moved her hand in a gesture approximating a wave, still clearly astonished at her surroundings.

Elizabeth checked out the instruments watching the dials spin and the numbers climb. She adjusted her seat to see the horizon and sighed, sinking deeply into the leather. She reverently touched the panel in front of her and mumbled as she took in the beautiful plane.

"Does Sheila meet your approval?" Darcy questioned while hands glided over various instruments, switches, and knobs.

"You have a flight attendant?" Elizabeth exclaimed.

Darcy chuckled deeply, shaking his head and jolting Elizabeth into full awareness of just how ridiculous she must appear.

"No, the plane. I named her Sheila. The first time I took her out, Bingley and I ended up in a weird Australian pub, so the name sort of stuck."

"I've always wanted to travel," Elizabeth said, a sort of passing sadness moving over her eyes quickly. "My father hates traveling and, of course, my mother becomes a nervous wreck, so we tend to stay around here."

"Maybe one day, I'll take you there." The words hung heavily as he considered their meaning. "You'd enjoy it. Good food," he said before he could stop himself.

Elizabeth examined every aspect of the cockpit, looking behind her and watching his movements like a hawk. After a few minutes, Darcy pushed the intercom button and Elizabeth heard his low, smiling voice from the headsets.

"Welcome to Darcy Airlines. I'd like to remind you that this is a non-smoking flight and keep seatbelts fastened at all times unless the captain has turned the seatbelt sign off. There's an exit, so please find the one nearest you and be aware that it may be behind you."

Elizabeth continued to look around, amused by Darcy's entire speech.

"Bennet?"

"Yes, Captain?"

"Didn't you say you needed practice?"

He doubted Elizabeth Bennet had ever moved so quickly in her life. She had said that before pilot training, she had only been able to fly a small Cessna. He considered her excitement at the mere prospect. His pulse quickened as she flashed a smile at him. He schooled his features and began a technical discussion about the plane before they rolled forward for takeoff.

After a few minutes in the air, between explanations and discussions about the Beechcraft's features compared to Cessna or Gulfstream, Darcy recommended that Elizabeth plot the short flight to Rosings.

Elizabeth nodded and held up her watch and grabbed the map and began to chart a path for the next few turns. She converted nautical miles to time and noted threats, like tall towers and windmills. She watched her surroundings as they traveled past them and began to give Darcy directions regarding speed changes in order to hit the turns at the time she had marked, adjusting that speed based on landmarks for her turns. Darcy provided appropriate feedback and complimented her work.

"Make sure you hit your last point perfectly, plus or minus five seconds. Your IP won't care how well you fly unless you can hit that last point."

"Wow, really? That is fantastic advice. I thought overall perfection of points was more important. Thanks. I'll change my process for that."

She scribbled notes into her book and continued practicing, adjusting with her new information.

They passed the time discussing the finer points of Elizabeth's practice. Darcy was captivated at her quick intelligence and the rate that she absorbed her studies. Elizabeth was incredibly bright and despite Darcy's wild imaginings of her physically, he never had imagined a brain to go along with her body. Female pilots had a reputation for being poor pilots. In Darcy's experience, there had always been at least one that reinforced this thinking. Now, he was beginning to repent his prejudices toward her and other female pilots he knew.

Before either was truly ready, they touched down at the short airstrip at Rosings. His aunt's home conveniently boasted of a private runway for her own plane.

Aside from his aunt, whose district housed bases from every military branch, eight other government members including two senators, two congressmen, two Department of Defense officials, and two civilian businessmen representing base contractors were members of the Commission. They had each visited bases, or like Senator de Bourgh, had sent aides to visit all bases which had been put forward for closure. At this stage, they would take testimony from interested parties before sending the list to the President. After the President's signature, the approved list would make its way to Congress. Should Meryton be approved for closure, not only would pilot training be transferred to one of the other three training bases, clogging up those pipes, but Longbourn City would be drastically altered. Housing prices would plummet, contractors would be out of jobs, and the town would most likely die.

A large, opulent stone building loomed as they approached and landed. The grounds were pristine, although almost alien in their exacting perfection. The hedges were uniform, and the tall trees were pruned to circular perfection. Elizabeth wondered aloud at the small army of gardeners that must roam the grounds and how she was obliged of Mr. Collins' praise of Rosings' grandeur so she was amply prepared to be appropriately astonished.

Darcy could feel tension wash over him as he neared the hangar. Not only did he have his own testimony to worry about, but he had family to deal with as well. Catherine de Bourgh could be described as cantankerous at best and a heinous bitch at worst. Family lore said she had married Louis de Bourgh to gain power and prestige within her senatorial district. Uncle Louis had been rich, and the former Catherine Fitzwilliam needed cash and influence to further her political aspirations. When she had first been elected to her seat in 1979, there had not been a female US senator in five years. Only eleven women had proceeded her in the Senate since the first female senator was elected in 1922, a mere two years after women's suffrage. Aunt Catherine was a formidable woman with firm convictions. She thrived in a man's hostile world and had become hardened by it.

Darcy knew Elizabeth did not suffer from lack of confidence and was successfully navigating a similar world in pilot training. He had watched her study and was impressed by the strength of character she possessed. She had chosen to remain kind and swim gently through the torrents of harassment using her wit and intelligence as her weapons, proving her objectors to be wrong instead of bulldozing through the oppressors as his aunt had. Darcy knew Catherine would see that choice as weakness instead of wisdom and would reject Elizabeth because of it.

Darcy was anxious to see Anne again. Aunt Catherine had practically adopted Anne Montserrat. They had been engaged—before his father had died. Anne had been a longtime friend of the family. Blonde hair, vibrant blue eyes, and a tall, slim frame. Just before they became engaged, Anne began working for Catherine and also began to change. Where once a kind and gentle soul had stood, now a mercenary assistant took her place. Anne was married to the job; she would never leave her phone, constantly watched the news, and slowly left Darcy as well. Eventually, their relationship was a shell of the friendship it was, and he would never call it companionship. When Darcy's father had passed, Darcy had to call her four times and send texts before she returned his call. It was then that Darcy knew it was over. Anne had been furious. But in the intervening years, they had formed a sort of truce of easy companionship with each other. Darcy now viewed Anne almost as a cousin but never again as a wife. Unfortunately for Darcy, Aunt Catherine had never forgiven him for calling off the wedding and tried to force Anne down his *eligible bachelor* throat every time he visited. Anne never contradicted her boss and adopted mother, leaving that nasty task to Darcy.

The plane smoothly taxied into a hangar and a caretaker opened the door and then pulled their suitcases out of the cargo hold. Before she deplaned, Elizabeth turned back to him and said, almost shyly, "Thank you. For all of this. You have been a great help. And surprise." Before he could respond, they were escorted into a dark sedan and chauffeured to the back of the house. Darcy led the way, taking the porch stairs two at a time and pulling open the wide, wooden doors. Darcy strode through the entryway, Elizabeth followed warily into the large living room where Catherine herself was seated in a great arm chair, holding court, flanked by Collins, an agitated Anne, a few other assistants, Charlotte Lucas, and his cousin, Colonel Richard Fitzwilliam.

"Fitz! Fancy seeing a boy like you in a place like this," Richard exclaimed.

"You know I hate that nickname." Smiling, Darcy gripped Richard's extended hand.

ELIZABETH NOTED THE LARGE, dated tapestries on the walls, the gaudy gilt-framed paintings. She was surprised when the colonel enthusiastically addressed Darcy by his first name.

Elizabeth started as Senator de Bourg spoke. "You must be Lieutenant Bennet. Well, Lieutenant, let's have a look at you."

"Ma'am?"

"Step forward, step forward. Why are you making me squint?"

Elizabeth looked around at the faces around her, none of which looked as if anything unusual was going on. She stepped forward and gave a slow turn before defiantly facing the woman.

"Now, you should have been told why you are here, to give

testimony as to the continuance of Meryton Air Force Base. What can you offer to these discussions?"

"Well, ma'am, I have an intimate understanding of the businesses that are highly affected by the base. Also, I am a current student pilot myself."

"Let me introduce you to the rest of the group providing testimony"—gesturing to the others. "Mr. William Collins, you know, as I believe he mentioned he stayed in the inn run by your family. Charlotte Lucas, you know as well. My assistant Anne Montserrat and standing there beside William is my other nephew, Army Colonel Richard Fitzwilliam. The rest are aides running in and out as I have about fifteen here at my local office. And a few that have travelled with me from DC as well as the aides to other commission members."

"Thank you, ma'am. It is a pleasure to meet you all."

"Why do you keep calling me, ma'am? Don't you know that is abominably rude?"

"No, ma'am. My mother raised us on manners and expected us to call all of our elders 'sir' or 'ma'am', ma'am."

"Young lady, I do not like your tone."

"I am sorry, ma'am. That was never my intent."

The snickers from Captain Darcy and the colonel only added to Elizabeth's discomfort.

Elizabeth was shocked to hear: "William, Anne looks lovely today, doesn't she?"

Darcy barely glanced at the fashionably dressed blonde assistant before blushing, clearing his throat, and turning to Richard.

"And why have you joined our illustrious company?"

"Can't let you have all the fun, can we, Fitz?"

Darcy's jaw tightened. "I hate that nickname."

"I know. Makes it all the more fun. By the way, Georgiana is doing well. Talked to Mom today and she asked me to pass it on."

Lady Catherine interjected, "How is Georgiana? Does she still play the piano? Does she have a good teacher? She must practice you know. You never get anywhere without practice. Of course, practice does not make perfect, but perfect practice makes perfect. She must strive for perfection in every note. I never learned, but I am sure that if I had, I would have been truly marvelous. So would Anne, if she had ever taken lessons."

Elizabeth smiled at the ridiculous woman, settling in anticipation for what she imagined to be a preposterous, diverting evening ahead. Oh, how her father would have enjoyed such an ensemble of characters. He was forever saying, "For what do we live, but to make sport for our neighbors, and laugh at them in our turn?"

Mr. Collins decided that the room's decibel level was not high enough and that this was the most appropriate time to begin his obsequious mutterings. He began in a dull mumbling that was unanimously ignored by everyone, except Charlotte. Charlotte looked at Collins, nodded in appropriate places and strangely seemed to pay attention to Collins' ramblings.

At long last, an aide came in and announced dinner, and the group moved to an incredibly formal dining room. The dining room made Elizabeth feel that they should all be elaborately dressed, with the men in tails and women in gowns and gloves. She smiled at the image of a large ball and an image of Darcy in a well-tailored jacket and cravat crossed her mind. *Must stop watching period dramas with Jane.*

The dining room featured a long table, set for sixteen. Catherine, of course, sat at its head. Two enormous gilt centerpieces displayed huge bouquets of flowers that were impossible to see around. Catherine directed the seating at the table, putting her aides farther away from her and the newest arrivals nearer... *For interrogation?* However, Elizabeth noted she sat Anne at her right and Darcy at her left. Elizabeth was seated next to Darcy.

Lady Catherine began a furious cross-examination of Darcy.

"William, Richard tells me Georgiana is enjoying living with his parents, is this true?"

"Yes, Aunt Catherine. She enjoys the school in Matlock. As Richard shares guardianship with me, it's nice for Georgiana to be close to family."

"Well, when you marry"—she looked poignantly at Darcy, then Anne—"Georgiana is welcome to come here and have private tutors like Anne had before university."

Darcy seemed to suppress a shudder and Elizabeth noticed a vein in his neck which seemed to twitch as he chewed. "No matter my marital status, I'm committed to the air force for at least three more years, so Georgiana will stay in Matlock."

"Of course, Rosings is much closer to you now, is it not?"

"It is, Aunt, but she and I prefer her living at Matlock."

Richard chimed in. "Aunt Catherine, you would not want to rob my parents of their enjoyment? They love to dote on Georgie in their empty nest years. It's difficult with Preston and I out of the house and still no grandchildren."

"Preston should have chosen his wife more carefully. Pity she can't give him any children."

Elizabeth hid her repulsion that anyone could suggest such a thing! And this ordering people about and the ridiculous demands on those she deemed in her purview made Elizabeth privately dub Senator de Bourgh, "Lady Catherine", as if she were nobility and the rest were her subjects. If she was to be dictatorial, she might as well get a proper title out of it, and she smirked to herself at her little joke.

"What do you find so amusing, Lieutenant Bennet? Please share it with us. There are few people in more need of amusement than I in these troubling times."

"Nothing, ma'am. I was just enjoying this close family meal."

"Tell me about your family."

Elizabeth cleared her throat. "I am the second of five daughters—"

"Five? My word, didn't your parents realize what causes children?"

"I'm sure they did, and they must have enjoyed it."

Richard coughed into his sleeve, earning him a pounding on his back from Anne, and even Darcy's sober mask appeared to crack. Lady Catherine, however, looked appalled that anyone would ever speak in such a cavalier manner.

"My, you give your opinions quite decidedly for one so young. How old are you anyway?"

"I turn twenty-two later this year."

"And you are already a student at Meryton? I thought the average student was twenty-four at the very least. You must have acquired a bachelor's first...hmm, and then all these budget issues from the House...causing a year or two of delay with the students on casual status."

"I graduated in only two years and went straight through to my pilot slot. I knew precisely what I wanted since I was a girl. I found that the most direct path." Senator de Bourgh nodded her approval.

Charlotte said, "Lizzy has always wanted to be a pilot. I could tell you story after story of her plane obsession."

Darcy's dark eyes seemed to crinkle in amusement as she popped an olive into her mouth.

Dinner continued in much the same vein. Anne uttered not a word. Collins used every utterance to compliment Lady Catherine. Darcy and Elizabeth answered prying questions with the occasional comment by Charlotte. And Richard joked with everyone. Lady Catherine observed the whole party from the head seat, inserting her opinions where they were neither wanted or needed, and seemed satisfied with the entire, awkward affair.

CHAPTER 16

*ith the abundance of aides and commission members, the home was packed with men and women in dark, conservative suits. Elizabeth, Mr. Collins, and Charlotte were accommodated rooms in a bungalow on the property while Richard and Darcy stayed in the mansion.

Elizabeth woke early, her habit of arriving early to work getting the better of her. As the first testimony would not occur until that afternoon, she decided to take the day off from studying and explore the grounds in such a fine spring weather. As she luxuriated in this rare decadence of lazing abed, she recollected the last twenty-four hours with Captain Darcy and how she had almost forgotten to dislike him. She could not regret his generosity with his plane or offering her training advice inflight. Or how amiable he had been in the car ride. Or during dinner. But then she recalled Wickham's disappointments and how he had called her inept and a "seven", and the bitter waves of distaste rolled in like the tide. And yet...she could not deny his handsome eyes did seem to follow her...and he did seem to... Confused by the enigma that was Captain Darcy, she groaned and got out of bed, opting for a run to clear her head.

There were several paths through the acres of grounds and Elizabeth found the path leading around the perimeter of the park appeared to be the most natural of the overly-manicured trails. She slowed her pace, breathing in the fresh air and enjoyed the green space around her. The wildflowers had just started to peek their heads out and Elizabeth loved seeing the bluebonnets bloom around the trees. Stopping to catch her breath, she closed her eyes and stood still for a moment. She breathed deeply and let the sun warm her face.

A twig cracked, and she snapped her head over her shoulder to see Darcy running up the trail towards her. She put her hands to her heart and he raised his hands in the air at her obvious surprise.

"Morning." He offered an embarrassed, lopsided smile.

"I was just out for a run."

"Same. And how's it going?"

"The flowers"—she gestured to the view before them—"I didn't think about it being spring until this morning. Something about being holed up in windowless rooms or flying thousands of feet above it all."

Darcy smiled showing a flash of even white teeth.

"I remember those days. I can show you a better path."

Matching his long stride to hers, side by side down the trails, Darcy showed her various vistas from Rosings and commented in a deep, steady voice on some of the unfamiliar plants. They talked about nothing of great importance, and she liked to see how the spring air seemed to renew them both—a welcome change before what would surely be a stressful afternoon. Elizabeth was once again surprised by Darcy's ease and pleasant conversation and sneaked glances at his athletic calves and flat stomach.

Eventually, they wend their way back to the bungalow and leaving her at the front door, Darcy jogged back to the main house.

TAKING the mansion stairs two at a time, Darcy kept up a quick pace back to his room. He opened the door, startled, as Richard leapt out in surprise. With quick reflexes, he punched Richard in the gut. Richard gripped his stomach.

"Richard! Why are you in my room?"

Darcy's question was met with wheezing laughter.

"Waiting for you. Wanted to ask about your testimony today. Are you ready for it?"

"I'm not concerned. Honestly, it's been a nice break after the desert."

Richard plopped down on Darcy's bed and started going through his night stand drawer.

"Are you planning on testifying for or against Meryton?"

"Well, I'm hoping to avoid any decisions, personally. It has the most flying days with the fewest weather cancellations, but there is nothing in that town and much too far to a city to keep morale at a decent level. There's really nothing for a bunch of twenty-year old guys to do. Mexico stopped being an option years ago, and as a result, there's too much fraternization with underage civilians. The schools are lacking, there's no stores other than Wal-Mart and Ross, only fast food restaurants, and no entertainment options unless you consider movies for two dollars quality time."

"But what about the town itself? Won't it suffer negative consequences from the base closure?"

"Most likely, but if the government is going to close bases, why should one town be held above the others? Obviously, any town would go under within a matter of years while local business that cater to the military will find themselves out of business in months. If it comes down to Meryton, I wish them well, but the fact of the matter is that the other training bases could handle the extra student load and the student and instructor morale would be significantly higher. There would also be better training continuity if we cut down the number of bases, so the students would be more controlled and have better curriculum management."

"Interesting. I'm sure you're right. Aunt Catherine asked me here to simply discuss the financial side of training and answer questions regarding assets. I'm sure an Air Force officer would be better, but she finagled the commission somehow to let me testify. Probably hoping I convince you to marry Anne. Does she not understand that marrying your crazy ex-fiancé is one, unlikely, and, two, completely unhealthy?"

"Please, let's not talk about Anne. I'm sorry, but I'm not going to marry her to save her from her crazy life. Aunt Catherine is getting thrown in the loony bin if she thinks that is *ever* going to happen. Who do you think we call to find something like that? Would my first shirt have psych resources?"

"No idea. I guess I'll start looking around for a good facility. One that has good food. Crazy people deserve good food."

Richard patted Darcy gently on the head.

Darcy rolled his eyes and took off his shirt, glancing about the room for his towel.

Darcy hopped in the shower while running down the list of tasks he needed to accomplish. He sighed thinking of his run with Elizabeth as he dried off and wrapped the towel around his waist. *This would be the longest week ever at Aunt Catherine's.*

"You still here?" Darcy asked as he stepped back into his room searching for his uniform.

"It's over there, in the wardrobe. I moved it to sit down on the bed while waiting for you." Richard pointed and started opening and closing dresser drawers in the room.

"What on earth are you doing?"

"Just looking around."

"You shouldn't do that."

"Well, I appreciate your sensibilities, but I want to see what the old dragon keeps in your room. It's much nicer than mine."

Darcy grunted in reply and smoothly buttoned down his

shirt. Richard continued. "How does Elizabeth Bennet figure into all of this? I gathered she's a student, so why is she here? Shouldn't she be piloting around?" Richard waved his hand through the air like an airplane and went back to rustling through drawers.

"Her father owns a local bed and breakfast which frequently houses pilots and visitors for graduations and the like. Collins decided it would be good to hear from her since she has seen both sides of the base."

"And what does she plan on presenting to the commission?"

"I can only assume she'll say to keep it open."

"What will her family do if Meryton closes?"

"No idea. The father seems to be indolent toward his business, relying mostly on the mother and the daughters to run the place. The mother is a good hostess, if a little quirky, you know the type, constantly flitting from topic to topic. Every time I've seen her she seems more concerned with her youngest snagging an officer than anything resembling sense. Great cook though. The three youngest are ridiculous. Honestly, only Elizabeth and her older sister, Jane, are respectable."

"High praise coming from you."

"Well, Bingley is seriously dating Jane, so I guess there are *two* witnesses to their respectability," Darcy said, tucking in his shirt.

"So, Elizabeth...is she single?" Richard asked while now going through Darcy's wardrobe and evaluating his clothing.

"Don't even think about it."

"Why? She's smart. She's pretty. She mocks Aunt Catherine to her face—an admirable quality in any woman. Besides, I'm stationed so far away, it won't even matter."

"Richard, just...don't." Darcy could only hope he kept the desperation from his voice.

Richard stopped his snooping, stunned. Darcy swore he could hear the gears turning in his cousin's head.

"You... You like her?" Richard wondered aloud. "Wait." He

began strutting around the room like a proud camo-covered peacock. "Darcy." He whirled around and pointed. "You *like* her!"

Darcy felt his face burn. "No"—grabbing his tie from the bed and bungling the knot several times—"I just don't like when you talk about using and losing women like that."

Richard roared with laughter that echoed around the room. "Sure you don't, Fitz. You must like her a lot!"

"I don't." Darcy fumbled with the silver button on his coat.

"Why, it must be the reason you've been so distracted lately." Richard whistled and looked at Darcy's face. "You've got it bad, Darce."

"I don't have anything. Besides, it's impossible anyway. I'm not going to marry someone in the military—deployments and joint assignments. All the dual mil couples I know might end up in the same state but not in the same city. It's impossible."

"Marry—?"

"Our family would never approve. She's from a miniscule town. Her family is absurd. It's impossible." Darcy ran his fingers through his hair in frustration causing it to stick up at odd angles.

"Why would you care what the family thinks?" Richard smiled widely. "William and Elizabeth sitting in a tree—"

"Stop it."

"K-I-S-S—" The rest of Richard's taunting was cut off by a shove.

After wiping tears of mirth from his eyes, Richard leaned back on his elbows and his expression turned grave.

"All right. All right. You don't have to beg. I will help you win the fair maiden, because based on that speech, you are going to need help." He bowed his head and flourished his right hand in a courtly manner.

"I don't need your help."

Ignoring his denials, his cousin continued. "Does she know you like her?"

Darcy looked askance at the thought. "I hope not!" Richard

smirked at this capitulation. "Not very professional of me to hit on her in the plane, is it? You want to get me kicked out for sexual harassment? Doesn't the army make you sit through those lectures? It needs to be a Green Dot space! I'm sure there is something they'd say about instructor-trainee relationships."

"This is precisely *why* you need me. Darce, don't take this the wrong way—"

"Why do I feel like I should be taking whatever you say the wrong way?"

"Didn't anyone teach you not to interrupt your elders? Don't take this the wrong way, but you have no game when it comes to women."

AFTERNOON SEEMED to approach quickly during her run, but the day progressed much more slowly for Elizabeth after that. Elizabeth had passed the last hour in the company of Mr. Collins and now wanted nothing more than to give her testimony and return to Meryton. At least Charlotte seemed happy. Elizabeth was awed by Charlotte's cool acceptance of Collins' fawning speeches.

Elizabeth, dressed in her service blues, walked to the manor house with Mr. Collins, who kept a blistering pace in both discourse and stride. Elizabeth's toes were already feeling pinched within her shining black pumps when they entered Rosings and she was again struck by the garish display of wealth. They meandered the hallways until an aide directed them to what Elizabeth suspected had been a ballroom. A large chandelier lit the raised platform where the nine members of the commission sat at a white cloth-covered table. She was directed to the second row of seats behind two tables facing the commission.

Glancing around, she reminded herself not to fidget—with little success. She shifted nervously in her chair, smoothed her hands over her pinned hair, and tapped her heel on the tiled floors

—then promptly ceased after an aide in a pant suit shot her a very nasty look. At last, she was called to the main stage and sat in front of a microphone at another white cloth-covered table.

The nine members of the commission looked down at her as she looked up at them. The distance seemed to grow larger the longer she looked. There seemed to be an unbearably protracted pause while an aide handed out papers, and then Senator de Bourgh's voice blasted over the microphone.

"This commission has been put in place by the President to determine which bases should be placed on the list for possible closure. At this time, we are hearing testimony from some hand-selected parties which may have useful viewpoints which could affect this commission's decision." Senator de Bourgh looked down at her paper as if to see who was to be deposed first. "Lieutenant Bennet. Please state your name for the commission's record."

"Second Lieutenant Elizabeth Bennet."

"Where are you from?"

"I live at Longbourn Inn, a small bed and breakfast—a few miles from Meryton Air Force Base."

"What do you do for employment?"

"I am a student pilot out of Meryton Air Force Base."

"Do you have any questions about your purpose here today?"

"No, ma'am."

"Let's begin. Senator Flores, you have ten minutes for questions."

Senator Flores began with questions regarding the local housing market and the general interests of the locally employed work force. A program manager, Mr. Sullivan then asked several questions regarding the numbers of civilian contractors versus military officers for pilot training instruction. How many businesses catered to the military? How would Longbourn be affected? Could the morale difficulties experienced by officers including lack of social activities, lack of specialty health care, lack of shopping opportunities and restaurants, and lack of higher educational opportunities, be easily remedied?

The interrogation continued in the same vein for over an hour. Her voice parched, the small crystal glass of water in front of Elizabeth was refilled three times before she was finally dismissed.

Returning the way she came, her brain was exhausted from pulling facts and opinions through the recesses of her mind. She could only hope her honest testimony would help her town. Elizabeth could relax for a while as she was not expected back in company until that night for another dinner at Lady Catherine's table. She wondered if they would require more testimony from her on the following day.

She walked out into the courtyard and eventually into the gardens of the manor. Finding no one was in sight, she took off her shoes. Her stocking feet touched the cool grass and she let out a deep sigh of contentment. *Alone at last.*

"Good afternoon." An unfamiliar voice from behind her caused Elizabeth to whip her head around, bringing her high heels up in her hand, ready to pummel the creep who had slinked up behind her.

The colonel from the night before, turned his hands up in surrender, laughing. "Jumpy much?"

Elizabeth slowly put her shoes down. "Oh, Colonel! Why would you sneak up on a person like that?" She quickly put her shoes back on, causing an already humiliating situation become hysterical as she hopped about trying and failing. She was forced to eventually lean on Colonel Fitzwilliam's arm as she placed damp, grass-covered stocking feet back into her shoes.

"I'm sorry. I just assumed you could hear me approaching. Honestly, I can't regret it. Being nearly pummeled to death by your shoe has been the most amusing thing that's happened to me in weeks."

The colonel's laughter continued to ring through the gardens and Elizabeth, whose nerves had finally eased, joined him.

"May I walk you home, Lieutenant?"

"Of course."

The two meandered their way through the wooded areas and chatting about Elizabeth's family, schooling, her ambitions in the jet, and their mutual love of the military. Elizabeth thought it was one of the most pleasant conversations in a great while. Richard was charming. And vivacious. And charismatic. Elizabeth could not help but compare him to Captain Darcy.

"When did you meet Fitz?"

"In the fall. He came to a Drop Night just before I started training."

"And?" Richard smiled at her and she smiled back.

"Prepare yourself for something dreadful. He stood in a corner and didn't acknowledge anyone. He didn't talk to anyone, order anyone a drink, or do anything but lurk about the walls."

"He has such a hard time mixing with new people."

"I find that unlikely. How does a man—an officer in the air force, a pilot, from a prominent family in New York—suffer social anxiety?"

"He never had much opportunity growing up."

"Maybe he should take your aunt's advice and practice."

Richard laughed at her jest but sobered. "I'm sure he should. But don't hold too much against him. When he was twelve, his mom died not long after his sister Georgiana was born."

Elizabeth raised her eyebrows in surprise at this new intelligence.

"Car crash. His father was never the same after that. Don't get me wrong; Uncle George was an incredible guy. Great leader, awesome uncle, everything William has ever wanted to be, but George kind of died right along with her."

"I've heard of people dying of a broken heart. I guess that really does happen."

"Poor Darcy was stuck at home with a colicky infant and the ghost of a father. He stepped up and took care of the family."

The two rambled the garden each in silent in their reflections. How completely awful it must be to lose half of your family, thought Elizabeth. With four sisters, a loud mother, and an impertinent father, Elizabeth would never understand the silence that must have surrounded Darcy at Pemberley. She began to wonder if this was the reason he was so serious and sullen.

Eventually, Elizabeth broke the silence.

"I'm very sorry for your family's loss. That must have been horrible. I heard one time that you should only think on the past as it brings you pleasure. I have made it one of my life mottos. Maybe that would help him. Think of the good times, the times you laughed, rather than the times you cried. What was your favorite thing about your aunt?"

"Aunt Rachel? Let's see. My favorite thing? We would go over to Pemberley in the summers for 'cousin camp' as she liked to call it and we would have wild dance parties. Darcy, me, my brother, Anne—you met her yesterday, and another boyhood friend would sometimes join us. It was so fun. We would dance for hours sliding on wood floors and pretending to break dance. I loved every minute of it."

"What I am curious is how Anne Montserrat fits into all this? Is she a relation? And why does your aunt seem to want Captain Darcy and Anne to marry? They clearly do not suit."

Thus, the good colonel proceeded to tell her the family history. Anne Montserrat, who had once been a vivacious, active woman was now a pale, almost sickly-looking woman of twenty-six. Darcy had known her for twenty-two of those years. At four, she moved about a mile away from Pemberley. They had grown up together playing and riding bikes between their houses. Anne was a few years younger than Darcy, but every summer when Richard came to stay, Anne was there. She had always been a dedicated student. Years later, when Darcy was home for summer break from college and Anne had just graduated from high school, there childhood friendship had developed into something more. Little Anne had blossomed, and Darcy seemed to have fallen in love with her. They were engaged within six months.

Anne had met their aunt Catherine on a trip to Washington DC, and her interest was piqued. She went through Harvard on a scholarship from the de Bourgh family and was later hired on as Catherine's personal aide. Long work hours began the demise of their relationship. She spent all night looking things up for the senator, making travel plans, answering calls and texts and emails. She spent more time with her phone than with Darcy and when he joined the military, it was the death knell to their engagement. Darcy broke it off after graduation from pilot training and their relationship had been relatively rocky ever since. Catherine de Bourgh always expected a reconciliation, but it was obvious to Richard that Darcy avoided Anne. Anne, too, had seemed to have moved on. Though she flitted from short-lived relationship to relationship, Anne Montserrat was married to her work and the management of Rosings.

Enthralled by this disclosure, Elizabeth thought they reached the little cottage far too soon for her own liking and thanked the colonel for accompanying her. She had enjoyed his company profoundly and wondered if there could possibly be more to the colonel.

CHAPTER 17

*D*arcy hated being at Rosings. Darcy appreciated hard work, but his aunt's sycophantic aides disgusted him. He thought they gave his aunt an inflated sense of worth and pride. He believed that where there is true superiority of mind, pride will always be under good regulation, but his aunt had been overly puffed up about her own worth for years. Aunt Catherine was domineering and demanding. With Catherine required to head the commission and host the many inhabitants of Rosings, Darcy thought he should seek his ex-fiancé out for a private discussion. He felt awkward that they had not spoken past pleasantries.

Anne had a spacious apartment on the second floor overlooking the grounds of Rosings. In a turn from the décor in every other part of the house, tall windows framed with light curtains allowed shafts of sunlight to pour in. Anne had always loved the outdoors and fresh flowers were on every available surface. Darcy knocked lightly, tapping a little rhythm on the door. After hearing a soft "come in", Darcy walked through the door. He was greeted by the scent of those flowers and Anne, sitting on the bed.

"How are you?" she asked in a mild voice. Darcy wondered if

149

constant subservience to Catherine had taken its toll or if she was just used to speaking quietly in meetings.

"Well. And you?" Darcy smiled at Anne and sat on the chair across from her.

"About as well as can be expected. No one has been here forcing me to take a break or eat or whatever nonsense while I'm busy working. I can always get so much more done when Catherine hasn't sent someone to take care of me."

"I'm glad to steal a moment up here at all. I feel like Aunt Catherine has me watched."

They both laughed lightly. Darcy grabbed Anne's hand gently and she touched his cheek before dropping her phone on the bed next to her.

"A little bird told me you're seeing someone."

"Well, that little bird has a big mouth and would be wrong." Darcy could feel the heat rise up his neck and behind his ears.

Anne rolled her eyes. "Will, you don't need to be embarrassed. You're allowed to have a girlfriend."

Darcy was stunned by her candor, but he hardly knew what *he* thought of Elizabeth.

"I don't have a girlfriend."

"But you like her right? What's her name, Benning? Banner?"

"It's Bennet."

Anne rubbed her hands together and he was reminded of the Anne of his youth.

"Why do I get the feeling you have some sort of epic plan?" Darcy laughed.

"I only have one plan, actually. I want you to be friends with Elizabeth Bennet. I like her. I enjoy how she stands up to Catherine. And she is smart. And witty. And kind. And she was amazing in her testimony this morning."

Darcy blinked at her. "Excuse me. I think I misheard."

"You have never misheard a thing in your life."

"Elizabeth Bennet? Why would you want me to be friends with her?"

"Well, I just told you. And maybe because she seems perfect for you? Maybe because you need someone? Any of these reasons enough?"

"I don't need anyone."

Anne rolled her eyes. "Everyone needs someone, Will."

"I have Georgiana."

"Who hasn't lived with you in four years. Let's not talk about the fact that she's still a baby."

"She's sixteen."

"But that's not the kind of companionship I am talking about anyway. And you know it."

"You don't even know Elizabeth." Darcy stood up and started to pace around the room. "Why do you think she's so perfect for me?"

"Let's see"—Anne began pointing at her fingers and ticking off her main points. "She's beautiful. She's obviously smart. She manages your aunt's interrogation, which in retrospect, probably should have been my first point. She has a job, so she can't be after you for your money. She gets along with you and Richard. She was kind to me. She's polite. Shall I go on?"

"No, I get it. I get it."

"Will, you need someone. And Elizabeth Bennet is the best girl I've seen in a long time. I know I don't have much of a social life. And I know my priorities are different than yours, but I think she could be so good for you if you'll let her."

He had forgotten how well Anne could always read his mind.

"You've been in charge for too long. You've taken care of everyone else for so long that now you don't know how to take care of yourself."

Darcy sat down again, practically collapsing onto the bed next to Anne.

"What would I do without you?"

"Probably visit Rosings even less."

∼

SHE TURNED and winked at him before he could tell someone was holding her hand. His eyes panned between the couple's arms in slow motion before seeing Wickham's blue eyes and wide grin as he leered at Elizabeth. He watched the man's eyes sweep down Elizabeth's chest, then over her hips before Wickham pulled her roughly into his arms. She laughed as Wickham's arms slid down her back as he kissed her, his hands sinking lower and lower before—

Darcy woke the next morning as the sun peeked over the horizon, sitting up and gasping. His hands gripped the thick comforter and he could feel the sweat dripping down his forehead and his bare chest.

Like a lion in a cage, he stood and paced. He ached to be outside, away from his dreams. Rosings had always given him nightmares, but typically they were just of an angry Aunt Catherine rather than the woman he loved running off with the worst man in existence.

Love. Did he love her? He must. He had loved her from the first moment he had seen her. From the moment her brown eyes had flashed at him and her smile glistened across the room. He grabbed the shirt he had discarded when readying for bed the night before and pulled on his shoes. He needed to go for a run. He needed to be moving and figure out how to woo her. To win Miss Elizabeth Bennet.

∼

DARCY STARTED out immediately behind Rosings, but before he had gone too far, he steered himself towards the path he had shown Elizabeth the morning before. He ran for ten minutes before he heard someone singing incredibly loud and off-key. It took him a few moments before he finally recognized "Somebody to Love" by Queen, though Freddie Mercury was surely turning in his grave at the attempt. He listened for one turn more before the path widened and he saw Elizabeth. He called her name and waved awkwardly once, twice. He finally gave up before she turned her head just as he entered the clearing and jumped back and grabbed her chest with a little shriek. He slowed his jog and watched as she ripped the buds from her ears.

"You should have said something!" Her cheeks flushed with embarrassment.

"I called you several times." Darcy laughed. "It wasn't until that last Elvis hip shake there that I realized you had music on. Two thumbs up, by the way."

"Well, next time, call louder." She placed the buds back in her ears and quickly ran off, back along the path. He easily caught up and jogged next to her.

"Do you need something?" She removed the right ear bud as she ran.

"Do I have to need something to enjoy a run here? I believe I showed you this road, so maybe I should ask you the same question."

"I needed a run. I don't understand how people can be so cooped up all the time."

"Me either. I was outside all the time as a kid and before college. My parents were always looking for me in the barns or in the orchard. I'm sure if they could have put a homing device on me, they would have."

"My mom hates it too. She thinks my running isn't very lady-like. 'Real women do not sweat, Elizabeth, they glisten.' She just doesn't see that I'm so much happier when I'm out. I feel relaxed when I can't afford to relax any other time."

"You relax in the air." Darcy did not ask; his sentence was

declarative. A sound statement of fact rather than a ventured opinion.

"Flying is different. Especially these days. I can't afford to be less than number one."

"Flying should be where you're home."

"It is, but I guess it's hard to be at home when I know I'm being graded on whether I did my dishes."

Darcy smiled. "I can certainly understand that. Pilot training kind of pounds it out of you. But, do you remember the first time you flew? Do you remember that feeling of soaring through the sky, feeling like Icarus?"

"Have you flown too close to the sun, Captain Darcy?" She raised an eyebrow at him without breaking her stride.

She had no idea how close he was to his sun. If he continued orbiting in her company, he soon would not even need wings to soar. He felt it every time she shot him his favorite impertinent glance.

"How have you found Rosings?"

"Rosings is lovely. I've enjoyed getting to run about the grounds. Though some of the company..."

"Not everyone here is so bad. Richard likes you and Anne told me that she would like to be friends."

"Lucky for you, you get to stay with them. Mr. Collins is about to drive me batty."

"He is rather...uh...unique." Darcy looked at Elizabeth with raised eyebrows and shrugged his shoulders causing her to laugh.

"It is nice that Charlotte and Mr. Collins get along so well though. You can't imagine how hard it is to find someone at home."

"Hence the morale problems."

"Well, of course, to you, with your plane, it must seem incredibly close. Near and far are relative terms. It is possible for a woman to live too near her family."

"Yes, exactly. I don't think you would want to always be near Longbourn."

"Well, I did join the air force."

He could see she longed for adventure and he wanted to show it to her. He wanted to see her smelling the salt from the sea or the wind as it flew through her hair on top of a mountain. He had had plenty of adventures in his career so far and even at Pemberley, he could travel and do as he wished. As they ran together, Darcy could not stop wondering what it would be like to be on an adventure with someone like her by his side.

"You finished?"

Elizabeth had stopped running and was standing with hands on hips, beads of sweat at her temples, looking thoughtful. "Oh yeah. I wanted to go in and take a shower before noon in case we get called back in today."

Admiring the way her hair curled around her face, rebelling against her ponytail, he walked her back in companionable silence, broken by an occasional observation about the grounds or a question about the house.

After Elizabeth closed the door behind her, Darcy strolled back to the main house. He looked at the edifice in front of him and noticed his aunt on her grand balcony glaring down at him. He knew his aunt too well and could only guess her thoughts upon witnessing his exchange with Elizabeth Bennet.

CHAPTER 18

*M*r. Collins had been ordered to the mansion early in the morning by Senator de Bourgh. Enjoying a *Collins-free* morning, she teased Charlotte about how well she looked playing house. Charlotte had relished being away from home, puttering around the cottage, and enjoying the domesticity of it. Though not required, Charlotte had taken four years of home economics classes through high school and in her first year of college had completed fifteen credits of family home and consumer sciences. Elizabeth could never understand her friend's obsession with keeping hearth and home but to each her own.

"Oh, Lizzy. It is a pleasure running my own home."

"Which would make much more sense if it was actually your home."

"It's Mr. Collins home. Did you realize? He told me yesterday. I thought this was just a guest cottage. Mr. Collins said that it was at one time a rectory but had since been converted into a home for Senator de Bourgh's top aide, which happens to be Mr. Collins."

That explains his genuflection toward Lady Catherine. How much sucking up did he have to do to get that job? Elizabeth grinned over her coffee.

"I didn't even realize he was the top aide. Apparently, Senator de Bourgh has come to rely on him, so she never wants him far away from her."

"Bully for Mr. Collins."

"I know you look down on him, Lizzy, but he is a decent man."

"He's ridiculous. I've never seen anyone so subservient."

"Hush. You aren't better than the rest of us just because you can fly planes or because your dad makes more than anyone else in town."

Bristling at her friend's outburst, Elizabeth said, "I don't see why it matters or why we're even fighting about it for that matter. Mr. Collins is objectively strange. Once this is over, we can all go home, and life can just go back to normal."

"Lizzy, Mr. Collins and I are engaged."

"Engaged? To be married?"

"Heavens, Lizzy. What kind of engaged did you think? Engaged to go to the grocery store? Engaged to find an appointment with a realtor?"

"When on earth did you even have time to get engaged? We've known him six months, but really only seen him for maybe two of that. Also, we've been here, like, two days! What did he propose with? String? Did he just have a ring lying around?" Agitated, Elizabeth began to pace around the small room. Charlotte, however, sat still, coldly still, in defense of herself.

"I'm not romantic, you know. I never was. I only want a comfortable home, and considering Mr. Collins' job and prospects for the future, I am convinced that my chance for happiness with him is just as good as most people when they get married."

"But, but he's ridiculous! He doesn't know when to be quiet. He's rude. And he's long-winded. Why on earth would you ever want to saddle yourself with someone like that?"

"So, he talks a lot! Do you think it miraculous that Mr. Collins should be liked by anyone, simply because he's disliked by you? Yes, he's not entirely sensible. He can be irritating but so can I. So can we all! I know that whatever emotion he feels for me must be imagined, but I have never thought much of men. Or marriage, for that matter. Listen to me, though. I'll be away from Meryton. I'll never have to stay in that tiny town wondering when some young pilot will whisk me away. I'm twenty-seven years old, and I realize that is by no means ancient, but I'm only getting older and no twenty-two-year old hot shot is going to want me. Look at me, Lizzy. I know I'm not pretty like you or your sisters. I'm plain at best. I haven't finished school. I've got nothing, really. But maybe this way, I'll be happy." Silence filled the room and then— "And I want you to be happy for me."

Elizabeth stopped pacing and pulled her friend up to her and the two embraced as best friends do. "Of course, I will be happy for you. I guess I always pictured we'd end up living near Long-bourn our whole lives. What will I do without you, Charlotte?"

Yet, the dull ache in her heart told Elizabeth their relationship had forever changed. She could never sacrifice her emotions for the stability of a home or to escape from her parents. Charlotte had lost some of her shine in Elizabeth's eye and while they would remain life-long friends, Charlotte had lost Elizabeth's respect. Elizabeth was a romantic, always convinced that she would most likely never marry, but if she did, she would only do so for love.

The air was filled with tension, and eventually, following halted attempts at conversation, Elizabeth went to get dressed and return to the commission's tedious questions. She was unsure how she would tolerate her afternoon with equanimity after the news she had received but determined to make a good show of it. She wanted to protect her town and the people she held most dear. The closure of Meryton Air Force Base would kill her community and she could not stand for it.

"LIEUTENANT BENNET, I would like to see you for a moment."

Senator de Bourgh's shrill voice beckoned her to a large sitting room just inside the front door of the mansion.

"Yes, ma'am." Elizabeth's shiny, black heels clicked against the marble tiled floors as she made her way to the couch across from the winged arm chair which held *Lady Catherine*. The woman wore a red skirt and jacket which contrasted with her stark white hair. A flag pin embellished the lapel of her suit coat, emphasizing the power she held over Elizabeth. Taking in the senator, in all this state, Elizabeth sat up straight and eyed the woman directly.

"You can be at no loss, Lieutenant Bennet, to understand the reason I summoned you here. Your own conscience must have told you."

"No, ma'am, I cannot account for the honor at all." Elizabeth wished she had been standing so that she might have curtseyed. In her highly diverted mind, somehow, in the moment, it seemed a natural response.

"Lieutenant Bennet. I am not to be trifled with. However insincere you may choose to be, you shall not find me so. I have been described as frank and sincere and, in times like this, I find it wise not to depart from it. A report of the most alarming nature was delivered to me by Mr. Collins not one hour ago. I was told, Lieutenant, that you, Elizabeth Bennet, are seeking to be united with my nephew, Captain Darcy. Because I know it must be a horrendous lie, I instantly resolved to make my feelings known."

This was news to her! While she had only begun to daydream about Darcy, she had told no one of her inklings.

"If you believed it impossible to be true, I am surprised you took the trouble to tell me." Elizabeth felt her cheeks blushing in both surprise and scorn for the senator and her assumptions.

"I insist on having such a report contradicted. Of course, you realize that Captain Darcy is in every way your superior. Not only in military rank, but in social standing, wealth, and class."

"Detaining me from accomplishing the task I have been assigned here would confirm any suspicions rather than deny them, surely? Besides, I don't know that I believe that this rumor even exists. I don't know that I would take the word of Mr. Collins over the word of someone who is touted to be in the purported relationship."

"So... You want to pretend to be ignorant of it? Of course, I'm sure you started it in an attempt to trap Darcy. Bring ruin and shame on his whole family. Do you know that this rumor is being circulated throughout the halls of Rosings? Why, even Anne, has mentioned it."

"I have never even heard of it. Surely someone would have approached me about it—"

"I am—"

"Especially considering our ranks. He is an instructor for God's sake! We can't just be together without completely destroying our careers! Why would I do that? And if you don't believe that I wouldn't risk his career, then why on earth would I risk my own?"

Elizabeth prided herself on remaining calm in the face of adversity but felt like she was about to lose her temper. If the haughty Senator de Bourgh was anything, she was delusional and starting trouble for reasons she knew not why. If word got back to the Wing that Elizabeth and Darcy had anything but a professional relationship, her future might be sorely affected.

Seemingly satisfied in Elizabeth's vehement denial of the relationship, the senator eased back against her padded chair.

"Do you swear there is absolutely no truth to these rumors?"

"I do not have to answer these questions. In fact, I refuse to do so. I won't continue to sit here and be attacked over something I have no control over."

"Lieutenant, I insist on being satisfied. Are you and my nephew in a relationship?"

"You have declared it to be impossible."

"That is how it should be. However, I know women like you, Bennet. Women who use their arts and allurements to make men forget what they owe to themselves and their families. Women, from small towns, who use their bodies to get what they want when their brains won't suffice. You might have drawn him in."

Lady Catherine's disgust-filled speech filled the room and it held there for a moment.

"Even if I had, I would be the last person to confess it."

"Do you know who I am, Lieutenant? I am not accustomed to being spoken to this way. I am almost Darcy's nearest relation in the world and I am entitled to know all of his concerns."

"But you are not entitled to know mine, ma'am." Elizabeth stood furiously out of her chair, the slow burn within finally spilling over. Taking long strides to the door, she stopped upon hearing the senator's cool, smooth tones—the voice of someone who had been corrupted by too much power.

"Let me be perfectly clear. You and Darcy—can *never* take place." Senator de Bourgh nearly snarled. "No, never. Captain Darcy is engaged to Anne. Now what have you to say?"

Elizabeth pivoted about to face the woman still imperiously seated.

"Only this. If he is engaged, you can have no reason to suppose he would ever toy with me."

"Lieutenant Bennet, I expected to find you a reasonable young woman. Do not believe that I will ever recede. You are not excused until you have given me what I require."

"And what is that? Ma'am?" Elizabeth stood, hands on her hips as her chin rose in defiance.

"I want you to leave him alone."

"Senator, there is nothing you can do to convince me to do more than I am already doing. Your nephew is a big boy and fully capable of doing what he wants to do."

"He is testifying against Meryton and you *will* lose your home." Elizabeth felt the blood drain from her face as Lady Catherine stretched back like a cat who had just killed the mouse she had been toying with.

"What—?"

Catherine looked her up and down, seeming to evaluate that final blow.

"You heard me. Naturally, knowing that Meryton is bound for closure and your family for destruction, you would cling to the first man you thought could support you. Is Pemberley to be polluted by you and your outlandish relatives? Mr. Collins told me tales of inappropriate behavior, chasing pilots, wild conduct at parties, bad manners, and more!"

Elizabeth, suddenly introspective, thought of Kitty and Lydia and their outlandish behavior that she had begged her father to curb. She thought of her mother shrieking about the house in a fit of nerves. Mary's preaching and awful piano performances split through the headache building at her temples.

"Ma'am, you have insulted me in every possible way and can have nothing further to say. I will see you during my testimony."

Elizabeth spun and listened to the echo of the clicks of her heels as she walked away. Away from that hideous woman.

When Elizabeth entered the grand commission room, she immediately took a seat in the back. She understood the stakes but not until this moment did she fear the senator's unwieldy influence on Elizabeth's future. If there had been a line in Vegas on what she expected to occur today, she would have lost a tremendous fortune.

That morning, Darcy had been sweet. In fact, she would even say that she could see herself falling for his dark eyes and easy smile. They had flown together. She had seen the sun on the horizon shining through the cockpit and sensed Darcy completely relax with her. He seemed reserved in company, and could be a pompous, stuck-up jerk, but during their run... Had she imagined seeing his mask lift? That had all changed when the senator said Darcy was testifying *against* Meryton. She felt sick as if he had intentionally manipulated her feelings. Wickham was obviously correct. Darcy and his entire proud, arrogant family, including his aunt, did not deserve her consideration.

And Charlotte. Engaged! To Mr. Collins. Why on earth would anyone accept such a sniveling, sneaking worm? Mr. Collins who ran back to his boss with every gossip report. A boss who walked on him like the doormat he was. How would Charlotte live with him? Or, the better question, why would Charlotte ever consign herself to the toadying man?

The commission called Elizabeth's name before she was finished thinking about the strange turn of events. As she made her way down the aisle of chairs to sit in front of the microphone, trudging through the muck and mud of her thoughts, and fell into the seat, already exhausted.

"Lieutenant Bennet"—Senator de Bourgh's voice echoed over the microphone and Elizabeth felt the vibrations in her skull as she spoke. "This commission has only a few questions left for you before we make a final decision on the proposed closure of Meryton Air Force Base."

Her mouth felt dry and her palms sweaty. She wiped her hands on her skirt under the table.

"There has been testimony that there are severe morale difficulties at Meryton. What can be done to correct them with no activities nearby, few young people in the community, and few outdoor opportunities?"

"It is my experience that students do not have enough time during their studies for this to be a valid concern, Senator. I have found that beyond flying and studying academics for flying, I have just about enough time to run every day and sleep. It is my personal opinion that this should not be a concern for this commission."

"And what of the instructors, contractors, security personnel, and other permanent party? Should they not be included in the commission's purview?"

"I do not believe we join the military to be entertained, ma'am."

"It has further been said that our other current training bases

164

could handle the additional student load and conjoining the Meryton students with those bases would in fact lead to better training continuity. The commission would like to hear your defense for keeping students at Meryton."

"I profoundly disagree. Meryton boasts the most flying days in the country. We have good weather. It doesn't rain. It stays sunny and warm. Student pilots need good flying days and Meryton is able to provide them. I don't feel qualified to speak to training continuity, but as pilot training is a nationwide program with a highly specific syllabus, I feel that better continuity is a weak argument for the redistribution of twenty-five hundred students and extensive personnel."

Lady Catherine looked at Elizabeth from her perch on the stage. Her eyes looked identical to a lion's about to pounce. Elizabeth had seen it once on an animal documentary. Elizabeth quickly imagined her crouching low before the killing strike.

"Lieutenant Bennet, one last question. How do you feel about fraternization between instructors and students?"

"I believe we must all do what is best for us, but we need to ensure that students are properly mentored without fear of repercussions."

Lady Catherine looked down her nose and smiled, a look that made Elizabeth reassess all her answers.

"Lieutenant, you are dismissed."

Blood roared through Elizabeth's ears as she stood up, politely nodded to the committee and made her way back to her seat. She could hardly hear the committee as they each took a turn speaking regarding her testimony. Elizabeth's mind raced against the imminent fear of abject failure to find something more that she could have said or a turn of phrase that would have helped. It was as she found herself sitting once more in the back of the room looking at the blurred faces of the members that Lady Catherine spoke once more.

"It is my opinion that Meryton Air Force Base should be placed on the list for closure. All those on the commission in favor, please say 'aye'."

A chorus of "aye" reverberated around the walls and Elizabeth felt nothing but hate in her heart for Captain Darcy and his imperious, imposing aunt. In a single weekend, they had dragged her halfway across the state and managed to destroy not only her friends and family's livelihoods but her professional reputation as well.

Elizabeth stood up in a rage and stalked out of the room, heels clicking percussively against the floor. She needed to be outside, to see the sky and feel the sun. Elizabeth had always been comforted by nature and that was what she needed now when her heart was at its heaviest. She had failed, and she would return home to give the news to her family. Her father would be upset, her mother furious. She needed to take the last few peaceful moments she would have before it was time to leave.

CHAPTER 19

*D*arcy paced about in his service blues. He had given his last testimony immediately after returning from his run with Elizabeth and his elation had stayed with him through the afternoon. Aunt Catherine had told him that Elizabeth's would be the final testimony and he had nervously waited outside in the garden for her after extricating himself from the commission room.

He had thought the entire Bennet situation over and had come up with several solutions. One thing was certain, he loved Elizabeth. Completely. Hers was the first face he wanted to see in the morning and his mouth practically begged to taste hers. To feel her body as it pressed against his in a deep kiss of wanting and accepting and giving back in return. The problem at hand was that, at Meryton, or any base for that matter, a relationship between the two of them was impossible. She was a student. He was an instructor. There was very little he could do to work around that, unless of course, they were married.

Elizabeth was the most beautiful creature Darcy had ever seen. She was intelligent, witty, and loved flying as much as he did. She understood his world better than anyone he had ever met. Over the months that Darcy had known her, thoughts of her were never far. In his mind's eye, he could see her curls cascading down her back and her eyes flashing at him dangerously while they debated something meaningless.

Darcy had volunteered for deployment to avoid her, but over the last few days in her presence, he knew that he had really been running from the depth of his feelings. He had never felt this way about another person before. She would be a perfect wife, a perfect sister for Georgiana, a perfect lover, a perfect mother. He could not contain his excitement, and so, he paced.

Soon he glimpsed her quick pace down the path to where he stood. Her eyes were down, and her fists clenched. As she approached, he stepped into her path, smiling. Elizabeth glanced up, clearly surprised. She took a step back but said not a word. Instead of making a sound, she paused, set her jaw and walked around him. After walking silently beside her for several minutes, he was anxious for the words to come, but he knew he must.

"Elizabeth, I wanted to catch you. I've tried so hard not to say anything, struggled against it, even, but I have to tell you. You've got to let me to tell you how much I love and admire you."

Elizabeth was astonished but she refused to let him see it. And then, she stumbled over a crack in the sidewalk, made an attempt to speak, flushed, stuttered again, and finally fell silent.

Darcy felt confident she was attracted to him. He had seen all the signs. He had admired her blushes when they talked and how she looked at him when they were not speaking at all.

"Elizabeth, I have attempted to repress my feelings. I even ran away to the desert in order to avoid facing them. These last few months have been horrible. I have fought against my better judgement to avoid fraternization, my rank, and my family. Some of my family will obviously disapprove and the obstacles they might throw in our path may be impossible to conquer. Of course, there may also be significant consequences to your training because of our relationship, but I feel that, even without flying, we could be incredibly happy."

Her color was high and eyes unreadable. "I don't understand what you are saying."

"I love you," Darcy blurted.

She looked away and her shoulders straightened.

"Sir." She paused, her eyes fixed on the ground. She shifted her weight from one foot to the other. The pathway was silent but for the sound of birds, and Darcy was apprehensive for her response for the first time.

"Elizabeth? I want to marry you."

Stammering, she said, "Captain. I thank you for your feelings toward me. But I must admit that I cannot now nor do I think I could ever love you in return."

Darcy's eyes widened, and his mouth dropped. *Nor do I think I could ever love you...* He looked away, his eyebrows knit together in concentration. *I thank you for your feelings for me...I could never love you...* His head snapped to face her once more, his eyes meeting hers as they blazed back and then quickly looked to the ground next to them. *I could never love you.*

"I am sorry to have hurt you."

She could not meet his eyes.

"I can tell that this conversation is not what you were expecting. I promise I would never mean to intentionally hurt you."

She would not look up at him.

"I can reasonably hope that your feelings will change quickly, though as you say, you clearly have enough reasons not to like me at all, I'm sure you'll be able to get over me quickly."

Look at me damn it!

She began to walk away before Darcy grabbed her arm and turned her to face him. He was gentle, but firm, and without words, he demanded her attention. Struggling to maintain his composure...and feared what he might say. Elizabeth pulled back and defiantly faced him until he found his voice.

"That is all you're going to say? I should ask why you'd reject me, but I guess it doesn't really matter!"

"Do you honestly think I could ever love someone who has ruined not only my family, but my friends, and my hometown? Everyone I know will be affected if Meryton is closed and you testified against it. Senator de Bourgh just placed it on the list for closure and now I am responsible for going home and telling my father how you are responsible for the death of his business and the loss of his home. Do you deny it?"

Darcy clenched his teeth. "I do not."

"How could you?"

"If a base has to close, I believe Meryton would be a good selection."

"Why would you ever think that?"

"I've watched the base and the community objectively. Meryton could close tomorrow and the community could live on, but even if it couldn't, the people could move on."

"You didn't look close enough."

"Those were my observations and I testified truthfully. I thought honesty was perhaps something you could respect."

Elizabeth stepped closer to him.

"And what of Lieutenant Wickham?"

"Wickham?" A wave of hatred roiled through his chest.

"What excuse can you give for your behavior toward him?"

"You're interested in him?"

"He told me what had happened to him."

Darcy snorted his derision.

"So, this is what you think of me?"—nearly nose to nose with her, he exhaled loudly.

He looked longingly at her and for the first time realized how very close they were. His gaze flicked to her lips. Their chests rose and fell in near unison as his pride warred with the greater emotions of love and hate, despair and desire.

He consciously released her arm that he had been grasping as a life line and took a step back.

"I'm sorry, Lieutenant, for taking time away from your busy schedule. We leave tomorrow at eight. Your bags will be brought to the air strip fifteen minutes prior and I'll make sure they're loaded. I will see you tomorrow."

He spun on his heel and walked further away from Rosings and away from Elizabeth. Aimlessly wandering the grounds for several hours, he attempted to school his thoughts and process what had been said.

The rain started about two hours into his solitary excursion. Richard did not look for him until well past dinner; he finally found Darcy, soaked, sitting on a bench near the roses.

CHAPTER 20

*E*lizabeth returned to her room and wept. She wept at the realization that they could never be. In the last week as she had come to know him better, she believed that she might have misjudged him—that he was not the beast she thought him to be but maybe her prince charming. But the senator had confirmed her original estimation of him and she hated being proven wrong.

Her night was very much the same as her afternoon following a brief phone call to her parents with the dreaded news, resulting in a headache and emotional exhaustion. Blessedly, Mr. Collins was busy, ingratiating himself to Lady Catherine's concerns. Charlotte found Elizabeth dabbing her eyes and attributed her melancholy to the placement of Meryton on the closure list.

The next morning, she arrived at the air strip at a quarter to eight. She was dressed in jeans and a t-shirt and paced, her sneakers squeaking with each step. Darcy showed up at exactly eight, signaled her to the cockpit, and they took off. Half way through the flight, he broke the silence.

"If you'd like to practice again, please, go ahead."

Elizabeth looked at him, but Darcy's expression was hidden behind a pair of aviators. She had a sudden impulse to cup his cheek and force his eyes to look at her but brought out her study materials instead. The aircraft provided smooth turns that cut through the sky like eagle wings. She loved the exhilaration of twisting into the sunshine and feeling the push of the turns on her body.

Elizabeth flew without comment from Darcy and they kept up their silent flight until they touched down. When the plane came to full stop, Darcy turned to Elizabeth.

"Elizabeth"—the way he said her name made her shiver involuntarily. His deep voice was almost a prayer and soothed her. "I wrote you a letter. I hope you'll do me the honor of reading it."

With that speech, despite his deception, Elizabeth's heart melted a little, and she opened her mouth to speak before Darcy reached over her to open the door. She stepped out to allow him to climb onto the ramp and then jumped back into her own seat to gather her things. She watched him walk away.

She sat for some minutes before a knock on the canopy door startling her. She saw Jane's blonde hair.

"Jane! Why are you here? I thought Captain Darcy would be taking me home."

"He called last night. Said you were upset about the commission. And asked Charles and me to come meet you."

"That was very nice of him."

"It was. Lizzy, I have such exciting news for you. We're engaged!" Jane held up a manicured left hand sporting a magnificent round, solitaire diamond ring. Elizabeth grabbed her sister into a hug.

"Jane! I am so happy for you! If there is anyone in the world who deserves to be happy, it is you."

A flame of red hair poked in the cabin doors. "I'm inclined to agree."

Elizabeth brought Bingley into a hug and only released him when his smothered voice suggested getting some lunch.

"We could go to Subs and Clubs. It's just across the way," Jane said.

"Perfect. Let me grab these bags and I'll meet you ladies in the car."

"I am so incredibly happy for you, Jane. I don't know what to say! How did he propose? When did it happen?"

"It was perfect. Last night, I was over at Netherfield—Caroline was out getting a manicure—and we had just sat down to have a glass of wine and he just blurted out, "Will you marry me?" Except I didn't understand what he said because he said it so fast, so he had to ask me two more times before I finally said 'yes'. He was so nervous! He pulled my ring out of his pocket and that was it."

"Did Mom just die?"

"I don't want to talk about it. Let's just say, she was ecstatic. I don't know if I've ever seen her so excited about something before in my life. She's already got about seven binders full of wedding planning and it's only been one day. Sorry I didn't call you about it, telling Mom took so much time that I couldn't and by the time I could this morning, you were already on the plane.

"S'okay. I really can't tell you how happy I am for you." Elizabeth smiled but could feel that only her mouth moved—the smile did not reach her eyes.

"Are you okay, Lizzy? Did something happen?"

Well, I was proposed to by a rich, handsome man that I was just starting to like, but he lied to me and is awful, so I rejected him, then was stuck in a tiny cockpit with him all morning. Elizabeth shook her head as she opened the car door and sat in the back.

"Nothing, just disappointed with the results of the committee."

"I'm sure you did your best."

Did I? Should I have asked him why he testified against Meryton? And

*his face when I mentioned Wickham. Knowing they have bad blood, should I
have not brought it up?*

Bingley opened the door of the truck and hopped into the seat behind the wheel.

"Where to, ladies?"

Elizabeth put her own feelings in a private corner of her mind to go back to after they went home.

"Subs and Clubs. Jane was just telling me all about your proposal. Can you tell the story one more time? I want to hear every single detail."

Jane gushed about how he had proposed, with Bingley filling in essential details. They talked about tentative wedding plans and Jane warned Elizabeth of their mother's excessive joy.

"Mom hasn't been this happy since Lydia was born."

"I bet the only thing that could possibly make her happier would be you asking her to provide the meal for your rehearsal dinner."

Charles blanched at Jane. She stroked his arm and laughed lightly. "Lizzy, you know she'll do that anyway. I doubt we will be able to make a single decision about our wedding without Mom providing a reason that she should be able to do whatever it is. I don't doubt she's looking to ordain Dad as a minister as we speak."

Arriving back at Longbourn, Elizabeth immediately excused herself to her room, unable to talk about the commission yet. She threw her luggage on the floor and pulled out Darcy's letter. She stared down at the stationary and consciously released the breath she had been holding.

"Let's see what he has to say for himself."

My dearest Elizabeth,

*I have longed to speak to you in the most loving of terms. I promise to
refrain from doing so, but please allow me this one address. Don't be*

worried that I will propose again. I know that for the happiness of us both, we should forget what happened yesterday afternoon. I will do my best to avoid you so as not to cause you further discomfort. Should we be thrown together for work, you can be assured I will maintain the utmost professionalism.

You laid two offenses at my feet yesterday. The first, that I testified against Meryton in total disregard of your family, friends, and community. The second that I ruined the prospects of Lieutenant Wickham.

I gave my honest testimony when queried about Meryton. I provided no testimony whatsoever for or against the closure of Meryton. I testified to the low morale situation of Meryton and that the other training bases could take on the load of the student pilots. I was not asked any questions regarding the off-base community and I did not bring up any personal acquaintances or possible negative consequences of the base closure. My testimony was nothing other than truth.

SHE CLENCHED her fists at the idea that William Darcy had not even given Meryton a chance. How long had he lived there? A few months? It was preposterous that he should be charged with giving testimony after so short a time. Her fists soon unclenched, however, when she accepted he was clinically correct. Meryton could be closed and the American population at large would never feel sorrow, regret, or sadness at its loss.

At every party I have attended, every officer I know has been accosted by civilian women who are looking for their ticket out and often do not consider the potential aftermath of a relationship. I have seen women scorned by the officers and turn bitter toward them, with officers facing the community consequences as Longbourn protects its own. This can be no different from any small town near a military base but there you have it.

I am not sure what George Wickham exactly accused me of, but I have known him long enough to understand what the usual grievances might be. George is the son of my father's best friend. George's father was one of the best of men. He was loyal, a hard worker, and industrious leader who helped my father in his businesses and in the running of Pemberley. George was raised with me at Pemberley. We grew up together. We attended the same private schools even. During our teenage years, George and I began to drift apart. I studied hard, managing my social life with my academics. George, on the other hand, chose to run with a very different crowd. Often, he would ask me to cover for him or loan him money to get himself out of bind. By college, we were on completely separate paths. I could never tell my father how Wickham acted. I couldn't disappoint him that way. Wickham drank and caroused...as many do in college, but Wickham took it to a whole different level of disgusting behavior. Suffice it to say, Wickham is one of the most base men I have ever had the misfortune to know and I would never recommend his friendship to anyone.

You see, George was left a large inheritance by my father and a position in my family company which would have set him up for life. He was given the money immediately and offered the position. When his own father died six months after mine, Wickham declined the position at Pemberley. He said he was going to go to law school, but I didn't hear from him for three years. I don't know where he lived or even how, and I wasn't upset. I assumed he was getting his law degree.

He called me up out of the blue, demanding the job he had given up. He told me that he had no money and that everything in his life was going wrong, which I had no difficulty believing. I stood firm and told him that the position had already been filled and that I did not intend to hire him for anything else. I knew what kind of man he was. You can hardly blame me for turning him away. We avoid each other even now. Especially now.

All this would be forgotten, if not forgiven, but last summer, just before I moved to Meryton, Wickham did something I cannot possibly forget or forgive. Elizabeth, I don't know if you know, but when my father died Colonel Richard Fitzwilliam and I became co-guardians of my sister Georgiana until she turns eighteen. She is still in school and as both Richard and I cannot be near her, we hired a nanny to live at the house and look after

her well-being, take care of her when we could not be at home. We wanted
her to be in the home she has always known and not follow her bachelor
brother or cousin around to our military duty stations, and go to her own
school, be near her friends, etc. We didn't want my father's death to further
disrupt Georgiana's life.

Last summer, we hired a new woman, her name was Mrs. Younge,
seemed fantastic: her references were impeccable as was her training. And
Georgiana took to her immediately. Last summer, I rented a beach house for
Mrs. Younge and Georgiana for a few weeks. But it wasn't until later we
found out that she was friends with Wickham.

While at the shore, George and Mrs. Young "ran" into each other and
after the happy reunion with my sister, they spent a lot of time together. As
it turns out, George conspired with Mrs. Younge to convince Georgiana he
was in love with her and they should run away together. When she is
married, she is entitled to an inheritance of more than two million dollars.
She was only fifteen! No doubt you can see how easily a young,
impressionable teenager might be tricked into believing she was in love.
Blessedly, she told me of the entire plan. I had leave and planned to visit
with her at the beach and was able to surprise her a day earlier. It was then
that she told me of her secret engagement. You can guess how I acted. Suffice
it to say, I found Wickham, ran him out of town with threats of statutory
rape, and immediately fired Mrs. Younge. We were lucky. He never violated
her and denies any wrongdoing that I could tell the police or the air force
about, but the threat of reporting him was enough to scare him off.
Georgiana has been living with Richard's family in New York since that
time. Wickham's target was obviously Georgiana's millions, but he cannot
be trusted if he would prey even on such a young girl. I must ask you to keep
this private as she is still so young.

WICKHAM HAD ENGAGED in salacious gossip. Indeed, he was
the one to start it. No one had heard anything negative about
Darcy until Wickham had slandered him at every gathering in

town. Darcy had been rude to her but nothing more. Generally, in fact, he was the picture of polite society. With the notable exception of Drop Night, Darcy was helpful and frequently kind. By all accounts from her friends in T-38s, he was an excellent instructor and endeavored to help the lowest ranking students learn. How humiliated he must have been to have to admit his shortcomings as guardian of his sister and his own father's misplaced belief in Wickham.

I have written the truth. I don't know what lies he has told you, and as he has convinced those much closer to him of worse, I am not surprised that you should fall prey to those lies. I wish I could have told you all of this personally, but I could not keep my emotions in check yesterday to do so. If you would like any other evidence, you can talk to Colonel Richard Fitzwilliam. I know that your poor opinion of me may color this story, so I would beg you to talk to Richard.

I am hoping to give this to you tomorrow morning at some point. God bless you.

Forever yours,

William Darcy

THE LETTER FELL to her lap, her heart and head warring with each other as she ran through every emotion. Hurt. Offense. Sorrow. Embarrassment. Anger. Shame.

Elizabeth re-read the letter several times that day. Stirred by his beginning endearment and despaired at the idea that she would never hear "my dearest Elizabeth" in Darcy's deep, rich voice.

Elizabeth was taken aback that her musings, her antagonism toward Darcy had changed completely. She found that she desired his approval. Instead of disgust at his treatment of Wickham, she found that she esteemed Darcy for protecting his sister as best as he knew how.

Contemplating how to fix everything, she stood at her bedroom window, looking out onto the garden. She was not sure how she could possibly manage it, but she was determined to try.

CHAPTER 21

*D*arcy arrived back to work, single-minded on the tasks of his day. He was flying with a student at eleven but before that he would need to complete annual computer-based training. He wished he had more to look forward to than mind-numbing slides. After his flight, he would fill out his grade sheet and have time to return emails.

He quickly made a checklist and went to work with the efficiency that came naturally to him. When he completed the first four items on his list, he stood to take a break. He strode out of his shared office to the scheduling desk where he promptly volunteered for every cross country flight he could for the next several months. When he had to give up a cross country to another instructor, he volunteered for long out and backs and every additional duty he could think up.

Darcy could keep the visions of the beautiful Elizabeth out of his mind if he was busy, but at nights or when he did not have enough to entertain his thoughts, she crept in. He had grown used to the idea of her at his side or running with him down the avenue near the house. Worse, her frequent presence in his thoughts as he flew unnerved him as he sailed through misty clouds and twisted in his patterns. Days later, he found himself sitting tensely on the couch while thoughts of Elizabeth tortured him. Hushed voices from the kitchen soon floated into the room and stirred him from his contemplation of sparkling brown eyes.

"Jane, I'm telling you. Darcy's been acting strange, even for him. He's gone more often than not, and when he isn't, he shuts himself up in his room. I've barely seen him for longer than ten minutes here or there and I live with the man. I just don't understand what changed. He looks miserable and tired, and I just don't know how to help him."

"I wish I knew what to tell you. Lizzy's been the same way. She's been studying for her formation solo. I know it's a difficult ride, but she never studied so hard for any other flight. I wonder that something didn't happen when they were both gone."

"But what could have happened? The commission hasn't even officially submitted the closure list, so it can't be that."

Darcy's jaw dropped. The commission had not submitted the list? Classic government speed. He should have assumed. If that was the case there was still time, still hope. His mind raced.

"Maybe Darcy liked Charlotte Lucas?"

Darcy made a face. There was silence and then he heard laughter.

"Of course, you're right. Absurd. But, for a long time I hoped that he would like Caroline so that we could really be brothers, but...well, you've met Caroline."

More laughter and then—"Hey, you remember George Wickham? I saw him in the flight room today while I was with a student. Apparently, he is dating someone named Mary King. Do you know her?"

"Mary King? I do. It is a small town, you know. She went to school with my sister Mary, so she must be nineteen or so. She's a pretty girl, and an uncle died a few months ago and she supposedly came into a huge inheritance. Enough to buy a house or something. I don't remember the exact amount, but I remember Kitty and Lydia moaning about it."

"Well, I'm just glad he's away from your sisters. I don't like him."

"Lizzy said much the same thing, which surprised me. I know he was a favorite in our house until just recently, though Kitty and Lydia still talk about him and Captain Denny almost non-stop."

"William?"

Darcy started, nearly jumping out of his skin. He spun his head toward the speaker and saw Caroline in another flamboyant orange dress.

"What are you doing?" She tossed her keys on a side table.

"Nothing. I was just heading into the kitchen for a glass of milk. I didn't hear you come in."

"I'll get it for you."

Everything came with a price in Caroline's mind and Darcy was not willing to pay. "No, I'll grab it." He strode through the kitchen door, greeting Bingley and Jane before pouring himself a glass of milk he had not wanted and headed to his room. He locked the door of his room and was free to think miserably about Elizabeth once again.

CHAPTER 22

*H*onestly, it doesn't matter to me where the wedding is because Colonel Forster's daughter, Abby Joe, invited me to go with them to Brighton Beach. Colonel Forster has some sort of exercise nearby and Abby Joe would like me to go as her particular friend. I won't be here for the wedding, so I won't have to go watch that tubby marry poor Charlotte before she is flattened like a pancake."

"It's not fair!" shouted Kitty.

"You're just jealous because you weren't invited."

"Who is Colonel Forster?" asked Elizabeth to Jane.

"He is new in the intel wing. His daughter is eighteen too. Not sure about their story, but they met Lydia at a party at our aunt Evelyn's house and they've become quite close friends."

"I miss so much when I'm studying," Elizabeth said dryly, picking up her books and setting them out on the newly cleared table.

The two youngest Bennets continued to bicker. Mary looked on the activity with disapproval before picking up a book of sermons and began to read out loud. Jane and Elizabeth shook their heads.

A feeling of disquiet nagged at Elizabeth until much later that afternoon. She was concerned for Lydia. Lydia was known for being the reckless girl from Longbourn. Elizabeth resolved to speak to her father about it and perhaps rein in Lydia's summer plans.

She found her father in his office.

"What can I help you with my dear?"

"I wanted to speak to you about Lydia."

"Such a silly girl."

"I just found out that you are letting her go to Brighton Beach with the Forsters."

"There will be no peace in this house if I don't."

"Dad, she's out of control."

"Colonel Forster is a sensible man. I'm sure he will make sure Lydia doesn't get into any real trouble. It is my hope that this trip will show Lydia exactly how insignificant she really is."

"You don't think this is her ticket to *Girls Gone Wild?*"

He waved the thought away. "I am happy to have the noise reduced in this house by letting her."

"Just tell her to be careful."

"I will, but only because you said." Mr. Bennet winked at Elizabeth. "And how are you doing these days?"

"Just studying. Seems that's all I do."

"It seems that way, but I think you will be surprised how fast it goes. William Lucas said that in pilot training the days seem like weeks and the weeks seem like days."

"That is exactly how it feels. I'm sure one day I'll look back on everything fondly. But right now, it's a blur."

"Now, Jane has Charles Bingley."

"She does, and they are so happy."

"It does a girl good to be in love, Lizzy. You can see it in Jane's eyes. Now, Charlotte. It is time for you to be struck yourself."

Elizabeth rolled her eyes. "Okay, thanks, Dad," she said sarcastically.

Her father laughed.

"What about that Wickham fellow? You seemed to get along with him well."

Shaking her head, Elizabeth decided that Wickham's history with the Darcy family was not her story to tell. "Thanks. But no."

"You know, happiness in marriage is just a matter of chance. Look at your mother and me. We started out head over heels in love. We've raised you girls well, but I don't know that I would call us happy. Look at Charlotte. She can't be marrying Collins for his good sense."

"Then I guess I won't get married. I only plan to find a husband if I am truly in love with him."

"A rarity these days. I'm glad. I'd like to keep you to myself." Mr. Bennet pulled Elizabeth into a hug before she returned to her books.

FANNY BENNET WAS NOT PLEASED with her second oldest daughter. Lizzy had always been a foolish, ungrateful child. This was yet another example. Mr. Collins had come to Longbourn to extend an olive branch to Longbourn during this uncertain time. Was it her fault that his version of an olive branch was to look for a testimony amongst her own daughters? Was it her fault that his sights had fallen on Lizzy? And was it her fault that Lizzy was too stupid to know how to make herself pleasing to a man? A man who had influence with Senator de Bourgh? But no. Instead of doing her duty as she had been taught, she had tramped off and got Meryton closed—and even lost a conquest like Collins to the plain, old, spinster Charlotte Lucas, of all people.

Fanny Bennet spent much of her day in her darkened room nursing disappointment, hurt feelings, and an anxiety born of having no customers for her inn. What would they do if the base closed and had to close the inn? How could they ever replace the home she had spent the last twenty-five years building or replicate the stellar reputation of the table she kept.

After she had worked herself up to her boiling point, she made her way out of her room, down the stairs, and found Elizabeth sitting at the dining room table surrounded by papers covered in maps, checklists, and numbers, everything she hated.

"Lizzy." The word was hissed as a curse.

Elizabeth jumped and turned to meet her glare.

"You are a traitor to your family."

"Mom?"

"You should have put yourself forward."

"What?"

"To Mr. Collins."

"He's disgusting."

"Most men are. I fail to see your point. My point, however, is that you should have protected your family, had you been nicer to him."

"I was nice to him. Treated him with respect like everyone having business at the base," Elizabeth said dismissively and turned back to her work.

"Don't you turn your back on me, Miss Lizzy." Elizabeth flung up her arms in a shrug and spun around to face her mother.

"Mom, I've got to study. My check ride is only a few rides away. I have a cross country coming up and I need to be at the top of the class. I can't just sit at home flirting with sycophantic weirdos in the hopes that somehow everything wrong with Meryton will be fixed and we will all be saved. I have a job, Mom! Why can't you just be proud of me for what I'm doing?"

"You are just like Phillip," her mother murmured blankly. She shook herself, her anger flaring up as quickly as it was lost, then flitted out of the room before another word could be said. For several minutes Elizabeth wondered what her mother had meant because her father's name was Thomas.

CHAPTER 23

The sizzling July sun dawned over Meryton, warmer than usual, but Elizabeth never noticed. When she was not studying or in the dim, windowless flight room, she was flying and too busy concentrating to notice the sweat as it ran down her temples and clung to her back. She insisted her flight suits were washed after every flight, despite what the rest of her flight mates did with their own. Upon entering the squadron building, a distinct male odor offended her nostrils before she became enveloped in a near frantic state of work.

Her first stop every day was at the scheduling desk. The flight schedule could never be trusted more than a day out and even that was subject to change. Weather, plane maintenance, flight cancellations, mishaps, and tower difficulties could alter *everything* at a moment's notice and the scheduling desk made it happen.

Today, only a few changes had been made. Elizabeth noticed that despite original plans, Lieutenant Wickham would be partnering Captain Denny for a flight instead of herself, while she was to join Edward "Uncle" Gardiner for a cross country over the weekend.

Elizabeth was quite pleased with this new information. Lieutenant Colonel Edward "Uncle" Gardiner was one of her favorite instructors. He and his wife Madeline lived in the Cheapside neighborhood of town and owned a small business in stock trading. The Gardiners had never been able to have children of their own, and as a result had habitually "adopted" young student pilots into their family. They gained a reputation for kind, compassionate mentorship to the students and solid instruction to every class of new pilots as each came through Meryton's doors.

As a reservist, Uncle Gardiner had more time available for business pursuits and was known to share trading information with students during their flights. She had quickly learned never to ask questions about retirement as her first flight with him rapidly descended into a lesson on the topic. Now that she regularly contributed to her Thrift Savings Plan, she was hopeful that her instruction would be conducive to her pilot career.

On the first Friday morning of July, Elizabeth arrived in the briefing room excited for the trip. She had been told by a friend that Uncle Gardiner always liked to tour whatever area they wound up in during a cross country and Elizabeth was excited to find out what she would get to see.

"Morning, Bennet," Uncle Gardiner said as he strolled in the room and deposited himself into an open office chair.

"Morning, sir." Elizabeth's face broke out into a smile. She simply could not help herself.

"We're going up to Rochester."

Elizabeth's smile faltered a little. "New York?"

"That's the place. Squadron commander wants us to participate in a quick air show up there and we are going to tour the lakes."

"Are there lakes in Rochester?" Elizabeth had rarely been outside of Texas and knew little to nothing about central New York.

"Just outside, the Finger Lakes, they call them. They're these long, skinny lakes and I hear the scenery thereabouts is stunning."

"When are we leaving?"

"Next Thursday. We brief at nine."

The two left the room and for Elizabeth it seemed like they were back in the same attitude for her brief within a blink of her eye.

Elizabeth and Uncle Gardiner went over her flight plans before stepping to the jet. This trip was much farther than the typical cross country, but it was Uncle Gardiner's last before retirement and he intended to make it special. Elizabeth was grateful as well for the extra time to practice. Soon she would have her final check ride in the T-6 and would be given a slot either in the T-38 fighter trainer or the T-1 heavy trainer and she desperately wanted to do well and move on to T-38s. *Fly fast and loud, shoot through the sky like a blazing star.*

Uncle Gardiner showed Elizabeth various sights from the air and was an excellent instructor. He made corrections when necessary, but they were thoughtfully addressed and praised when amended. He showed her techniques she had not seen before and kept the flight fun, which Elizabeth had missed desperately during her pilot training. The last flight she had enjoyed was with Darcy and she refused to think about that time, just as she willed herself to refuse to think about the man himself.

Elizabeth landed the plane at Rochester Airport, a smaller airport with a few national airlines. Their small part in the regional airshow took place that afternoon. Elizabeth met thousands of people and presented the T-6 to every one of them. She held small children on the ladder where she was quizzed on every knob, dial, and switch. By the end of the day, she was relieved to hop in the small rental car with Uncle Gardiner and move toward their hotel. They drove an hour, eating on the road, before finally stopping at their inn.

Elizabeth noticed the small sign over the entry way: "Lambton Inn" in scrolling script on a crisp, white sign.

"Are we in Lambton?"

Uncle Gardiner pointed to the sign and said, "Jewel of the Finger Lakes."

"I think I know someone from here."

They checked into the quaint inn and agreed to meet in the lobby at eight for breakfast and to tour around.

Her small, well-appointed room smelled like pine and strangely reminded of Darcy. She threw her bag on a chair near the bed, unzipped her flight suit, and sat on the end of the bed to remove her heavy boots. Not long after she had pulled on her pajamas, she dozed into a fitful sleep.

In the morning, she appeared downstairs for breakfast in jeans and a t-shirt, carrying her bag.

"All right," Uncle Gardiner said while viciously stabbing a bite of scrambled eggs, "I talked to the guy at the desk and he said that Pemberley is open for tours, so we'll stop there first and then I was thinking about just driving down the 96 and stopping for lunch somewhere before we have to head back. Sound like a plan, Stan?"

"Did you say Pemberley?"

"You know, Bennet, I heard you were pretty smart, number one in your class, but the last few minutes really have me doubting your intellectual prowess."

He smiled, and Elizabeth let out a nervous laugh before biting into a bagel.

"I just didn't know that Pemberley was up here. Isn't that Captain Darcy's home?"

"Darcy, yeah, that's the fellow. They open up the house for tours and so I called just now and scheduled a tour. It's one of the oldest homes in the area and the winery and orchard have been owned and operated by the family the entire time. According to the desk manager, it's one of the nicest homes in the country."

"Of course, it is," Elizabeth murmured to herself. *Darcy's house. I can't gallivant around his house like a freaking tourist!*

After paying the bill, they headed to the rental car. "I was, uh, thinking..." Uncle Gardner turned his ear toward her, grinning. A little louder, she said, "Maybe we shouldn't go."

"Oh really, Bennet? Why?"

"I just think it must be awkward to have tourists wandering around your house. Don't you think?"

"Of course, he won't be there. Besides, didn't you say you know him?"

Uncle Gardiner opened the car door for her.

"I do."

"What? You don't want to go because you know the owner?"

"Doesn't that make it kind of weird to you?"

Uncle Gardiner smiled widely. "Nope."

They stepped to the car and Uncle Gardiner searched for his charger to plug in his phone while entering the address into his GPS app. Elizabeth lowered herself into the passenger seat and pulled on her sunglasses to accept the inevitable. She was going to Darcy's house.

Every color of green streaked past her window. The dark green of the pine contrasted beautifully with the lighter greens of hickory and oak trees. Large beech trees provided shade to grass covered rolling hills. Quaint farmhouses dotted the landscape and wide, flower covered meadows gave way to barns and large plantation-style homes. *So different from Texas. So green. You can barely see the road for all the trees.*

They turned left at the "Pemberley Woods" sign and entered a wide drive. The park was large, and they drove through a beautiful wood, stretching over miles.

Uncle Gardiner pointed out sights but Elizabeth's mind was too full of admiration for conversation. They gradually ascended for half a mile and found themselves at the top of a large hill. Through a gap in the trees, her eye caught Pemberley House. On the opposite side of the little valley was a large stone building standing on rising ground and backed by a ridge of high, woody hills. Along the front, a small stream swelled into a large pond with beautifully landscaped banks. Elizabeth had never seen a place for which nature had done more.

They parked along the winding front driveway and all of Elizabeth's apprehensions of suddenly visiting Darcy's house returned. She drew in a breath and recited to herself that Darcy was flying over Meryton and would not be home. Relaxing, they knocked on the door and waited.

A small, wrinkled woman of middling age answered the door. Her face burst into a smile and her wrinkles grew deeper, but Elizabeth's heart was warmed by the woman.

"Good morning. You must be Colonel Gardiner."

The entry hall was the perfect combination of class and elegance. Deep, carved wood accented the high ceilings and large open windows allowed brilliant light to fall on a tall staircase.

"This way," Elizabeth heard the woman say before turning and beckoning them in.

"My name is Mrs. Reynolds. I've been the housekeeper here for more than twenty-five years and have loved every minute of it."

"Is the family at home?"

"No, ma'am."

At this, Elizabeth calmed down and decided to enjoy herself.

"Right this way. Pemberley is the oldest family owned and operated winery in the country, having been founded in 1750. The Darcy family emigrated from the county of Derbyshire in England and initially farmed the land. You'll see a drawing of the original plans here..."

Mrs. Reynolds took them through a stately dining room, a comfortable sitting room, a large chef's kitchen, and a colossal library. Elizabeth, who had never seen a library in someone's home, dawdled among the shelves, running her hand along spines of books. Several minutes passed before Elizabeth came to the startling realization that she was alone and could no longer hear Mrs. Reynold's voice.

She walked down the corridors, occasionally uttering a half-hearted "hello?" and peeking into rooms surreptitiously. At the third doorway, she turned to glance inside and bumped headlong into a man in jeans and a long-sleeve button-down shirt. She knew it was him before she looked up to his face.

"Elizabeth?" Darcy looked almost as taken aback as she was, but somehow, he seemed more composed than normal. He smiled. A smile that sent shivers down Elizabeth's spine.

"Darcy?"

She turned to run. Except her feet did not cooperate. She was looking into his expressive eyes. She could feel herself staring, but she could not look away. Her hands fidgeted at her side and finally she brought them in front of her to fret.

"She told us you weren't here."

"No, I just got in on leave. I needed to take care of some business," he said, still smiling down at her.

"I am so sorry. You weren't supposed to be here." *Why couldn't she think of anything else to say?*

"It's okay. I haven't even seen Mrs. Reynolds yet."

He reached out and touched her elbow, suddenly very aware of his touch and the heat that spread from her arm to the rest of her body.

"I want you to meet my sister."

"I don't... Maybe I should... I think..."

"Come on." Darcy slid his hand down Elizabeth's arm to lightly capture her hand and led her down the hallway and through a series of doors.

Light, airy piano music pulled Elizabeth's feet further into Darcy's home and she struggled to form a comprehensive thought. Elizabeth trailed Darcy into a room where she was greeted by a willowy, blonde teenage girl—a stark contrast to her dark brother. Her piano playing slowed as Darcy entered and then stopped abruptly when she saw Elizabeth.

"This is—"

"You must be Elizabeth!"

Stunned, Elizabeth sought an appropriate response and eventually nodded.

"I've heard so much about you! I can't believe you are here! William has told me all about flying up to Rosings. I am sorry for anyone who has to spend time any time with Aunt Catherine. You should know that no one likes her."

"Georgie!"

"Well, it's true," Georgiana said quickly and then stopped, blushing furiously.

"I have two sisters that are your age." She crossed the room to shake Georgiana's hand. "We will have to find something to talk about when your brother is out of the room."

Darcy interjected, "Who are you here with? Are you on a cross country?"

"Uncle Gardiner! I have to find him." She started toward the door.

"Wait. I'll go." He left the room and Georgiana reached out for her hand, pulling her to the piano bench.

"Do you play?" Georgiana asked eagerly.

Elizabeth touched the keys and looked almost longingly at the music. "Very poorly. My parents put me in lessons when I was ten, but I hated my teacher and only took about a year before I quit. It's a pretty small town, so there were no other teachers. I practice every now and then and can play some simple songs, but I really am not very good. My sister Mary is the pianist in our family. She practices all the time."

Georgiana smiled. "You'll have to play with me. Or sing. Do you sing?"

"I'd like to think I sing much better than I play."

Silence ensued, but it was a friendly sort of silence. A peaceful moment between the two as they thumbed through music companionably.

"Do you like my brother?"

The question walloped Elizabeth's peace. She shifted uncomfortably. "He is always...very...kind."

"But do you like him?"

Her throat felt taut as she struggled to say anything coherent. She was saved when the man in question came striding into the room with Uncle Gardiner.

Uncle Gardiner gave Elizabeth a thumbs up. "Darcy's invited us to stay for lunch and some fishing in his pond out there."

To her amazement, a great weight lifted from her and was replaced by pleasure. The faces in the room reflected the same back at her.

Darcy and Uncle Gardiner left to find fishing tackle a moment later.

"So, Georgiana, what shall we do while the men are otherwise occupied?"

"William said you came for a tour. Did you get a chance to finish?"

"I got lost after the library—"

"I'm so sorry you were lost!"

"No, it is completely my fault. I lingered far too long looking at all the shelves."

"Well, let me show you the gardens and the tasting room. I think those are typically next."

"Do you give the tours?"

"Oh no, Mrs. Reynolds has always done it, but William has always made me take a tour at least once a year to ensure I remember the history of the house and can answer any questions for visitors. I've never worked here, typically the family starts working at eighteen, so I've only done some preliminary studying to understand the nuts and bolts. I'm sure William has told you all about it."

Desperate to change the topic from Darcy, Elizabeth tried another tack. "What other family works here?"

"Oh, no one. It's just William and I, but my father and his brother both worked here and their parents and aunts and uncles, of course. William told me you have a big family though, so that must seem odd."

"I have four sisters and my parents, of course."

"That would be absolutely amazing—I'm sorry, I shouldn't assume things—"

"No, you aren't assuming anything. Most people have good relationships with their siblings. I do with most of my sisters. Don't worry about it."

"I can't imagine how wonderful it must be to always have a friend nearby. I bet you borrow each other's clothes and brush each other's hair! Much better than having a brother more than ten years older."

"It sounds better when you put it like that, but you're leaving out the fights and a lot of screaming and bickering. Besides, can you imagine sharing a bathroom with that many women? Believe me, not an ideal situation. One brother, though, you don't have to share anything. You've got it made. I'm sure you want for nothing and he is just the sweetest brother anyone could ever have."

As Georgiana showed her the tasting room and various wine casks and tasting glasses, Elizabeth thought on all that Wickham had told her about the Darcys. It was clear to her that Georgiana was not arrogant. Georgiana craved female attention and needed frequent reassurances. Being with her that morning, Elizabeth was reminded of her sisters. Georgiana was less exuberant than Lydia, much more like Kitty. For the first time, Elizabeth was grateful for her mother, silly and ridiculous as she was, for she had always been there to speak to and give advice. Seeing Georgiana, absent from that female mentor in her life, Elizabeth was relieved to have never felt unconfident about her place in the home.

A couple hours later, when the gentlemen returned from fishing, they found the girls on the terrace being served lunch by Mrs. Reynolds. Eyeing their pant hems, muddy from the bank of the pond, the girls laughed as Mrs. Reynolds exclaimed, "Gentlemen. Please. Take off your shoes before coming in the house! Six inches of mud does not need to be trekked through those floors."

CHAPTER 24

*D*arcy had rarely enjoyed fishing more than with Gardiner. He had only heard of him and was a little wary to meet someone who had a second job in day-trading. Darcy was responsible for a vast amount of investments and he was pleasantly surprised to discover the extensive knowledge Gardiner possessed. After their conversation, he had left with new and interesting investment possibilities and planned to ask Gardiner to assist him in diversifying portions of his portfolio.

Set to admire the gardens nearby, the terrace always enjoyed the rich fragrance of whatever was in bloom for the season. Peonies, freesia, and roses combined their scents to deliver a heady, wild fragrance while the songbirds sang sweetly. Darcy sat across from Elizabeth and smiled contentedly. He had so often dreamt of Elizabeth at Pemberley that this reality was too much emotion to hide. Elizabeth laughed and teased. If Darcy's heart had not already been lost, he would have fallen hard.

Goat cheese with crisp pears, French dip sandwiches, and caramel pecan tarts were laid out in succession by Mrs. Reynolds. Darcy noticed that Elizabeth took special care to thank Mrs.

Reynolds for all her attention. Mrs. Reynolds winked at him before bustling back into the kitchen, humming quietly as she returned to her duties.

"So, Elizabeth, how do you find pilot training? It must be so difficult being a woman in a field dominated by men." Georgiana took a bite of her sandwich.

"Well, I guess I always wanted to fly. Did you ever have those dreams where you fly in your pajamas? I suppose I just didn't want those to stop. I grew up in Longbourn, and Meryton was just a step away and the pilots always seemed so confident, really going places, you know? I guess I never thought about the fact that I didn't really see any women."

"Do you know about the WASPs? They were so amazing. William told me about them a few months ago and I've been reading about them. They stepped up in a time where flying was a man's job and did it just as well if not better than the men. It's a shame they didn't get the credit they deserved."

Elizabeth's jaw dropped and her eyes met his quickly before returning to look at Georgiana with a small smile at the corner of her mouth. Darcy cleared his throat and addressed Elizabeth.

"An even better example of women doing a man's job is Wally Funk. She was part of Mercury 13 space program and even scored higher than John Glenn in her astronaut testing."

"The program was cancelled—"

"But she paved the way for Eileen Collins to pilot the space shuttle in '95."

"She was also the first non-military flight instructor."

"That's right. And soon, you'll be there, walking in her footsteps as an instructor."

"I've got to get through UPT first."

"Elizabeth, do you really think you won't make it through? Top of your class, excellent instincts. I'm sure every one of your flight mates would kill to be half as good as you."

"He's got a point, Bennet," Uncle Gardiner said while lifting a glass of water to his lips. "Poor Chunk would sell a kidney to skate through academics like you do."

Elizabeth smiled at Darcy, her eyes bright. *She's certainly not looked at me that way before.*

"Can I show you around the garden, Elizabeth? Gardiner, of course you are welcome to join us."

"I am fine right where I am. I want to see if Mrs. Reynolds has any more of these little tarts. I don't think I've had quite enough."

"I'll go find her." Georgiana stood and walked back into the house.

Darcy held out his arm and watched as Elizabeth walked to him tentatively. He motioned toward the stairs and together they started down the garden path.

"I'm surprised you told Georgiana about the WASPs. I didn't think you had a terribly high opinion of them." Elizabeth stopped to investigate a flower, turning her back to Darcy.

"You changed my mind. I had never thought of them as anything but a quick footnote, like I had told you, but after your passionate defense of their historical influence, I educated myself and came to appreciate them. Georgiana has my aunts, but no mother to look up to and I want her to look up to women that go above and beyond what they are handed. I want her to look up to women like you."

Darcy stopped to face Elizabeth. He swallowed, nervous that he was pushing his luck. She had smiled at him and he did not want to ruin what small peace they had gained.

"Elizabeth, I would love it if we could become much better friends. I know I sometimes speak before thinking, or worse, I don't talk at all and appear taciturn. Bingley always teases me for brooding. Anyway, now I'm rambling. I just want you to know that despite what I have said and done in the past, I have a very high opinion of you."

Darcy searched Elizabeth's face. Her head was tilted slightly and her eyes were narrowed but searching his own. He could see her eyes bounce back and forth between his, but he held his gaze steady. He held his breath and noticed that her own chest was rising and falling faster and heavier than normal. He took a chance and moved his arm down to slip his hand around hers, enjoying the way her whole hand fit within his. She licked her lips and he noticed her eyes drop ever so quickly to his own lips before returning back to meet his eyes. He lowered his head and could feel her body move towards his as she rose onto her toes to meet him.

And then her cell phone rang.

Elizabeth gasped and jumped back as if burned. She felt her back pocket, where the lyrics by Train continued loudly. She held up a finger to Darcy, shrugging her shoulders and mouthing "sorry" before she answered.

"Hello? Jane, what's up?" He watched as her brow furrowed and she pushed the phone closer to her ear.

"She did what?" She turned away from him, her feet slowly pacing the path.

"How do they—?" She put her hand on her head. "Where is she?" Her hand moved to her hip. "Let me know." The phone dropped from her ear and she pushed the end button. She took two steps forward and then stopped.

"What's happened?"

"Lydia," Elizabeth whimpered, a flood of tears overwhelming her. He gathered her into his arms and held her as she sobbed.

"Has something happened? An accident? Is she okay?" He cupped Elizabeth's chin and met her eyes, searching for answers.

Elizabeth shook her head, shoulders trembling.

"Elizabeth."

Elizabeth raised her gaze once again.

"You must tell me so I can fix it."

"Lydia..."

"Tell me."

Her phone chimed, signaling a text message. Instead of words, Elizabeth handed the phone to him. Pictures of one of her younger sisters assaulted his eyes. They were scandalous, horrible photographs showing that her in sexually suggestive poses. In several of the pictures, Wickham stood near her, in equally offensive postures.

"Where are they?"

"Not at Longbourn. These are from Jane. Bingley showed them to her and she alerted Dad to Lydia's stupidity. Apparently, they've been passed around for the last two days throughout Meryton. My father's been looking for Lydia with the police, but there's little since she's eighteen now. She and Wickham have run off together. No one knows where they are. She has no money, no connections. I'm afraid she will be lost forever."

"This is my fault. I should have told your father. I should have told the whole town. I should have talked to the base commander. I should—"

Elizabeth touched her fingers to his lips gently. "No. I should have told my sisters that he was not to be trusted. It's my fault. I won't have you blame yourself."

One tear slipped from Elizabeth's eyes and he wiped it away with his thumb.

"We can figure something out."

Elizabeth sniffed loudly. "What are you going to go find them and beat him up?" She laughed weakly. "Lydia is eighteen and while this is certainly the stupidest thing she has ever done, there's nothing exactly illegal about it, is there?"

"That isn't a bad idea. He deserves it."

"Listen, I appreciate your concern, but this is already too big. If Bingley has seen them so has the rest of the base. The world." She sighed. "I need to get home to figure out how to salvage any part of her reputation. Damn her! I have to call Dad."

Elizabeth slowly turned and walked away from him, all the

while muttering the depressing possibilities in front of her.

～

GARDINER AND ELIZABETH BENNET had immediately left Pemberley to fly back to Meryton. Darcy sought out Georgiana to explain and say that he would be back soon, that he would make sure all would be well. He called his cousin Richard as he walked to the small hangar on the property. Fortunately, he was at Matlock, only twenty minutes away, visiting his parents.

Richard was quick to arrive, chomping at the bit for a fight with Wickham. With time on their side, they quickly jumped into Darcy's Bonanza and took off for New York City. Before his usual hang outs at bars and the red-light districts of various boroughs, they thought to check in on Wickham's friend Mrs. Olivia Younge in Hunts Point. Darcy would start there.

The four-floor walk-up was in a part of the city that Darcy would never have let Georgiana walk through, night or day. Trash littered the ground along with the brown, red, and clear stains of unidentifiable liquids. Burnt out, hollow apartments left a shell of what the neighborhood had once been. The pervading stench of urine and body odor lingered in the air as Darcy took the stairs two at a time and pounded his fist against the grey metal door.

Darcy heard the slide of a lock and the scrape of a chain from the other side before the knob turned and a wary green eye peeked through the crack of the door.

"The fabulous Mrs. Younge. Long time, no see." Richard pushed the door open, causing the thin woman to stumble. Darcy grabbed her and brought her close, ignoring her wreaking breath and rotting teeth. *This is what meth looks like.*

"You know, I've missed you. You know who else I've been missing? My good friend, George. You wouldn't know where he is, do you?"

She shook her head, unable to wipe the shock off of her face.

"Captain Darcy?" A small voice caused him to spin about and face a frightened Lydia Bennet. Barely dressed in a stitch of clothing, she covered herself modestly with one hand and twisted her long hair with the other.

"Lydia, you must come with me. Is Wickham here?"

"Right through there." She pointed. Darcy looked her up and down assessing for any harm that might have come to her. Aside from being provocatively dressed, if one could call her fashion choice clothing, he could not see anything wrong with her.

Richard quickly slid past Darcy and into the room. He caught Wickham with one foot out of the window and on the fire escape, but a quick punch to the kidney stopped all Wickham's thoughts of a quick escape. Richard kicked him in the side for good measure.

Richard said he would take care of Wickham and Darcy assumed he would be quite pleased with himself when he had finished the job. He thanked Mrs. Younge with a nod, draped his jacket over Lydia's shoulders, grabbed her hand, and led her down the stairs.

"Where are we going? I want to go home."

Before walking onto the street, Darcy looked down at the teenager.

"Do you know what could have happened? Your family has been worried sick. What on earth were you doing with him?"

"He told me he loved me and would take me away. He told me we'd live happily ever after, just like I've always dreamed." Lydia's eyes filled with tears.

"You're married, are you?"

"Well, we were going to be as soon as Georgie could get money together. Instead, we decided to have our honeymoon here while he called some friends who owe him. Have a little honeymoon here first. He took me to see the Statue of Liberty." Darcy rolled his eyes at Wickham's lies.

"He did, did he? Did he introduce you to his children all over

209

the city? Or to the men he owes money to that will kill him if they ever find him? Did you even think about what would happen to a lieutenant that doesn't show up for work on Monday?" Despite his best efforts, Darcy could not keep the note of desperation out of his voice as it steadily grew louder.

"He told me he quit."

"Lydia, it is a blessing to be naïve, but in this case, you are simply stupid."

Darcy watched the wheels turn as myriad emotions flashed on Lydia's face ending finally in defiance.

"I loved him."

"Oh, I'm sure you did. But your family is frantic. You're lucky the police aren't already involved."

"He said he loved me."

"He used you. When he's done with you, he'll sell you to the highest bidder."

Darcy hit his mark. He watched the words as they hurt her, her pretty face falling into despair.

"How do you know?"

Darcy did not look at her. "He uses everyone."

Darcy led his young charge through the streets while ordering an Uber to come and collect them. They rode to the airport in silence. Darcy was furious at Wickham and indignant for the teenager beside him, mourning the loss of her first love.

While they waited in an airport lounge, he broke the news about the photos to her. "Do you know perverts are looking at pictures of you? Elizabeth received a call from Jane. There are pictures of you in some, uh, compromising situations that have been going around."

"Going around?" Lydia broke into hysterical sobs, shoulders shaking. Darcy's heart went out to the foolish girl. Darcy thought briefly about calling Elizabeth to tell her he had been successful but decided that the entire tale should come from Lydia herself instead of him. He was an outsider. Instead he sent a brief text stating that Lydia was with him and they were returning to Meryton.

When Richard joined them two hours later, it was clear Wickham was not with him.

"It's been much too long since I punched somebody. Leadership really is tiring." Richard collapsed himself into one of the airport's uncomfortable plastic chairs, legs sprawled lazily in front of him.

"Lucky you," Darcy replied drolly.

"Where is he?"

Richard chuckled and using finger quotations said, "Busy filling out paperwork to transition to Air National Guard as a convenience to the government. There will be a sixty-day approval time, but we can hopefully cut that down. Then he will be out of Meryton forever and your life forever. I have some friends in the office that approves those applications who was very happy to hear from me. You remember Reinhart? From school?"

"Max? Yeah, I liked him."

Lydia interrupted. "Why would he want to do that?"

"So that I don't call his commander to immediately charge him with desertion of duty, kidnapping, and any other charge I feel like adding to the call. He didn't want to be court martialed for some reason."

"But he didn't desert. We were on our honeymoon."

Darcy snorted. "Lydia, you have to be married to go on a honeymoon."

"Don't worry. He'll have enough trouble with the pictures floating around," said Richard.

It was at this point that Darcy determined it was time to depart. They guided the blubbering girl to Darcy's Bonanza and started their checklists. It would take a few hours to reach Meryton and then a drive to Longbourn.

While flying later, he let himself consider the happiness he had felt with Elizabeth in his home. She had fit so well. It was as if she had always been there. While he had dreamt of the occasion, the reality had been so much more than he could have hoped. He worried she would never come to him now that he was party to her family's shame and that thought was more devastating than when she had rejected his proposal.

CHAPTER 25

*E*lizabeth wished the T-6 was faster. She swore the propeller had stopped turning and that they were somehow stalled, unable to move forward. The ground seemed stationary. She checked her instruments again and confirmed that she was moving and not going in slow circles like she had imagined.

She replayed her phone call with Jane: "Charles was over at Longbourn when he got the text from his flight's group text. I got it from Charlotte who said someone else had sent it to Sir William. Father got them only moments after Charles and, Lizzy, I don't think I have ever seen him so. He huffed about the living room for a bit and then locked himself in his office. Even Mom wasn't allowed in. We could hear him yelling at Sir William on the phone, but we could never quite make out what he was saying." She felt desperate to know what had been done to find her. She thought furiously through ways to stem the tide of photos already all over the internet.

Thoughts of Darcy mixed with all her worries. She could hear his deep laugh and see the beautiful home that could have been theirs. What was she thinking to have rejected him? He had seen the danger of association with George Wickham. His testimony to the commission: she could see the wisdom in his words there as well.

Lydia needed to have been brought to hand years ago. She had told her father not to let her go to Brighton Beach. She had never thought to pair the word "lazy" with her father before, but indolent, uncaring, and languid seemed to be apt descriptions of him now. Lydia was his silliest daughter and he should have checked her behavior before it became so dangerous. Who else would have run off with a man nearly twice her age? Not only older, but also an officer deserting his post by running away with her. Elizabeth knew that in school they were cautioned against going with men they did not know, but had Lydia been too busy flirting to take note of those warnings? The pictures were the worst part. Lydia would be a laughing stock at Meryton. Regardless of Wickham's fault in the crime, Lydia was clearly enjoying herself when those pictures were taken. They had been sent to everyone Elizabeth knew. She could not see how her reputation and the reputation of her family would not be affected. Lydia had not only ruined herself but had shamed the entire family. These pictures and stories would follow Elizabeth throughout her career—she would be whispered about forever with pictures of her sister and that disgusting man.

When the T-6 rolled to a stop in Uncle Gardiner's spot and the fire hoses sprayed him down in celebration of his final flight, Elizabeth plastered a smile on her face. She even sprayed him with champagne another helpful lieutenant had brought out to her. This was an important milestone in Gardiner's life and she was determined not to let her misery affect his moment. As it was, Uncle Gardiner smiled and engaged himself happily in the party in the Heritage room.

Elizabeth ate pizza and jalapeno popcorn and drank a soda, all the while consumed by dark thoughts of how she would ever show her face in this building again. She felt self-conscious, like everyone she met had seen her sister's pictures, but she smiled and gave short answers and then busied herself by picking up trash from around the room.

Eventually, Uncle Gardiner gave her a quick debrief, told her to keep her head up, cuffed her on the shoulder, and she was able to leave. The drive home was pure torture and she decided to stop at Netherfield in the hope of meeting Jane before facing her over-exuberant mother. Her flight suit was sweaty and felt heavy on her body, her boots like iron weights as she got out of the car.

She knocked on the door and Caroline, draped in a burnt orange blouse, smirked.

"Hi, Caroline. Jane said she was here."

Charles poked his head into the hallway behind Caroline.

"Lizzy! That is what you like to be called?" He fidgeted and continued. "Or maybe I should probably call you 'Elizabeth'."

Elizabeth beamed at him, his awkward stumbling was the best thing that had happened to her since lunch. "Of course, call me Lizzy." Side-stepping Caroline, she hugged him. "You are almost my brother after all."

Caroline rolled her eyes and threw on a fake smile.

He led Elizabeth into the kitchen to find Jane sitting at the table.

"Lizzy! I'm so glad you're here. This business with Lydia…"

"Tell me what's happened. Darcy texted and said he was bringing her home, but that's all I know—really nothing more than when I called from New York—"

"Oh, was awful. But Charles has helped put the word out that Lydia is interested in modeling. Thankfully, her poses were only risqué and on the angles of the photos, you might think the photos were staged and she had clothes on despite looking nude, otherwise I don't know that anyone would have believed us. We told them all that Wickham was helping her with her poses and had accidentally sent them out on a group text."

"Did that work?"

"I'm not sure, but it seems to be helping. Hopefully, they won't see Lydia as a uniform chaser, although it wouldn't bother me one bit to see Wickham locked up."

"Bravo, Jane. That is the most unforgiving speech I've ever heard you make."

Jane bobbed her head in a mock curtsey and Bingley spoke.

"So far, it seems like people believe us and Lydia just looks young. And naïve."

"Which she is..."

Elizabeth smiled, grateful for Jane and her fabulous Captain Bingley. Now that she had the level-headed assurances of Jane, Elizabeth felt she had the fortitude to withstand her parents and less composed sisters.

Her phone beeped, and she looked down to see a text from Darcy. "Just landed in Oklahoma City. We should be in Longbourn by morning. I need to stop here for mandatory crew rest."

Darcy found her! Damn that Lydia. He was bringing her home. How had he done it? Where did he find her? How did he find her? She was wild to know. *Why hadn't he just called?* She stared at his text and could only respond: "I have no words. Thank you seems hardly enough." Questions agitated her mind and she felt herself drift into autopilot. She shared the welcome news with Jane and Bingley and headed home, exhausted.

On the way to Longbourn, Elizabeth rolled down the windows and let the breeze blow through her hair and rushed over her sweaty flight suit. She couldn't wait to take it off and stand in the shower. And yet, her mind was filled with Darcy. The fresh air filled her with a longing to be near him and breathe in his earthy scent. She longed for the gentle pressure and feeling of safety from his arms around her. When she turned into the drive, she emptied her brain of Captain William Darcy and geared herself up for the onslaught of her family's reactions. She took one deep breath and exited the car, grabbing her bag from the trunk.

She pulled open the door to the sound of silence. She dropped her bag and took off her sunglasses. She found Mary lying on the couch and reading.

"Hey Mar."

Mary waved one hand in response but did not look up from her reading.

"Where is everyone?"

Mary pointed to the dining room.

"Thanks."

Elizabeth, ignoring the total lack of greeting from her middle sister, continued into the dining room to see her parents and Kitty at the table, eating quietly.

Mr. Bennet looked up when he heard her boots thump in the doorway.

"Lizzy, my girl! Would you like some dinner? Your mother's creation is excellent tonight."

Mrs. Bennet blushed. "It's just a little ragout. Nothing very exciting. I decided simple was best tonight."

Elizabeth wondered if this was, in fact, her home. She looked about again and took a second glance at those seated at the table as if to confirm that, yes, this was indeed her family.

"What's going on? Why is everyone so calm?"

Kitty sent her a pleading look and said, "Our parents have gone mad. Please, help me."

Elizabeth smiled at that—"Well, I'm not really hungry and I need a shower"—but she sat down.

Kitty asked if she could be excused and her father relented. It is doubtful that anyone in the Bennet family had ever witnessed Kitty move as fast as when removing herself to the living room.

"That girl should try out for track," her father said satirically.

Suddenly, she noticed that no one had spoken of Lydia's whereabouts.

"Has Lydia called yet?"

"Darcy called about a couple hours ago to say that they were

LEIGH DREYER

returning, but they would need to stay overnight in Oklahoma City. Something about FAA regulations."

"He's been flying too long today, so he has to rest for twelve hours."

Mrs. Bennet shifted uncomfortably in her chair at the mention of her favorite daughter. In the past, this kind of news would have sent her to her room with anxiety. Elizabeth was deeply impressed by her ability to stay in her chair and face the reality.

"What are we going to do? I've seen the pictures."

"So, has everyone, Lizzy. They made their way around the school and online. There is no way to be rid of them, but Bingley and your sister have done an admirable job stemming the tide of gossip. Have you seen Jane?"

"I stopped by Netherfield on the way home."

"Then you know what they've done and the story we're using. You were right to warn me, Lizzy. Wickham was not a man to be trusted." A pause hung in the air as Elizabeth waited for her father to continue. "Of course, Kitty is very upset. She's been informed that strict rules are going to be enforced from now on and Mary is full of righteous validation. She said she knew all along that Lydia was wild."

Small squeaks came from Elizabeth's mother who had covered her face to sob.

"There, there." Mr. Bennet touched her shoulder. "So, my dear Lizzy, how was the air show?"

"It was great, Dad." She scooped a spoonful of ragout onto her dish. "It was interesting to see all the questions people had about the plane."

"I'm sure it is different for those people to see inside a military plane, isn't it?" her mother asked.

"Yeah, most of them had never heard of a T-6 before. They didn't know that military planes used propellers."

It was awkward that her parents asked about her trip, especially given the latest news. And she had never seen such tenderness between her parents who normally teased, fought, or ignored each other. It was strange but also touching to witness.

"Well, and if that isn't enough news," said her father, "the commission is sending their report to the base and on to the President."

Elizabeth sat up at this. "Already? Can they do it so soon?"

"It seems Captain Darcy contacted each commission member personally and told them that he strongly suggested they keep Meryton open. He said that with as many flying days as there are here that they couldn't afford to lose Meryton if they wanted to keep their pilot slots full."

Elizabeth could not be more surprised by this news. However, since the situation with Wickham, she had come to regard Darcy as one of best people she had ever known. Still, she *was* astonished that he had gone to so much work. Not only had he changed his opinion, but to contact those commissioners meant going through red tape and assistants for hours before ever being able to actually speak to someone. *When had he done it? Why did he do it?*

Elizabeth was nearly overwhelmed by her gratitude and the knowledge that between her own stupidity and what her sister had done, somewhere in Oklahoma, Darcy might be thinking ill of her. She sat sullenly thinking about the loss of the best man she had ever known.

For the first time in a long time, Elizabeth had hope for the future of her younger sisters, for the marriage of her parents, and even that Lydia might be fixed before she sustained more permanent damage. Elizabeth's only despair after dinner that night was that all hope for Darcy was gone.

LYDIA WAS RETURNED to Longbourn the next morning by Darcy seemingly no worse for wear. He walked her to the door and, despite a bombardment of questions of how she was faring, the current location of George Wickham and how they could ever repay Darcy, he stayed quiet, answering in short, precise sentences. He left after effusive thanks from Mrs. Bennet and a handshake from Mr. Bennet. Elizabeth only nodded to him grimly as he stepped out onto the porch and made his way to his car.

Elizabeth could barely look at her sister, so ashamed that she would follow a man ten-years her senior—how irresponsible and reckless and repugnant. Elizabeth was equal parts horrified that she had ever thought of Wickham as a better man than Darcy and that her sister clearly did not have the sense to see her wrong-doing. Lydia rambled about her misadventure with little repentance and dramatically expressed how Darcy saved her, jolting Elizabeth from her own deliberations.

"What about Captain Darcy?"

"You know. He and his cousin stormed in, punched George, and then Darcy took me to the airport. I was so nervous. My weekend had gone nothing like I had expected, and George had been so upset when they came in the apartment. I didn't see what they did with George, but from what his cousin insinuated on the flight back, I can't imagine he feels very well today."

Lydia frowned as if she had been the witness to a great tragic moment and then sighed. "And it was awful the entire time, especially in Oklahoma. Captain Darcy made me stay in my room and then taped the door shut like I was on a high school field trip. Can you imagine the nerve? He said he didn't want me to escape? Where was I going to go? I didn't have a car. It was just the absolute worst. Never mind I didn't have a phone charger and couldn't even text Kitty and tell her all about my trip. He went on and on about how Wickham was so bad, as if I hadn't already figured that out? I know he sent out those pictures, but maybe that was some kind of mistake. He told me he wanted them to remind him of how pretty I was and about our trip."

"You do see how awful it is that Wickham took you to New

York without telling your family?" Elizabeth utilized every bit of self-control that she possessed in order to remain calm.

"Meh, it all worked. No harm done." And then Lydia winked!

"Lydia! Wickham is a hideous man. No gentleman would take a teenager away from her family."

"I'm an adult now, not some child. Besides, I told Kitty before we left. I didn't see the harm in going to New York."

It was at this unfortunate moment that Mr. Bennet had decided to come check on his youngest, wayward daughter.

"Kitty!" He boomed. "You knew? This entire time you knew? Do you know how scared we were? How much danger Lydia was in? She could have been killed! She could have been sold into something far worse than death!"

Kitty and Lydia's eyes widened at this intensely negative view of the aftermath of Lydia's choices.

"Kitty, because you knew and did not tell, you are nearly equally responsible for everything this family has been through. You lied to me by omission. You will be receiving the same punishment as your sister. Both of you are clearly not prepared for adulthood and will be home studying proper behavior with your mother and educated on weightier topics by myself. Lydia, you'll be lucky if I don't have you finish out your senior year in military school! Mary will help you in your spiritual journeys, and you can pick up more responsibility from Jane and Lizzy in the running of Longbourn. You will not be allowed to attend a party, hold a phone, or do anything other than go to and from school until I have come to the determination that you are no longer a danger to yourselves or others."

Mr. Bennet looked down on the stunned faces of his youngest children, nodded, and left the room.

SOONER THAN EXPECTED, life was back to the new normal in

the bustling home and inn. Mary read, Kitty followed Lydia in her whining about her "prison sentence", Jane had eyes and heart full of love for Charles Bingley, and Elizabeth studied. Her mother, a far cry from her behavior before Lydia's sudden disappearance, was helpful and provided Elizabeth with solitude and snacks for her studies, frequently asking questions and marking Elizabeth's progress with words of affirmation and sincere affection. As her mother's least favorite daughter, Elizabeth was not sure what to make of these changes, but she appreciated them in the days leading up to her next formation ride.

CHAPTER 26

$\mathcal{E}$lizabeth tugged at the sleeves of her flight suit scrunched near her elbows to her wrists. The day had dawned clear and bright, the sun blazing brilliantly over the horizon.

Today was her formation check ride. She would be flying six feet away from another aircraft going two hundred miles an hour. She had flown in a group of two planes for the last few weeks and done it well. It had been her favorite part of pilot training thus far. Her heart raced at the exhilaration of being so near another plane while shooting through the air. At six feet away she was perfectly safe, at four feet away the propeller of the T-6 would slam into the wings of the jet next to her, dropping them both out of the sky. She loved the aerobatics and the tingling electricity of sharp turns and precise movements. It required all of her concentration and was incredibly liberating. While she maintained a laser focus on piloting, in many ways she was able to let go and relax. Formation was one of the most difficult points of pilot training. When she had first heard it, her courage rose. She was never one to be intimidated and while she lacked complete confidence in her abilities to be excellent, she was excited to perform as well as she possibly could.

Flight suit perfect, Elizabeth fidgeted with her hair, checking the band and pins were still in place. She strode cheerfully to the scheduling desk before she became crestfallen. Next to her name in the schedule was "Lieutenant George Wickham". Elizabeth went to business attempting to change instructors, doing everything she could with the scheduler on duty to move her to another. She could not tell him why without revealing what had happened to Lydia and after fifteen harrowing minutes, Wickham remained her instructor.

Elizabeth tightened her jaw, feeling her teeth push together. She tightened her fists, her nails pressing crescents painfully into her palms. She could not express her loathing for Wickham without screaming, so she would maintain her composure. If she had learned anything from Darcy, it was to don his mask of cool, calm, and collected indifference. She slipped his overly-confident composure on as if it was her own and walked to the briefing room, head held high.

Wickham sat in a swiveling, black office chair, legs propped on a desk and chewing gum loudly. His handsome face twisted into a winning smile that Elizabeth recognized as one that had won over many a lady, including herself. Fortunately for her, she now only saw it for the grimace of the beast he was. Not only did he deserve to be in jail, he deserved far worse for the danger he had put her sister in.

"Morning, Bennet."

Elizabeth merely nodded in return.

"I didn't realize we weren't friends anymore."

Is he kidding? "Pffft. Aren't you supposed to be in the Guard now?"

"Paperwork will take at least sixty days. Haven't you been around air force bureaucracy long enough to know they can't move me without paperwork?"

"Let me guess, you convinced some airman to lose it at the bottom of the pile."

"Wasn't that hard, sweetheart. Airmen lose things all the time. The paper-shuffling bean-counters at the Wing can't be expected to keep up. Besides, I'm a great instructor. You think the squadron is happy to be stuck taking over my flights until they get a new guy in here? Give me a break."

Elizabeth cleared her throat and looked pointedly away from him.

"Ready to brief?"

Elizabeth plastered on a winning smile.

"I was born ready."

They waited until they were joined by Wise and Remington. The female IP and male student came in jovially and smiled as they sat near Wickham and Elizabeth. Elizabeth had always liked Captain Wise, the two women got along famously when they had flown together, and it made her a little easy knowing that at least one of their instructors would be smarter than a single-cell amoeba.

Elizabeth proceeded to give the best brief of her life. Elizabeth and Remington laid out a flight plan they had created together. They outlined the maneuvers they would complete in fingertip formation and those they would complete in tactical formation. Elizabeth briefed energy management for the lead and number two ships and Remington presented the locations for each planned loop, roll, and clover leaf maneuver. When the two were quizzed on general knowledge, they shined.

"Did you notice the weather moving in?" asked Captain Wise after listening to the plan.

Elizabeth and Remington looked at each other before Elizabeth responded. "There are some thunder cells in the southern operating area, but Remington checked earlier, and we are in the northern area today, so we'll have to keep an eye on it, but it shouldn't be a factor."

Remington continued. "Weather slides are showing a possible

weather recall toward the end of our sortie, so we'll need to keep an ear out if the SOF calls a recall."

At long last, the brief came to an end. Wise and Remington left the room first, walking heavily down the hallway in their boots. Wickham and Elizabeth followed initially, but Elizabeth quickly left to join Captain Wise and began chatting happily about their weekends, leaving Wickham to himself as they walked through the squadron.

They checked in at the step desk and walked through the doors, waiting for the bus. Wickham approached Elizabeth and leaned casually against the wall.

"How are you, Elizabeth?"

"Lieutenant Bennet."

"Sorry, didn't realize we weren't on a first name basis. How's Lydia? She get home okay?"

Elizabeth suppressed a shudder as it slipped down her spine. She had been with him less than an hour and she was already tired of his velvet voice pouring over her.

"Let's just not talk until we have to. We need to fly. I don't need to chat about my family."

Wickham held up his hands in mock surrender. "Sorry, I wasn't aware that Lydia was off the table. I like her. We had a lot of fun when I showed her around New York." A snake-like grin crept across his face and his eyes glittered like a cobra's.

Elizabeth remained tight-lipped and examined the concrete under her feet watching the ants as they marched in their lines.

After what seemed an eternity, the plain blue bus picked up the group and drove them to their parking spots. Elizabeth and Wickham began their walk arounds and climbed up into the plane. Elizabeth nested and soon started her checklists. She started the engines and waited for Remington to check-in on time.

"Nuke 61 flight check." Remington's voice came over the comms crisply.

Elizabeth pushed the button and responded, "Two."

Remington continued, "Ground, Nuke flight checking in parking spot Bravo 42. Request taxi to the inside runway."

"Nuke flight clear to taxi runway 02 right via taxi Alpha Tango. Hold short on runway two right."

After receiving clearance from the tower, Elizabeth moved into position behind Remington and Wise into the hammerhead to perform their engine run-ups before takeoff. Elizabeth ran up the engine and performed final safety checks before getting onto the runway.

"Bennet," Wickham's voice popped over the intercom.

"Yes, sir."

"Your checklist is going to tell you to flip that ejection switch to dual. I want you to flip it to solo."

Elizabeth shook her head, her helmet swaying heavily on top of her hair. "Sir, that's not in accordance with standards or with the checklist."

"Yeah, I understand that." Wickham sounded annoyed. "As the pilot in command, I can brief non-standard and that's what I'm doing. Besides, I don't trust my life in any student's hands, especially yours. You can't keep control over your own sister, why would I want you to be in control over me?"

"I don't think it should be flipped, sir," she growled.

"I don't really care what you want, Bennet. Flip it. That's an order."

Elizabeth flipped the switch with an exaggerated flourish of her hand ending in a middle finger pointed at the jerk behind her, a bold move considering he could hook her for the protocol breach.

In unison with the other plane, Elizabeth took off and started her flight. They performed various formation maneuvers including loops, barrel rolls, and a clover leaf within a man's arm reach of each other. Then they proceeded on to practicing tactical formation, which spread the planes out to a mile apart. The two planes communicated with wing rocks where the lead plane showed the number two where and when to turn. As number two, Elizabeth would follow the wing rocks and then attempt a formation rejoin and come back to arm's length to the lead once again. Then the planes would switch, and Elizabeth would lead the maneuvers.

In the middle of Elizabeth's second tactical maneuver, the radio blared over her headset.

"This is Meryton Air Force Base weather recall. A storm is rolling in to all operating areas. Suspend operations and return to base."

Elizabeth looked at the sky around her for the first time, breaking her concentration on the formation flight. Deep clouds had gathered in the distance and she could see them beginning to build into the storm columns they had studied in academics.

Elizabeth spoke into her headset: "Guess that's it for us. Let's head back."

"I have the aircraft," Wickham snapped. The plane banked hard to turn and look toward Meryton.

Wickham then radioed Wise in the number two jet: "Nuke 61 to 62."

"Go ahead."

"I'm going to keep my student in the area for further training. We are going to split formation and coordinate for single ship return. I want you to go first and then I will follow."

"Roger that. We are going down to the bottom of the stack and coordinating for return at this time."

Wickham then climbed into the top of the area while Wise went below and coordinated their return to Meryton.

"Now I'm going to show you how to really fly. When you were doing your loops, you were way too cautious. You need to fly the plane and not let the plane fly you."

Elizabeth felt their adjoining sticks pull back hard as he pulled hard into a loop.

"Shadow those controls Bennet and see how a real man flies!"

Elizabeth held on through the G-forces of the loop. Near the top, she looked up through the canopy below her at the building weather. While, initially the clouds had only been visible to the side, she now noticed they had drifted into the operating area below them. As Wickham next pulled the plane into a tight roll, Elizabeth watched as the storm cell beneath them slowly built, beginning to encroach upon their area.

"Sir, I think we should return. I'm looking at the weather and we're approaching our Bingo fuel."

"Pay attention to my instructions. Are you even listening, Bennet? Who do you think you are? God's gift to aviation?"

His voice droned into a hum in the back of her mind as soon as the curses and insults about her person began. Elizabeth was too busy watching the storm columns build around them and watching the last remnants of clear sky disappear as Wickham's voice continued berating her over the comms.

"Clearly, you aren't listening anyway, so we'll just go back home."

Finally.

While coordinating a return to base, Wickham continued to fly the plane from the back of the area to the front dodging the rising columns of clouds. As they transitioned, radio call complete, Wickham then began quizzing Elizabeth about vertigo and what she had been taught during academics.

"Have you ever experienced vertigo?"

"A little on my dollar ride." Elizabeth then recounted the story and was not surprised when Wickham responded.

"That's baby vertigo. You were fine. Let me show you what real vertigo is."

Instead of doing a standard thirty degree turn to exit the area, still in the midst of the clouds, Wickham instructed Elizabeth to look outside while banking to ninety degrees and pulling the aircraft to exit. From here, he rolled it quickly back to level flight while looking at his instruments.

"Okay, Bennet. Are we level or turning?"

"I feel like I'm in a hard bank to the right."

"So that's vertigo. I can even see you leaning so far to the right that your head is touching the canopy while we're straight and level. This is true vertigo."

As he spoke, Elizabeth watched the clouds turn from bright, sunlit white to the darkest grey. A blinding light and a deafening crack sounded just outside the canopy in the clouds. The plane began to shake with the turbulence in the air and rain as it assaulted the canopy.

Wickham stopped mid-sentence in his vertigo instruction. He must have awoken from his personal high-five to the weather that had been building over the last fifteen minutes. He had overturned the aircraft in a ninety-degree turn directly into a thunder cell! Panic filled his voice over the comms. "Damn!"

The plane was thrown about by the up and down drafts of the storm cell. Light flashed and thunder roared around them and a deafening crackling began to assault the plane, and Elizabeth felt the impact as hail bounced against the wings and canopy. Wickham continued to fly by the seat of his pants attempting to keep the plane straight and level.

Elizabeth could feel that the plane was out of control. The seconds passed like years while silence broken by expletives sounded over her headset. Wickham began to mutter nonsensically over the radio, but Elizabeth could only make out the words "straight and level" over and over again like a skipping record player. The beats of her heart matched the beats of Wickham's mumblings and Elizabeth quickly began to breathe deeply. She pushed down her fear and looked to her instruments. When she finally viewed the altimeter, she noticed they were in a rapid descent in a ninety-degree bank turn.

"I have the aircraft."

She grabbed the stick and rolled the plane level according to the instruments before the stick was ripped out of her hands and violently banked back to ninety degrees.

"Straight and level!" she heard Wickham shout over the sounds of the hail, rain, and thunder.

Elizabeth attempted again to straighten the plane twice more, increasingly positive that Wickham was experiencing vertigo. Elizabeth looked at her altitude and saw she was at four thousand feet with an ever-increasing descent rate.

"Mayday! Mayday! Mayday! MOA 6. Nuke 62. Experiencing severe weather. Going down."

The jostling of the plane ceased as they burst through the edge of the storm cell and back into the white clouds of the clear sky. At this point, still in their ninety-degree fall, Elizabeth continued to struggle against the stick and Wickham's hold on it, watching the altitude drop.

"Straight and level. Straight and level." Wickham's mantra continued over the intercom.

Elizabeth fought against the stick, pulling as hard as she could against Wickham's. She watched as the altitude closed in on two thousand feet. She could see the futility of fighting against Wickham and she was coming closer and closer to the end of her ejection window. The plane was still sideways in the air and she could see the ground looming larger.

Elizabeth looked one final time at her altimeter and saw one thousand six-hundred seventy-eight feet altitude. Her vertical velocity indicator read negative nine thousand feet. She was low and going lower nine times faster than the average airliner. She was in a nose-down dive, screaming toward the ground. The plane was going to crash with her in it! She made the only decision she could.

"Bailout! Bailout! Bailout!" she said over the radio. She looked down at her instruments cognizant there would be questions about them. She quickly memorized them. Years later, she would be able to recite every number and the placement of ever needle and dial on the panel in front of her as her hands fumbled toward ejection.

Elizabeth wrenched up as hard as she could on the yellow ejection handle between her legs. The canopy around her shattered as the egress systems detonated the explosives in the glass. She heard only the roaring sound of her world igniting and a hollow screaming she could not identify. She felt the wind for the long-lasting moment before her seat fired up the rails and exploded one hundred feet into the sky. Her legs were grasped violently by restraints as she shot up, breaking them. Her eyes closed, she could only feel the wind rush past her. Her body twisted with the seat, her feet straining against the bounds. She weighed a thousand pounds. Her back, her legs, her feet were being crushed and she could feel her head in her lap. Her lungs screamed for air. She could feel the mask on her helmet ripping into her chin as the force of the wind tried to tear her helmet from her head. She grunted hard with the pain of becoming a human rocket.

The seat then punched away kicking her sharply in the back. She felt, rather than heard the crack and screamed in pain. She thrust forward while her head and feet flung back with the force of the jettisoning seat. Her eyes opened in fright at the sudden movement and she saw the seat fall away beside her. Then it was black.

As a girl, she had often had a dream that she could fly. She would run down the hallway at Longbourn and take off, arms outstretched and shoot into the air. Sometimes she would fly just around her house, in and out of her sisters' room. Other times, she would fly over to Meryton and join the jets as they flew doing loops and rolls before she would return to her bed. Most of her dreams ended peacefully with a gentle landing in the soft pillows and downy covers. Occasionally, her dreams would end with a sudden start and she awoke in a panic. When the canopy of Elizabeth's parachute inflated, she felt the pain in her shoulders, her eyes flashing open again, and she felt as if she had awoken with a frightening start.

As the parachute softened her blow and let her adrenaline

slow, the pain set in. The first five seconds of her ejection had been eternal. The next minutes were even slower. Elizabeth did not hurt, but she also could not feel. She felt disconnected physically and emotionally from her body.

When she could next think, she was moving too fast. The ground was coming toward her too quickly. She closed her eyes just before the impact.

CHAPTER 27

$\mathcal{D}$arcy stepped to the jet for a solo. The sun was bright and cheery, despite his personal feelings about that morning. While working with Richard to get Wickham's transfer to the National Guard to go through the bureaucratic cogs of the military, he had little time for anything. He had been unable to see Elizabeth and assure her of his unaltered feelings. He loved her. He wanted to tell her and instead, he was stuck dealing with the damned Wickham—again!

Darcy needed to fly. He needed to feel alive. Since dealing with Wickham he had felt dead inside. He loathed the man and everything that he had stolen from him over the years. There were the girls he liked in their school days, the money from his father, and now the peace of mind of Elizabeth and her family. Darcy wished he could have accompanied Richard in punching Wickham's brains out instead of escorting a naïve eighteen-year-old home. Georgiana had never put him through this much trouble, even when she thought she was in love with the scum.

The wheels beneath the plane turned as he taxied to the runway, waiting his turn from the tower. The plane hummed beneath him. Planes were all noisy, everyone he had flown. It was why you found so many deafened middle-aged men clinking glasses at retirement ceremonies speaking at slightly louder than normal levels. They were all meticulously instructed to wear ear plugs, but it mattered little. Planes were noisy, but to Darcy, planes were the quietest places on earth. The dull drone allowed him to stop thinking of the little things and only focus on the big. What was it that poem said?

"AND WHILE WITH silent lifting mind I've trod
   The high untrespassed sanctity of space,
   Put out my hand,
   And touched the face of God."

MAGEE HAD GOTTEN IT RIGHT. That was exactly how it felt. A quiet, hallowed place full of noise but somehow full of silence.

He pondered at the events since he had come to Meryton. He had learned that despite learning good principles from his parents, he had grown to behave with pride and conceit. He had decided that he was better than others because he had paid for better clothes, education, and "friends." If the likes of Caroline Bingley were all who wanted to be around him, he clearly needed to re-evaluate his actions. He had already spoken to the Base Closure Commission members and he was hoping he could now take care of Wickham, but he felt well on his way to having repented of the sins Elizabeth had thrust to his attention.

His flight proceeded like every flight before it. He took off, went to his operating area and flew. It happened that today he was in the farthest area from the base. A T-6 formation was to his right, a T-38 ride to his left. He practiced a few loops and rolls and thoroughly enjoyed himself watching as the Earth and sky spun in his view.

"All flights. We have a weather recall. Clouds moving into airfield. Return to base immediately."

Darcy frowned at the shortening of his flight but closely evaluated the previously sunny skies. The clouds that had turned grey with black centers were slowly overtaking the skies. He began to turn about, back toward Meryton and the safety of the airstrip when he saw it. A solo T-6 where the formation should have been. He looked closer and watched as another T-6 returned in the direction of Meryton while the solo faced the opposite direction and climbed into the clouds. That section of the sky was still friendly, sun rays bouncing merrily off the cotton candy above, but the ominous storm was approaching and coming in fast.

When Georgiana was five, she would draw white puffy clouds on blue backgrounds over houses, trees, and puppies. A yellow sun inhabited the corners of her creations and a purple Georgiana would be scrawled carefully, if unevenly, across the bottom. Darcy had begun flying thinking of those great marshmallow clouds as a bearer of happiness and good will, but as his skills grew, he learned that they could turn malicious faster than Georgiana could draw them.

The clouds that the T-6 had disappeared into were building quickly into a tower. Black, shadowed clouds built upon each other, climbing higher into the sky above their base. At the top of the mountain of storm the clouds evened out turning the entire peak into a smooth flat anvil. Texas weather was notorious for changing quickly, but the weather around Meryton was especially known by locals for opening a clear sky into a torrent of hail and floods.

"What on earth is that idiot doing?" Darcy muttered to himself before fidgeting with the radio, turning it to his area frequency.

"Controlling Agency Warn. Fitz 02. I have a T-6 aircraft off to my left flying through storm clouds. Are they in distress?"

"Stand by."

"Roger. I'll hold in the area."

Darcy held in his area doing great circles around the same area of ground waiting for the area agency to get in touch with the busy Meryton tower. The T-6 dipped occasionally below the clouds and then re-entered them just as quickly in a steep bank. Away from them as he was, he also kept his eye on the piling blackness above them.

Darcy watched his radar and followed the T-6 as it passed in and out of the storm. The plane's altitude fluctuated, though seemed to continuously fall steadily as he watched them dip and dive in the storm clouds.

I hope that's a solo flight. Otherwise there is an idiot instructor over there. Why on earth would you let a student fly like that? Did they not hear the weather recall? It's not that hard. Just go back. Darcy's thoughts continued to complain against the top gun ruining his day and making him hold while watching for him to come out of the clouds on the other side. After the pause where he saw the plane enter the storm lengthened into a moment, the moment into a minute, and the minute into what seemed like hours, Darcy's stomach began to knot. He continued watching the plane flying on the radar heading directly into the storm cell.

The time passed more slowly than any minute in his life. Darcy stared at the area where he saw the T-6 disappear, paralyzed with fright. Frightened he would miss the T-6 emerge from the clouds, he looked quickly at his TCAS radar to see the T-6's altitude plummeting rapidly toward the ground. He noticed on his weather radar overlay that they were flying in and out of the yellows, reds, and magentas indicating the worst section possible of the storm. He watched and waited for the white block representing the T-6 to come out on the other side, despite continuing to plunge. The tiny block rapidly ran through reds to yellows to greens on the weather display, losing altitude to just above two thousand feet above the ground.

Suddenly, Darcy's guard frequency squawked loudly. "Mayday!

Mayday! Mayday! MOA 6. Nuke 62. Experiencing severe weather going down."

Darcy's heart was in his throat in a large lump he was unable to swallow. *That voice. He knew that voice.* He glanced at his maps, MOA area 6... Which area was that? MOA area 6... It was next to him he realized. His heart sank into his stomach making him nauseous. Elizabeth was in the plane he had seen. His mind went through a slide show of potential outcomes and he did not appreciate that very few of them were positive. After cross checking with his weather overlay to ensure he was out of reach of the storm, he determined to stay in his area until he could watch the T-6 make it through the clouds and head back to Meryton.

He looked back outside watching and waiting at the low, white, non-threatening overcast sky and willed himself to be able to see through the clouds to the T-6 beyond them.

Darcy's radio popped again, and the voice of Elizabeth shouted.

"Ejecting!"

Darcy's heart stopped even as his Guard Radio started. Darcy banked his T-38 to look at the ground and the sky near him for the appearance of a chute. The damn clouds were still in the way. He began to orbit around the location of the tiny T-6 block on his radar. Finally, after a lifetime, Darcy watched as a T-6 escaped the overcast clouds, propeller spinning furiously. The plane was in a steep bank, only its blue underbelly visible. Darcy watched as the plane seemed to right itself and even pull up in an attempted recovery from the grasp of gravity. Darcy inhaled sharply as the plane crashed into the dirt and grass below and smoke began to rise from the fiery collision.

Ripping his sight from the impact site, Darcy scanned around him, looking for the parachute, the ejection seat, or any sign that someone made it out. He once again cursed the skies for keeping him from Elizabeth. He swallowed down the rising panic and went to his checklists.

Darcy, quickly recovering, called out on guard, "Any aircraft, any radio. Emergency. Emergency. Emergency. Fitz 02. I'm orbiting above Nuke 62's crash site in MOA 10. I heard an ejection call. Did not see any chutes. I'll be the on-seen commander."

Darcy next switched over to tower and repeated his call, then added, "Request a separate frequency to conduct CSAR."

"Fitz, switch to 246.8."

Darcy switched over and the Tower said, "Understand you are current commander for the crash. State your holding time and current situation with Nuke 62."

"My holding time is ten minutes. Situation update: One aircraft down, currently on fire. Coordinates: North 35° 25' 46.2" West 101° 28' 33.2" I don't see any chutes...No, negative. I see one chute. Coming out of the clouds. Pilot appears unconscious."

"Roger, continue to orbit as long as you can. We're dispatching emergency personnel at this time. Due to the storm, they'll be delayed."

Darcy watched the unconscious pilot as they hit the ground, hoping against all hopes that Elizabeth was well and alive.

Darcy orbited five minutes past his holding estimates, desperate for any sign that she might be alive. With the weather recall and storm cells moving in, he was eventually forced to return to Meryton and await word in the squadron building or crash himself.

Bingley, muttering platitudes, stayed by his side. Darcy was numb. He could hear the sounds of people as they walked in and out. He could feel the overly cold air conditioner after the heat of his flight. He could see the olive green of flight suits as they walked through the squadron. For the first time since he had met her, Darcy could not feel her presence. Darcy could not feel.

CHAPTER 28

*E*lizabeth's deep eyes cracked open before blinking in the brightness of the room. Darcy pressed her hand, sandwiching her small hand into his larger ones. He allowed himself only one moment before relinquishing his space to Jane who spoke softly.

"Lizzy. Can you hear me?"

Elizabeth only groaned in response and squeezed her eye lids tight.

"Lizzy," Jane intoned in a sing-song voice. "Sleepy head. Sleeping in the sun. How you ever gonna get your day's work done?"

Elizabeth stretched her legs beneath the sheet and then groaned again.

"It's time to get up. It's time to get up. It's time to get up, it's morning," Jane sang again to the tune of Reveille.

It was easy to forget that these women had been born and raised ten minutes from the base until they did something like that which was so profoundly military-influenced. Darcy smiled at the idea of Elizabeth waking up every morning to the sound of the trumpet blaring over the giant speakers all over the base.

Elizabeth cracked her eyes open once more and glanced warily around the room. She lifted one hand connected to her IV to her head and rubbed her eyes gently. Her color was much improved over the previous day when she had been so pale and grey. Darcy had not left her room that night after seeing her complexion. Despite Jane's objections and Mrs. Bennet's nervous worries for his own sleep, he had leaned back in the uncomfortable hospital arm chair or laid on his folded arms on the side of Elizabeth's bed. Mr. Bennet was clearly annoyed at his existence in the room and insistence to be included in his family's affairs, but Darcy ignored him and kept his watch steadfastly.

Keeping one swollen eye shut, Elizabeth's other eye glanced at the faces in the room. First, she clearly saw Jane who was stroking her hand reassuringly. Next to Jane was Charles. Elizabeth's mother hovered, fluttering nervously about the foot of the bed while her father seemed to ground her by keeping his hand at the small of her quivering back. Her eye moved next to Darcy, and, for the first time since she had awoken, her face relaxed and her roving IV hand dropped.

"William?" Her voice was scratchy with lack of use and water. It was clearly an effort to speak and the word had cracked in the middle. With a great clearing of her throat, she attempted again. "William?"

"I'm here, Elizabeth." He did not move closer. He did not touch her hand or her face. Instead, he stood just behind her parents, his low voice.

"I remember ejecting. What happened to Wickham?" Elizabeth said, her voice still rough.

If she had any questions about his fate, the immediate expressions of everyone in the room would have been proof enough. She merely pressed her lips together and nodded, throwing up a silent prayer for his soul.

Jane squeezed her hand again and Darcy watched Elizabeth fade away into her thoughts, her eyes beginning to water.

"Perhaps we should leave so Elizabeth can get some rest," Darcy said quietly, saving Elizabeth from speech when she was clearly overwrought with the emotion of Wickham's fate and her own injuries, her gratitude shining through the fleeting manifestation of thanks that flashed in her eyes.

Jane squeezed her hand once more in farewell and kissed Elizabeth on the cheek before leaving with Bingley. Mr. and Mrs. Bennet both touched Elizabeth's casted feet on the way out and Darcy strode to his post in the uncomfortable chair. He had just lifted his legs to rest uncomfortably on the box of an air conditioner vent and leaned his head back to attempt the semblance of sleep when Elizabeth's voice sounded once again from across the tiny room.

"William?"

"I'm here, Elizabeth."

"What happened?"

"You ejected. I didn't get everything the doctor said, but spinal fracture, broken leg, a few broken fingers, lots of broken blood vessels, bruising, swelling, dislocated elbow."

"And Wickham? Did he make it? Is he just in the next room?"

"Died on impact. Never ejected. The report will probably say something kind about how he went down with the jet, turning it away from a home or something similar, but it didn't look like he even tried. You guys were at an okay altitude when you went, but by the time I think he figured out what was really happening, it was too late."

Elizabeth nodded and looked back toward the small mounted hospital television playing with a decidedly green tint to the picture. Darcy heard a whisper, but it could have been Elizabeth settling deeper into her pillow and underneath her sheets.

"I'm sorry I didn't trust you from the beginning."

She closed her eyes and sleep quickly overtook her.

◠

DARCY HAD NOT EXPECTED to be woken up so soon. His hospital chair was pointed toward the window where he had been watching the doctors and nurses bustle in and out of the busy front door across the small grassy courtyard. There were the doctors who quickly walked to their cars and without a second glance left the hospital for home or clinic or wherever they went. He watched nurses on their break as they walked to the small picnic table underneath one of the parking lot's nicely placed trees. He watched family members come in and out carrying flowers or gifts for their loved ones. As it was, he had slouched deeply into the chair and gazed out at the clouds, blowing around in the light breeze that was a surprise in the oppressive, humid heat of the summer.

THE ROOM WAS NEVER QUIET. The constant beeping of monitors and IVs that needed to be changed, the shuffling in and out of nurses taking vitals or giving Elizabeth medicine, housekeeping removing the trash. Darcy attempted to drown out the dull laughter and droning discussions from the medical staff in the hallway by sinking down still further into his chair and pulling a spare pillow he had requested from one of the nurses up and around his ears.

A CHAIR SCOOTED out behind him and, before he could turn around, a familiar fluttering voice startled him. Mrs. Bennet drawled soothingly at Elizabeth's unconscious form.

"Lizzy...I'm so grateful you're here and not...not..." Darcy heard sniffling and stared harder out of the window in a desperate attempt not to hear what was clearly meant to be a private moment.

"You look just like him, you know. Your eyes, your smile. That funny crease you get between your brows when you're frustrated. You know, you really should stop doing that, you'll get wrinkles. I might have a cream to help, but that's not important. I'm sorry, I ramble when I get nervous, but of course, you know that. I just wish... but Phillip was never one for the life I wanted. Always had to be the hero..."

Darcy wanted to disappear. As it was, he smothered himself deeper into his pillow.

"I love you, Lizzy. I know I don't show it. It's just...hard... I look at you and all I see is him. I can't do it. My nerves, you know. They've never been good. That's why I love your father. He is so calm, probably too calm really, but I needed that. Phillip and I never would have worked out. I would have fretted my life away and instead I got to be with you and your sisters. I could never have given you up. I'm absolutely dreading when you move, Lizzy. I often think that there is nothing so bad as parting. I will be heartbroken."

A deep, reminiscent sigh drifted lazily across the room.

"Well, I told your father that I would just go out to grab a gallon of milk, so I suppose I should head back. I just wanted you to know, Lizzy. I just wanted you to know that I need you around."

Again, the scraping of a chair and shuffling of feet around Elizabeth's bed joined the chorus of beeping monitors before only Elizabeth's breathing could be heard. Darcy waited a few ticks before moving himself from his station by the window and came to sit in the chair vacated by Mrs. Bennet. He looked at the bruised, pale face framed by dark, matted curls and stroked Elizabeth's hand.

"I need you too, Elizabeth."

CHAPTER 29

$\mathcal{T}$he wedding of Charles Bingley and Jane Bennet occurred on a sunny day two weeks later. The happy couple had decided after Elizabeth's accident that life was too short and they wanted to spend every fast-moving moment together. Despite Mrs. Bennet's vociferous protests that there would not be enough time to pull together the wedding of the century, she once again proved herself as the consummate hostess and the county's best party planner by accomplishing just what she said was impossible. The bride was radiant in a white tea-length gown and the groom, handsome in his Mess Dress though clearly nervous as he stuttered through the ceremony.

All twenty-four prominent families of their small village quickly arranged their schedules in order to attend the wedding of the most beautiful girl in town to the most amiable officer in Meryton. The small stone chapel was simply decorated with simple bouquets of baby's breath on the rows of old wooden pews. The rainbow prisms of light from the stained glass shone down on the aisle runner casting the bride in perfect lighting.

The chapel seemed to hearken to a time when each family would have their own pew and a preacher would stand and deliver a sermon each week. After his parents had died, Darcy had never had use for religion, but watching Jane walk up the aisle to meet the man who stood next to him, Darcy solemnly reevaluated his position.

For the first time since his father had passed, Darcy prayed. As Jane took her slow steps to the light piano, Darcy raised his thoughts up to a God he had cursed in thanks for the gifts he had been given. He thanked god for this horrible assignment, for his friendship with Bingley, and the nerve of his friend to drag him to that Drop Night so long ago. He thanked God for the Bennets and their irresponsible ways which produced the amazingly vibrant and resilient woman he had fallen in love with. Before the pastor asked the congregation to be seated, he thanked God once again for Elizabeth's life.

The local pastor had known Jane since he had baptized her as a child and loved her as only a pastoral shepherd could love one of his sheep. He smiled down on the couple in front of him as he officiated with an indulgent, fatherly gleam in his eye. Darcy, who had stood up with Bingley, watched his friend's joy as he married the love of his life. Bingley, who had often spoken of his angel, positively glowed. Jane, who was naturally more modest, exuded love and kindness. She had a fine pink blush on her cheeks at the attention of the congregation during her vows but showed no hesitation and spoke them loudly.

Only Elizabeth's absence from the ceremony dampened the festivities. Jane, who had asked Elizabeth to be her maid of honor, chose to leave her position blank rather than replace her with one of the other sisters. For Darcy, the dream of her was still there, stunningly beautiful in a short pink dress walking down the aisle toward him. Her legs were beautifully athletic and tanned from her frequent runs, in perfect contrast with the rosy lace of the dress. Her chestnut curls falling past her shoulders and gathering gracefully down her back, begging him to run his fingers through it. Darcy had to blink and remind himself several times during the ceremony to pay attention and remember to present Bingley with the ring for Jane.

Eventually, Bingley dipped Jane into a romantic kiss and the wedding was complete. The guests and wedding party made their way to Longbourn where Mrs. Bennet had created the most delicious breakfast and cake that had ever been tasted in Hertfordshire County. Tarts, croissants, pastries, chocolate, fresh fruit, cuts of meat, freshly baked bread, coffee, hot chocolate, and tea were served by the Longbourn Inn's staff in large white tents on the grounds. Darcy awkwardly stayed to the side as Bingley was being greeted by his guests and he wanted to keep the new Mr. and Mrs. Bingley as the center of the festivities. After tasting the cake and giving his toast, Darcy quickly exited and drove as fast as he could, desperate to get back to the hospital and his Elizabeth.

Darcy strode purposefully down the hospital hallway, the smell of bleach assaulting his nose as he progressed to Elizabeth's room. The door was open, and he burst through without thinking. Elizabeth sat up in her bed, hospital gown slouched so that he could see the smooth curve of her shoulder. She held a mirror and was touching the nearly vanished bruising on her face tenderly as tears dripped down her flushed cheeks. Darcy immediately went to her and gathered her into his arms before her body racked with deep sobs.

He soothed her and shushed her as he had done for Georgiana when she was a little girl. He stroked her hair and rocked her gently, careful of her injuries. Most of all, he pressed her to him feeling how perfect her body felt against his.

"Elizabeth, you're okay. You're okay. It's okay to cry."

Through her weeping, Elizabeth blubbered, "Thank you. I'm so sorry."

Darcy laid her back, cushioning her into the pillows on the bed.

"Elizabeth, I love you. I know there will be moments when you're upset, but there is never anything to be sorry for."

"I don't know how you can love me. I'm broken and—"

Darcy quickly cut her off, placing his finger against her chapped lips.

"Never say that. You are perfect." He cleared his throat and traced the back of his hand against her bruised cheek. "I want you to marry me, Elizabeth."

Tears started rolling afresh down her cheeks. She shook her head.

"No."

"I didn't ask, Elizabeth."

"No, you can't. I'm broken and stupid and—the doctors say I'll probably be about a half inch shorter."

Chuckling at her misplaced attempt at humor, Darcy placed his index finger over her swollen lips.

"Never speak like that. You're beautiful and perfect and amazing and I love you."

Elizabeth looked up at the sincerity showing brilliantly on Darcy's face as he looked peacefully down at her. She could see her reflection in his eyes, the stark white of the hospital sheets, the darkness of her matted curls, and her pale face looking scared and alone. She dropped her gaze and played with the hem of her sheets.

"Why?"

He kissed her.

Eyes closed, Darcy felt the curve of her cheek in his palm and the sweet pressure of her mouth as she returned and deepened his overture. He stroked her errant curls as they fell over her shoulder as she pushed her chest against his. *God, how I love you*, focusing only on the sensations she made rise within him. He ended the kiss while he still could.

Elizabeth blinked up at Darcy's retreating face, smiling as he rested her forehead against hers, their noses touching softly. The tears returned to blur his face from her view. Her voice cracked, and she said, "I can't."

He did not back away. He felt her arms enclose him tighter as he pulled her closer to whisper. "I'll be here until you change your plans." He crooked his finger under her chin to raise it to meet him. "I won't let you stop me from loving you. Not for the rest of my life."

"The best-laid plans of mice and men often go awry," Elizabeth said dryly.

"But, you are not alone," Darcy quoted back at her sitting back and grasping her hand.

Elizabeth sniffed loudly and wiped her face on her hospital gown sleeve. She looked at him through red, moist eyes.

"I want to. I want to so badly. After your letter and"—she sniffed—"and Lydia...I love you so much, but I just...can't."

"Lieutenant Elizabeth Bennet is not one to back away from a challenge," Darcy said as she smiled. "Let me show you. Give me time."

Darcy was ready to get down on his knees there on the grimy, germ-covered hospital floor if it would only convince her to give him a chance. Before she could respond, he added:

"I admire and love you, Elizabeth. If your feelings are still what they were last April, tell me so at once. My affections and wishes are unchanged, but one word from you will silence me forever."

Haltingly, clearly full of thought and emotion, Elizabeth spoke quietly, "I can't now...but—"

"I can be patient. You've taught me to hope." Darcy's voice lifted higher with a hope he had scarcely allowed himself to feel. He kissed her hand gently before replacing it on the bed next to him.

He was unsure what his future path would be, but Darcy was sure of one thing, Elizabeth Bennet would be a part of it.

ACKNOWLEDGMENTS

I found the amazing world of Jane Austen inspired fiction shortly after getting married. I lived in Virginia and worked in DC and had about forty-five minutes on the metro every morning to read. I started with *Death Comes to Pemberley* and fell completely in love with the entire genre. When I had my son a couple years later, I nursed him at night and he got up all the time, so I had a lot of time to read. I found every Jane Austen Fanfiction (JAFF) novel I could find and consumed them. Two years later, I had my daughter and the night nursing began again. In December of 2016, my sister-in-law was looking for a book to do with her book club and I recommended Diana J Oaks (author of *One Thread Pulled* and *Constant as the Sun*) because she lives in the same area and I thought it would be so incredibly neat to have a book club with the author present. Diana ended up agreeing to do the book club and I drove six hours to attend with my sister-in-law. During that book club, Diana was incredibly encouraging about how she wrote her books and I was completely in awe. I later spoke with my sister-in-law and mentioned an idea of Darcy but as a pilot. My dad and my father-in-law are both pilots, and my husband is a pilot, so it was a world I am intimately familiar with and I thought it would just be fun to have them there. My sister-in-law told me to do it. So, I did. My first acknowledgement then, would be to both Diana J Oaks and my amazing sister-in-law Jessica Swaney.

Secondly, I would like to thank my husband who is incredibly supportive of anything and everything that I want to do. He has not only helped me in my speech pathology career and my work as a mother, but he gave me fantastic feedback and was my in-home expert throughout the writing process. He was willing to let me read him portions of the book before he left to go fly for the day and would tell me if my dialogue was good or if I made Darcy sound like a stay-at-home mom writing during nap time (sometimes writing is hard). He is the love of my life and the best dad I could ask for my children.

Thirdly, I have to thank my dad. I joke that my dad might love flying more than me, but I know I win by something akin to Olympic gold to silver medal proportions (you know—when the gold medalist beats the silver by .0001 second). Not only did he raise me around the air force, but he, like Darcy, flew the T-38. He beta-read many of the flying portions and had me correct things that I didn't even know needed to be corrected which was awesome. Not only that, he recommended different ideas for flying, was willing to request specific flight data for me from his friends in the T-6 area at work, and provided me with some excellent reading material. I also need to thank him for giving me the amazing life of a military brat and helping me fall in love with flying.

Fourthly, Monica Cook of Joyous Reflections Photography and Portraiture. Not only are you a good friend, but you are also so talented. Thank you for your work on the cover and marketing photos. Alishia Mattee, another amazing friend and talent: thank you for your work on the covers! Without you two ladies in my life, not only would I be bereft of some of the best friends a girl could have asked for on 3rd Street, but I would also have had such a difficult time instead of having the blast that I did. Also, on the cover, I must thank Danielle Rivera for the loan of her uniform. Couldn't have done it without you!

Lastly, I need to thank my amazing beta-reading, feedback-giving book launch team of wonders: June Rudd, Vaavia Edwards, Elizabeth Moynihan, Tonya Hutchison, Teisha Field, Courtney Rudd, Camille Dockery, Emily Dockery, and Megan Moynihan. You guys are amazing.

ABOUT THE AUTHOR

Leigh Dreyer is a huge fan of Jane Austen variations and the JAFF community. She is blessed to have multi-generational military connections through herself and her husband, who she met in pilot training. She often describes her formative years in this way: "You know the Great Balls of Fire scene in *Top Gun* ('Goose, you big stud!'), where Goose and Meg Ryan have their kid on the piano? I was that kid." Leigh lives with her pilot husband, a plane-obsessed son, and a daughter who will one day be old enough to watch romantic movies with me.

GLOSSARY

1. Instruments: various dials that a pilot looks at to ensure all is going well with the plane. This might include an altimeter (measuring altitude), airspeed indicator (measures speed), horizontal situation indicator (kind of a compass that keeps left and right always the same), oil gauges, etc. Think of checking instruments like checking the dials on the dashboard of your car on the road but with significantly more information.

2. F-22: The F-22 Raptor is a single seat stealth fighter jet. It has two engines and is capable of air attack (shooting other planes), ground attack (shooting objects on the ground), electronic warfare (can jam signals being sent), and signal intelligence (gathers communication or electronic signals in order to gather intelligence about them). The F in F-22 stands for "fighter". The F-22 is a stealth jet because it is difficult to track on radar. The F-22 can drop a bomb at Mach 1.4 (faster than the speed of sound) and accurately hit a moving target twenty-five miles away. The top speed is Mach 2.25 (or two and a

quarter times the speed of sound, one thousand five hundred mph) and the plane can cruise at faster than the speed of sound. Because the F-22 flies so fast and so high, pilots are required to wear specialized G-suits that can help them regulate their bodies for the speed, gravitational forces, and temperature changes.

3. Touch and Go: This is when a plane lands for an incredibly brief amount of time (touches) and then takes off immediately (goes)

4. Stick: The stick is what the pilot uses to push the plane up and down or to turn it left and right. Fighter jets and the C-17 (a cargo plane) all use a stick while cargo and tanker planes and most passenger planes use a yolk which looks more like a steering wheel.

5. Thrust: Power, like pushing the gas in a car, pushing on the thrust is more power, pulling back is less.

6. Checklist: This is a common thread throughout the book, but in the pilot world, everything occurs by checklist. There is a checklist for a walk around to ensure the plane is in flying condition. There is a checklist for take-off, landing, every emergency procedure, etc. A pilot's world is ruled by these checklists. In the Air Force, if a pilot has difficulties and does not follow check list procedure, they can be kicked out. It is vital they are followed to the letter to ensure the pilot's safety and the safety of the aircraft.

7. TMO: Traffic Management Officer. This office is responsible for all military moves including scheduling movers, shipping goods wherever they need to go, shipping cars, etc. Darcy would need to visit them, supply a copy of his moving orders, and then he would be able to schedule his actual move to Meryton through the office.

8. Tactical Approach: This type of approach is when a plane comes in to land faster and from a higher altitude than in a typical landing.

9. Pilot Instructor Training: Commonly referred to as "PIT" (pronounced pit), a training for those officers who will become instructor pilots—essentially teacher training for pilot teachers.

10. T-38 Talon: The T-38 Talon is the training jet which funnels pilots into the fighter program. The "T" in T-38 stands for trainer. These twin-engine jets have two tandem seats, one in the front (student), one in the back (instructor). They are sleek and pointy, made for flying fast and learning quick movements and maneuvers typically used in fighter and attack planes. Their top speed is Mach 1.3 or eight hundred twelve mph, which means they are supersonic or can go faster than the speed of sound. They can climb from sea level to thirty-thousand feet in one minute. Because they fly quickly, they use fuel faster and the typical flight times are less than two hours.

11. Bank: Stick out your flat palm, now turn the whole hand from straight (palm facing the ground) to sideways (palm facing the side). This is a bank. The wings of the airplane angle to the direction the plane should go. The plane then rolls back to straight up and down to continue flying straight again.

12. Roll: A roll is similar to a bank, except that the pilot uses ailerons: moveable, mechanical panels on the tip of the wing which allow the pilot to control the bank angle by increasing or decreasing lift to the wing

13. Tower: Refers to the Air Traffic Control Tower found at most airports and airstrips across the country and most of the world. The Tower is responsible for maintaining

control of the landing and take-off order of the planes in the area and giving planes coordinates for where to go to avoid mid-air collisions. Think of them as the policeman at a stoplight telling cars when it is there turn to go, turn, or stop.

14. Fitz 27, Dollar-05, Nuke 62: These are radio call signs used in the air. Typically, ground control assigns these names and numbers before take-off and typically have a system for doing so. Because this is a work of fiction, I based all "Fitz" call signs from Darcy's nickname. "Dollar" stands for Dollar ride, although typically, in the real world, this call sign would be something related to her squadron at the time (for example, all students in the Red Bulls squadron would be Bull-00). "Nuke", I used as an example of the squadron being the same sign, but you'll notice that the two planes have different numbers at the end (Nuke-61 and Nuke-62). The most famous call sign is Air Force One, which is the official air traffic control sign for the plane carrying the President. While most of us think of the large 747-type plane, if the President decided to jump into a T-6 or T-38 or fly alone, that plane would then be called Air Force One.

15. Five-mile Initial for the Overhead: Refers to specific vectors necessary in order to land at the correct time on the correct runway in the correct order.

16. Landing Gear: The wheels of an aircraft. For larger aircraft and some smaller aircraft, the landing gear is mechanical and can move up and store inside the plane. Other planes (crop dusters, for example) always have their landing gear extended. You can throw the landing gear down because there is a big switch in the cockpit to switch them from stored to extended.

17. Breaking Over the Numbers (In the Break): When

coming in for a landing, there are numbers at the end of the runway which indicate what direction you should arrive from when coming in for a landing. As a plane comes in, they fly over the runway at pattern altitude (however high they were flying before) and then turn to spend energy, lower gear, and descend rapidly to land after doing a quick circle. A typical pilot would begin their braking process about halfway down the runway (midfield), but a hot shot fighter pilot might brake right at the beginning of the runway or "over the numbers." In the break is the first turn in the circle before descending to land.

18. Taxi: Anytime the airplane is on the ground driving around, it is taxing.

19. Park: Just like in a car, an airplane parks at a certain spot. "Taxi to park" indicates that the plane is driving to its parking spot.

20. Fini-flight: In the Air Force, it is tradition that the last flight in any aircraft is called a fini-flight (for final flight). Members of the squadron bring out water hoses, fire hoses, champagne or sparkling cider and as the pilot gets out of the plane, they are sprayed until they are soaking wet. Sometimes the event is rather small with only a few people out to wish them well with hand-held, fire extinguisher-type spray hoses, sometimes they bring a fire truck and really let loose. Typically, the fini-flight also has some sort of celebration in the heritage room of the squadron, complete with toasts.

21. Air Traffic Marshaller: Personnel at the airport with the glowing hand-held cones. The cockpit of an airplane has limited visibility on the ground, so the marshaller directs the plane where it needs to go.

22. Call Signs/Nicknames: Throughout the book, there are several people who have different call signs like "Fitz"

and "Uncle." In the Air Force, many, but not all squadrons, hold "naming nights" wherein an individual would get a nickname from others in the squadron. Many of these nicknames border on the perverse or relate directly to experiences shared among the group. Some of my friend's names include: Cap, Fog, FNG, Ghost, Spanky, Snake, Chaff, and Two-Ball.

23. ABUs: Airman Battle Uniform or ABU is the camouflage uniform worn by the majority of Air Force personnel. They are a different style, cut, and fabric from the flight suit worn only by pilots and a few select other positions.

24. Officer Ranks: *The Best Laid Flight Plans* is all about pilots. In the Air Force at this time, there are no enlisted pilots (excepting a few in a specialized Remotely Piloted Aircraft program) and so the characters are all officers. The basic ranks structure from lowest to highest is 2nd Lieutenant (Elizabeth), 1st Lieutenant (Wickham), Captain (Darcy and Bingley), Major (Warby), Lieutenant Colonel (Richard), Colonel (Forsythe), Brigadier General, Major General, Lieutenant General, and General.

25. AFI: Air Force Instruction. These numbered regulations detail the rules and regulations of the Air Force. Each office in the squadron has multiple binders of AFIs that relate to their particular position. For example, a training office would have regulations related to training easily accessible.

26. Casual lieutenant: A lieutenant that has been selected for pilot training but has yet to start the program. Often these lieutenants receive "busy work" jobs within the squadrons to relieve some of the stress of the current staff.

27. Scheduling desk: Often a large, prominent desk/area in the squadron, the scheduling desk is typically manned

by one to three people who run the schedule of all the pilots flying at that time. The schedule may vary widely depending on a jet's maintenance status, the weather, the condition of the pilots, what particular pilots need, etc. Frequent changes are expected, and schedulers are often the best informed as to the goings-on of the squadron.

28. A-10: The A-10 Thunderbolt II, affectionately referred to as the Warthog, is a single-seat jet which is primarily used for close ground support for friendly troops, attacking armored vehicles and tanks. It is especially well known for its thirty-millimeter Avenger rotary cannon (giant gun on the front) that holds one thousand one hundred seventy-four rounds. Its maximum speed is four hundred thirty-nine mph which is relatively slow and often mocked by other pilots.

29. Instructor Pilot: a pilot instructor/pilot teacher. They are commonly referred to as IPs and are in charge of ensuring that the information on the syllabus, both academic and practical, is addressed for each student. There are two "types" of IP. One graduates from pilot training, goes on to fly another air craft, and then returns to become an instructor, like Darcy. The other, referred to as FAIP (rhymes with tape) or First Assignment Instructor Pilot, graduates from pilot training and then immediately goes on to pilot instructor training (PIT) and returns to pilot training as an instructor.

30. Drop Night: During pilot training, there are two big events that the students look forward to aside from graduation: track night and drop night. Track night is when a pilot tracks from T-6 (the beginning plane) to either T-1 or T-38 (in most cases, they can also go to bombers or helicopters, but it is rare) which determines

whether they will fly cargo/tanker jets (T-1) or fighter/attacker (T-38). Drop Night takes place just before graduation and presents each student with their official first assignment after pilot training. All students turn in a "dream sheet" that lists all the planes and bases they would like to be assigned to, after which those in charge of placement look at the sheet, the bases and planes available and make a determination of where to assign each student. At Drop Night, the students, along with family and friends, congregate to receive their assignment. Typically, the student is called up and the assigned plane is shown on a projection screen along with the base location. The nights often have themes. For example, "ugly sweater" is a popular theme at Christmas and the students wear related items.

31. Officer's Club: The Officer's Club is located on base and is a place where dinners, dances, and other events are frequently held. Originally, only for Officers, the clubs have now become inclusive of enlisted and officer personnel. At most bases, you can become a member of the club which has advantages like less expensive entry into events like Drop Night or graduation or invitations to additional functions. In yesteryear, the Officer's Club was exclusive and held significantly more prestige than the modern clubs.

32. Class Patches: Each squadron in the Air Force has their own patches, frequently having regular patches and "Friday" patches. For example, the real life 535th Airlift Squadron "Tigers" have a picture of a tiger climbing over a globe on a red background with the words "535th Airlift Squadron" and a yellow banner below it. This is worn on the pilot's shoulder and clearly identifies where they work and what plane they are associated with. Each pilot training class is responsible for creating a

patch that represents them. My husband's class patch had a picture of a woman on a plane in old pin-up style with the words "Man I Love Flying" and his class number underneath it. The students were easily identifiable to those on base and those familiar with the program could quickly understand where they were in the program. The base Meryton is based on has huge displays of old class patches in multiple locations on base.

33. T-1: The T-1 Jayhawk is the trainer jet for pilots who will be tracked to tankers and cargo jets. It has cockpit seating for an instructor pilot and two students and can carry four additional passengers. It looks like a little white business jet. The maximum speed is five hundred thirty-nine miles per hour.

34. DNF: Stands for "Do Not Fly." If a pilot "goes DNF," they are not allowed to fly until taken off of that list. Sometimes pilots go DNF for simple reasons, like a head cold or a broken leg. Other times, they are permanently placed on the DNF list for other more serious reasons, like mental health difficulties or blindness—something that causes them to be unable to safely fly.

35. FNG: Fucking New Guy. FNG is often placed on nametags when a pilot has not received a nickname.

36. F-16: The F-16 Flying Falcon is a single engine supersonic multi-role fighter aircraft. The F-16 is currently being flown by the United States Thunderbirds. F-16s can carry up to eleven various bombs, missiles, and rockets. It also carries a 20 mm Vulcan cannon for close range aerial combat and strafing missions. It can go Mach 2, or two times the speed of sound, can withstand up to nine Gs, and climb 50,000 feet per minute.

37. Nellis, Holloman, Shepherd, Creech: These are all
names of real bases throughout the United States.

38. F-35: The F-35 Lightening II is a single seat, single
engine stealth multirole fighter and is the most
expensive military weapons system in history, making it
incredibly controversial. As part of its stealth
capabilities, the F-35 is designed to have low radar,
infrared, and visual signatures. It reaches a maximum
speed of Mach 1.6+. It has one twenty-five-millimeter
cannon and a total weapons payload of eighteen
thousand pounds to carry a variety of missiles
and bombs.

39. Blues: the service blues or the blue uniform worn
frequently in the Air Force. Typically, pilots do not wear
the uniform more than once a week at the most and
having to wear blues is considered a punishment
compared to the comfort of a flight suit. When pilot
training students start out, they must earn the right to
wear the flight suit outside of flying and wear blues
daily. Once that right has been earned, it can be taken
away for misbehavior, frequent class failings, or other
occasions when the students would lose a privilege.

40. Butter Bar: The First Lieutenant rank insignia is a
yellow gold bar on the shoulder, affectionately called a
"butter bar."

41. Solo Ride: As the name implies, this is the first ride for
a student where no instructor pilot is present in the
cockpit and they are flying "solo".

42. Dollar ride: The dollar ride is the first plane ride for a
student. It gets its name from the tradition of handing
the instructor a dollar, frequently decorated and often
framed, to represent the occasion.

43. Cover: rectangular flight cap worn by pilots

44. NOTAMS: A "Notice to Airman" is a written

notification for pilots, advising them of flying-related circumstances. Pilots may need to be advised about facilities, services, or procedural changes or hazards before a flight in order to fly safely. For example, if Elizabeth had a plan to fly to Laughlin Air Force Base, she would need to know ahead of time that there was an air show going on and would be unable to land on the base runways. Then she can choose to adjust her plans accordingly.

45. MOA: Military Operating Area. Each base has a specific area that they work with, for example the Meryton MOA. These areas are broken into sections, which are confusingly also referred to as area. For example, the Meryton MOA may have ten numbered sections (e.g., Meryton MOA area 2) where planes are directed to air traffic safety.

46. Dash-1: The "owner's manual" for the jet. This three-ring book filled with hundreds of pages is divided into sections that list systems descriptions and operations, checklists and normal procedures, emergency procedures, crew duties, operating limits (i.e., how high or fast the plane can fly), adverse weather procedures, etc. It is called the Dash-1 because it is listed as T. O. (technical order) 1T-1A-1 or 1T-37B-1, they both end in -1. Pilots have these with them at all times in the cockpit and are required to know them inside and out. Anytime there is a checklist for takeoff, landing, starting up the jet, and emergency, etc., that checklist would be listed in the -1 and must be done exactly the same every time.

47. Stand up evaluation: This type of evaluations happens frequently throughout pilot training and requires a student to "stand up" in front of the class and perform a specific task while being quizzed by instructors. At this

time, the student may sit as they would in a cockpit and use a large print out of the cockpit, their -1, and their other lists they would carry into the cockpit in order to complete the tasks. During these evaluations, "evals", the entire class must sit at attention and watch the proceedings, while the instructors make it intentionally difficult in an effort to trip up the student and add pressure to the test.

48. Hog Log: a nickname for the maintenance log in which all maintenance on the aircraft is noted.

49. MATL: An acronym for Maintain Aircraft control, Take proper actions, Land

50. Snacko: the person in charge of purchasing snacks for the squadron. It also can refer to the location in the squadron that has snacks, like a breakroom in a normal office, but stocked with soda, water, and snacks.

51. Thunderbird: The United States Air Force Thunderbirds is the national air demonstration squadron. Flying the F-16 Fighting Falcon, the Thunderbirds perform at air shows around the world to demonstrate various feats of aerobatics and precision. They are the Air Force counterparts to the similar Navy Blue Angels team.

52. Step Desk: The desk located immediately before exiting the squadron to walk to an aircraft. The personnel who man this desk may have last minute information for pilots.

53. Comms: The communication system within the jet that the pilots use to communicate with each other through a headset and microphone in the helmet

54. Gs: G force is the force of the gravity working against a body. As the plane accelerates, these forces push down against the pilot and if they experience too much or experience them too quickly can cause the pilot to lose consciousness. In aircraft that experience detrimental

levels g-forces, pilots wear G-suits which help keep the body pressure stabilized and are taught techniques to help prevent negative effects.

55. Cessna: a brand of plane. There are many varieties, however Cessna's tend to be smaller two to four seat propeller planes.

56. IFS: Introductory Flight Screening or IFT for Introductory Flight Training. The name has changed several times in the past few years. Taking place in Colorado, this is a quick, twenty-hour course to screen pilot training candidates before they head to actual pilot training.

57. CAOC: Combat Air Operations Center. For the purposes of this book, it is

58. Sim: Short for simulator. In pilot training, the student performs the tasks for each ride in a simulator first and then in the actual jet. While sims are led by the instructor pilot, simulators are currently operated by contract government employees who are former Air Force pilots. Open sims are also available for students who need to practice.

59. First shirt: In the United States Air Force, the "first shirt" or "shirt" is a nickname for the first sergeant, a special duty—rather than a rank—for a senior enlisted member who is responsible for the moral, welfare, and conduct of the squadron. He is also the chief advisor to the squadron commander regarding enlisted personnel on topics including health, morale, discipline, career progression, professional development, etc.

60. Dual mil: Dual military. Both spouses are active duty military.

61. A current Air Force program emphasizing positive workplace relationships including no sexual harassment/assault, no hazing/bullying, etc.

62. Undergraduate Pilot Training
63. Formation ride: There is a series of rides or flights that occur as tests in the pilot training program. The formation ride occurs at the end of the T-6 program and consists of multiple tasks all within a plane formation with at least one other jet.
64. Mess Dress: the formal

EXCERPT FROM THE FLIGHT PATH
LESS TRAVELED

CHAPTER ONE

*S*econd Lieutenant Elizabeth Bennet felt the vibration of her seat as the propeller sprung into motion. She stretched her legs to move the rudders as she turned onto the runway. She could see the number one plane just in front of her and, as it began to roll forward, her left hand pushed the throttle and felt gravity pull against her as she took off. The sun beat down on the cockpit and Elizabeth felt sweat drip down her neck beneath her helmet.

Elizabeth loved flying, soaring from cloud to cloud. Sometimes she imagined she was in one of the old biplanes and could let the wind whip her scarf and her long dark hair behind her as she danced through the skies. When she was younger, she read a book about the wing walkers of the 1920s and had wanted to stand on the wings of a plane and feel the rush of the wind and sky around her. She took one long look out of the cockpit and watched the clouds form eddies as she rocketed past.

This check ride was important. It was the last bastion she had to conquer before she could track to 38s. She had wanted to fly the shiny, fast, sexy jet since she started pilot training and then move onward to flying jets in the real world. Maybe the F-22?

Maybe even the 35, if it was not still grounded by the time she graduated in six months.

She sighed deeply, feeling the moisture of her breath in the oxygen mask pressed against her nose, and then remembered where she was and what she needed to do.

The number one plane in front of her rocked its wings and Elizabeth pushed the stick firmly to the left, completing a roll and watched the world spin through the glass cockpit. Over comms, she heard a familiar instructor pilot, "Nice job, Bennet. Keep it a little tighter in the formation and watch your altimeter. Keep it straight and level."

Elizabeth unexpectedly felt nervous, but trained her mind back to the task at hand. She watched the number one, moved her wing a little closer to maintain tight formation, and watched for the next signal.

Abruptly, the stick was pushed forward and she strained against the metal to pull it back.

"Straight and level. Straight and level." A haunting echo began to repeat itself in her headset. She pulled the stick back again and again, pushing her legs against the plane straining the muscles in her things, her boots slipping on the metal surfaces.

"Mayday! Mayday! Mayday! MOA 6. Nuke 62. Going down," Elizabeth shouted into the radio. The harness pushed against her breasts while she threw herself into pulling the stick up from her horrifying dive toward the ground. She saw the trees getting bigger and bigger in her view and prayed hysterically for a miracle. She vomited into her mask. Through tears she searched her panel for the altimeter. Two thousand feet. She could only see blackness.

She had to get out of this plane. She did not want to die in this flying metal coffin. Before her mind flashed a vision of her crying mother receiving a triangular folded flag while her father patted her on the shoulder. She watched the uniformed soldier play taps while her sisters openly wept over a casket that contained nothing but charred bits of the former Lieutenant Elizabeth Bennet.

"Straight and level! Straight and level!" *Who was shouting at her? Did they not see her trying everything she could? Pull up, damn it! Pull up!*

She felt between her thighs for the yellow ejection handle. She had to get out of here. Where was the handle? She could not see. She felt again furiously groping the spot between knees, searching wildly. Her vomit-filled helmet blocking her chin from touching her chest and her eyes from the bright looped handle she was looking for. One hand continued to pull at the stick in a desperate attempt to right the plane and the other roved under the seat in an attempt to locate her only chance at safety.

"Straight and level! Straight and level," repeated the scratchy voice in her helmet.

The ground was coming too quickly now. Every movement of her body was strangely slow and halted. She desperately grasped at the stick and made another weak attempt to pull up, her arms exhausted from the strain. She screamed with the effort. She looked once more and closed her eyes, braced for the impact.

"Lizzy!"

The plane shook Elizabeth violently as they continued to shoot through the sky. Elizabeth pondered the movement of time and was surprised that it took so long for her to hit. It felt like she had been falling forever. Turbulence would never kill her. She was no flight attendant walking through the aisle serving diet cokes and pretzels. She was a pilot. She had studied for this. She just had to eject.

"Lizzy!"

Elizabeth screamed again. The stick simply would not budge. She could not find the ejection handle. She felt the plane rock and her mind jolted back to her vision of the dirt below. No more than ten seconds.

"Ten, nine, eight, seven, six, five, four, three, two, one."

Darkness.

"Lizzy!"

Elizabeth shook again. She must have hit. She waited for the scent of exploding fuel and burning flesh she knew would come and the sharp metallic taste of blood that would likely accompany it. She expected the crash to be painful, instead she felt like she was shaking. She felt the shoulder straps of her harness push against her as she continued to shake violently. Suddenly, she felt smothered by her helmet, her face crushed inside her mask.

Her eyes popped open suddenly to see Darcy's chest. Her eyes fluttered and her breath continued to come heavily, burning in her throat as she pulled away and felt herself fall back on her pillow with a soft *whoosh*.

"Lizzy?" He looked at her, his dark eyes creased in concern and a wrinkle appearing on his brow.

"I thought I was crashing," Elizabeth said hoarsely. Her eyes darted around to see her bedroom at Netherfield. The forest green curtains. The dark dresser. The flowers she had received in the hospital. The man looming above her. She could not quite understand how she had got there.

"What was real?" Elizabeth skin prickled as Darcy's deep voice vibrated in his chest as he spoke. She thought furiously, her head cloudy as the sensations of her flight stayed with her.

"The crash. I couldn't find the ejection handle. It wasn't there." She felt herself tear up. Hot wet tears, spilled down her cheeks against her will and she became furious at her inability to control herself. "It wasn't there! Who doesn't put an ejection handle in a plane? What kind of idiot was on maintenance? How on earth do they expect someone to survive without an ejection handle?"

"Honey," Darcy began, pulling Elizabeth to his chest. She pushed him away.

"Don't 'honey" me. I couldn't get out! How did I get here?"

Darcy leaned down to look directly into Elizabeth's eyes. They looked wide and vulnerable, like a deer in headlights. Darcy reached down to rub her arms gently, slowly pulling her petite frame against his chest.

"You got out. You're here. I've got you. You're all right. We're here at Netherfield. The crash was weeks ago, do you remember? You didn't want to go home for fear your mother would smother you. Jane and Bingley are married and are sleeping in the other room, or, uh, were. You were screaming, so I came, but I expect to see Jane any minute." Darcy pressed her against his chest and whispered into her ear.

"Oh, God." Elizabeth looked around. She was in pajamas sitting in her bed. Darcy was shirtless but wearing sweatpants. She suddenly remembered that they had a precarious arrangement wherein he knew she loved him and vice versa, but after one incredible kiss in the hospital, they had barely touched each other, both too anxious to give the other space and now on the first night out of the hospital, she had to ruin everything by freaking out. She was embarrassed. She was tired. She also realized with a sudden blush that maybe this old, ugly shirt from high school and yoga pants with a hole in them should be retired as her night wear of choice. She was frightened, but as she relaxed into him, the feeling of her body against his was the only bearable thing in her existence.

She slowly shook off the remnants of her flashback and her thoughts began to clear. Netherfield. She was at Netherfield. It was too stressful to go home to Longbourn Inn with her mother checking on her every ten minutes and her father shutting himself in his office to avoid her mother. Mary, Kitty, and Lydia were equal parts annoying and dreadful to be around, so Jane had been kind enough to offer her new home since Darcy would be there and Elizabeth had taken up residence directly upon release from the hospital. The hospital therapist had said to expect nightmares and flash backs. Thoughts of the dream brought back all the feelings of fear and a slow blush crept up her cheeks and into her hairline.

"I'm completely embarrassed. Of course, none of it is real. I can't believe I made you get up." She let out a long exasperated sigh and looked around the room, pushing away from him and combing through her tousled curls with her fingers. "Go back to sleep. You have to fly tomorrow."

"Elizabeth, it's no big deal."

"It *is* a big deal. You have to fly. You can't show tired after dealing with me being a baby all night."

Darcy shrugged. "It's an easy flight. Besides, I don't show till ten. I've got plenty of time." He stroked her hair gently, enjoying the feeling of Elizabeth in his arms. "Want me to stay with you a little while?"

Elizabeth's mind was calm as she inhaled his scent and felt the pressure of his arms around her, despite her complete mortification. She exhaled deeply and relished the quiet. Darcy's hand gently touched her hair, smoothing it from the frizz that had overtaken it from her thrashing and ran his hand down her back as he held her. She listened to his heart beat. She matched her breath to his, breathing deeper and slower than was typically her wont. Her eyelids drooped and she relaxed into his arms.

"Elizabeth?"

"Hmmm?"

"Want me to stay?"

"Hmmm..."

"That was not an especially helpful answer. Could you nod or shake your head or something?"

Elizabeth did neither as she nestled closer to his chest. Darcy felt her body relax against him and smiled. He pulled her close and leaned against the headboard where he was found minutes later by a frantic Jane. Darcy opened his eyes slowly and looked at her as she walked clumsily in the dark room.

Darcy pressed his finger to his lips and Jane nodded at him, slowing her steps as she entered.

"Is she back to sleep?" she whispered.

Darcy nodded.

"Go ahead and lay her down, I'll stay with her."

He gently moved Elizabeth's sleeping form onto the bed and

maneuvered himself out of her embrace. They needed to figure out their relationship soon, he hated leaving her like this. She sighed and snuggled deep into her pillow, her hair tumbling over her shoulders and fanning onto the pillow. Darcy looked at her again and waved to Jane before leaving the room as quietly as Jane had entered.

Jane lay down by her sister, grateful that she had the day off from work, and closed her eyes missing Bingley's warm presence. They had only been home from their honeymoon a week and while Charles understood Jane's need to care for Elizabeth, it was still difficult on their new relationship. Elizabeth had come straight to Netherfield, not even stopping at home for clothes. Jane had packed for her, enlisting Kitty's assistance the day she returned from Hawaii. Darcy had been insistent and Jane knew her parents would drive Lizzy crazy within forty-eight hours.

Jane closed her eyes and reviewed her list for the next day. She needed to clean as Caroline had refused to keep up with any task she thought would befit the "mistress of the house." She needed to sort out trimming the trees in the avenue on the road to the house because Caroline had neglected them the year before. Then she would need to take Lizzy to the doctor and get groceries... Caroline had not cooked a meal since the wedding. Jane added *"speak to Charles about his sister—again"* to her list.

Elizabeth kicked Jane and Jane grunted and moved over. She had forgotten Lizzy kicked. Thank goodness Charles slept like the dead and barely moved. Jane did not miss this particular aspect of her sister's many charms. Soon, Jane made herself as comfortable as possible and drifted off to join her sister in slumber.

Made in the USA
Coppell, TX
20 March 2022

75286470R00166